FOLLOW ME

RACHEL GRAHAM

GRAYSCALE
INK.

Content warning: This book contains scenes of coerced psychiatric treatment and British spelling, which may be distressing to some readers. Discretion is advised.

This is a work of fiction. Names, characters, places, and incidents either are the product of the author's imagination or are used fictitiously. Any resemblance to actual persons, living or dead, is entirely coincidental.

First edition printed June 2024

Published by Grayscale Ink.

ISBN 978-1-067011-50-5 (paperback)
ISBN 978-1-067011-51-2 (ebook)

Cover design by Rachel Graham
Cover image by Alexander Possingham

For all those who recognise that reality is but a story that we tell ourselves.

CHAPTER
ONE

I WOULD'VE GIVEN anything to not have my life. Those too-white walls that crept closer any time you looked away; that not-a-camera-we-promise dome on the ceiling; the high school aged blonde nurse who peered into my mouth as I lifted my tongue up, left, right, checking I wasn't harbouring any fugitive pills. As if I wouldn't down as many of those pills as I could get. They'd been my salvation. My damnation as well, but I'd been damned long ago. Probably in a previous life, based on how this one had turned out.

"All clear," the nurse chirped, then narrowed her eyes. "There's no more until three thirty."

My eyes bugged and I bit my lip to stop myself sending a snarky comment back that I wished she'd told me that *before* I took them.

I nodded instead, internally reciting my mantra. *Keep the peace, Lena. Be a good psych patient, till they let you out.*

The nurse flashed a fake smile and returned to the office without another word. With its window lined walls, the central nursing station was like a zoo exhibit. Nurses roamed around their enclosure, busy with their paperwork and phone calls and "team meetings" and anything except actually spending time with their patients. Better off drugging us and sending us on our way.

Fine by me.

I glanced at the little clock behind the glass and inhaled sharply. Nine thirty. Six hours until my next dose. Overlapping laughter and mumbled mocking rattled through my mind, the relentless chatter of my not-so-friendly auditory hallucinations like a hive in my head. I closed my eyes and exhaled the same breath. The voices would be quieter soon. *Here comes your sleepy-time spray, little bees, time for night-night.*

My wonderful, patient (excuse the pun) and best-slash-only friend Nia would have to come to my rescue and distract me for the half-hour or so until the meds kicked in. Save me from myself, and from making a scene where the nurses decided I better stay in this godforsaken place any longer than they already planned. A mocking shriek rattled through my skull, leaving sharp pain in its wake. I grabbed at my head, as if that would solve it. Those damn voices. My misery, their entertainment.

I trudged down the long, bland corridor toward the art room as the walls grew ever closer, still pressing my hand to my temple until the pain let up. The incessant mumbling remained, as always, but low enough that I could bear it. I dodged the various stains that decorated the carpet, vaguely wondering about their origin, and why they hadn't been cleaned properly. Why nothing in this place was ever cleaned properly.

Sure enough, Nia was in the art room, colouring another one of her geometric Buddhist drawings that supposedly got her in touch with her inner peace. Her puppy dog brown eyes lit up when she saw me, and my cold heart warmed at her enthusiastic grin and matching invite to the chair beside her.

"Got your drugs?" Nia asked as I crossed the room to take my plastic throne.

"Only the best," I said, though the uncoated pills had left their bitter taste in my mouth before I'd washed them down with the hospital's chlorinated water. That wonderful mix of flavour that I called "My Inadequacy."

I sighed as I pulled the chair out further and swiped aside some papers so I could lean on the table. "But I'm out now, till three thirty."

"Ouch." She grimaced. "I thought you were gonna cut back?"

I pouted, then flopped my arm flat on the table and dropped my head onto it. "I know," I whined, my mental horde harmonising with my pitch. "But…" I pointed to my head. It was only yesterday that I'd told Nia I was going to cut back to prove I was ready for discharge, but meds were the only thing that gave me any peace. She'd raised her eyebrows at me then, evidently not believing I could do it, but hadn't said anything. Didn't need to, either. Here was her proof.

Nia pouted as well, not mocking, just empathetic to my suffering. She pointed her pencil toward the array of papers I'd pushed aside, all with different images printed on them. "You wanna do one?"

My head rose and fell along with my arm's dead fish impression of a shrug against the tabletop. I wasn't any good at art. Wasn't good at anything, really. Didn't have any hobbies. No interests. What a bore-zo.

"I prefer just watching you do it," I said.

"You can have this one, if you want," she offered, her dark hair falling off its perch behind her ear.

"Thanks."

I meant it.

We both sat in silence for a while as I watched her work, her careful, natural strokes of the pencil shading from the outline to the centre of each shape. I could watch her for hours, feeding off her calm energy as she created something beautiful in this otherwise grim place.

The walls were covered in her art, so full now that the pictures had spilled onto the windows. A driveway ran up the side of the building like a moat, bordered by a wide strip of grass that led to a large staff carpark. The open space gave plenty of people-watching opportunities, all coming and going, while we were stuck in here. Not that getting out of here would cure my psychosis, but it sure would help with the boredom, and distract from the voices haunting my mind.

A fence ran from the end of the carpark out past the edge of where I could see, even if I pressed my face against the window. Based on the direction the cars came and went, I figured that was the exit to the hospital grounds. I'd come in by car, but got turned around once I was here. It was surprising they didn't give us a full view of the exit—it seemed the sort of thing they'd love to torture us with, that peek at freedom that would be forever out of our reach. Mine, anyway.

Until Aidan. My brother was the first glimpse of hope and stability I'd had in years. He had a flat for me to stay in, with normal people, living a normal life. He wouldn't kick me out like all the foster homes who deemed me "too much trouble." Aidan was my chance at getting out of here for good. Though at that point, I'd happily get out for evil. I just needed out, and to never return.

I put my elbow on the table and rested my chin on my hand to get a better view of Nia's picture. She'd added a calming mixture of dark and light blue, along with light green and yellow. Despite my lack of artistry, I thought red would make for a nice accentuating colour. Nia swapped to a red pencil, and I frowned at the so-called "coincidence."

"Alena?" Someone called my name, and it took a moment to register that it wasn't in my mind. I glanced up at the nurse in the doorway.

"You have visitors," she said.

Visitors, plural? Only my brother ever visited me, and he always let me know when he was coming.

"Is it Aidan?"

The nurse exhaled in irritation, half leaning out the door, wanting to be done with this interaction. "No, she said her name was Rose."

I locked eyes with Nia, sending her my confusion. I didn't know any Rose. Nia's face mirrored mine, and she lifted her shoulders in a slow shrug.

I did the same. "It's probably for someone else. I'll go look."

I followed the nurse to the visiting room. We passed the nurses' enclosure, and the two who were in there didn't bother looking up from their phones. From their office, the nurses could see directly into the dining room, lounge, and courtyard, plus right down the two identical corridors housing eight bedrooms and four shared bathrooms each. If they ever bothered to look, the line of view shot all the way down to the fire exit doors that teased us with our captivity—single doors that opened directly to freedom, but were always locked. Even the nurses' keys wouldn't open them—I'd asked.

The nurse unlocked the small visitors' room, home to two couches and two armchairs squashed so tightly around a central coffee table that you could barely move in there. She held the door open and I inched inside, a frown plastered on my face.

Not one, but three unfamiliar faces met me, belonging to an older woman, a girl about my age, and a middle-aged man, all dressed in their Sunday best, even though it was casual Wednesday. They all stood as I entered—the man bounded up with little regard for the poor old woman, who struggled against arthritic knees. The girl stood reluctantly, like she didn't want to be there. She certainly didn't want to be in her yellow flower-girl dress—she tugged at the hem awkwardly to keep it in place. It did look good on her, though. I wished I had a pretty dress to be uncomfortable in.

5

I glanced back at the nurse to tell her there was a mistake, I didn't know these people. The door slammed in my face, and I recoiled to stop from getting smacked in the nose. My eyes bulged and mouth dropped open. I shouldn't have been surprised. The nurses couldn't wait to be done with me. I'd have to remind them they had my permission to let me out any time.

"Alena," the older woman exclaimed, as if I were her most favourite person in the world. I turned to see her beaming at me, with her hand on offer to shake. "It is so wonderful to see you."

"Hi," I said, my tone reflecting my discomfort. The grins of the old woman and man were probably meant to be welcoming, but were the dead opposite. The girl turned the corners of her mouth up in a forced smile, as if she'd been told to play nice. She hadn't even met me and it was like she already hated me. The hive piped up to assure me I was correct. I squeezed my eyes shut for a second, as if that would make them go away.

"Dear, are you okay?" the woman asked, reminding me I had company who were now certain I was crazy, if the whole locked-in-a-mental-hospital part hadn't yet given it away. I faked a smile, like normal people would. It came out looking like someone was pulling my mouth from both sides.

"Good," she said. "My name is Rose, and this is Elly and Leroy." She gestured either side of her as she introduced the others, then held her hand out again for me to shake. She had to be in her late sixties at least, her skin dotted with sunspots. A tight up-bun pulled at her white hair, yanking her hairline back to give her a mini facelift. I stared at her outstretched hand, not returning my own.

"Hi," Elly said coldly, giving a small wave. She *really* didn't want to be there. Her mouse brown hair and brown eyes matched mine, and though she had more muscle on her and a tanned complexion, we could be related. Maybe it was just typical teenage angst and her attitude had nothing to do with me. God knew I wasn't exactly thrilled about being there myself.

The man, on the other hand, was way too enthusiastic. There was something off about him and his energy, like he wanted to get past the old woman and climb into my skin. I was grateful for the barrier she provided, and the table wedged between us.

"Hi Mary, I'm Leroy," he said in two excited breaths, bouncing on his heels, clenching and unclenching his fists.

My eyes narrowed. Right... as if Rose hadn't just introduced him, and already said my name. "Hi Leroy," I said slowly, before emphasising my name. "I'm Lena."

Leroy scowled. "No—"

"I knew your mother," the older woman said, cutting Leroy off.

I froze, every muscle in my body tensing in unison. The voices moaned, spurred on by my shock. "You what?"

Which one?

"Yes, when you were just a baby," she continued, repurposing her outstretched hand to indicate to the couch across from where she had been sitting.

My mother. My birth mother. I had barely known her myself, and this woman thought it was okay to casually drop that into conversation?

"How'd you know my mum?" I asked in the same bewildered tone I'd used in my first response to this revelation. I angled my body toward the door, as if that would give me some form of emotional protection against whatever other bombshell this woman might be about to drop.

Rose gestured again at the couch across from her. "Please, sit."

Overlapping groans and wails sounded in my mind, imploring me to get out, get out *now*. To spite them, and in somewhat of a trance with the hopes Rose might be able to tell me more about my mum, I slowly lowered onto the corner closest to the door. The visitors returned to their seats. Elly slumped into her corner of the couch, while Leroy shuffled on his seat like he was resisting the urge to launch off it and hug me. He fiddled with his hands. Stimming—that's what it was.

Rose smiled sweetly, pleased I had followed her direction. "We used to catch up for a coffee when you were just a newborn. I was very sorry to hear what happened to her."

"Yeah," I said dryly, somewhat relieved they'd had such an innocent meeting. I'd heard a bit from Aidan, enough to know that my being in hospital was a family trait, and was unlikely to turn out well for me. "What did you hear?"

Rose softened her voice. "Not too much, just that she had some... struggles."

That was one word for it. I glanced at Elly, hanging her head like she didn't want anything to do with the conversation, and at Leroy, who was grinning like a loon, completely out of sync with the tone of the room.

"She was a wonderful woman," Rose said, filling the silence before it grew awkward. "It's such a shame we weren't able to spend more time together."

You and me both.

"Can you..." I hesitated. The words had jumped out before I really knew I was going to say them, and my vulnerable self had shut them down almost as quickly. I swallowed, and fiddled with my hands, willing myself to ask more. Aidan didn't really talk about her—Cara—and I might not ever get such an opportunity again. I certainly couldn't ask Cara what happened. "Can you tell me more?"

Rose tipped her head in confusion.

"About my mum," I clarified.

Rose took a sharp breath in, then looked at me with those same pitying eyes the doctors gave me. Poor stupid, sick Lena.

"I don't really know what else to tell you. We caught up a few times for a coffee, she brought you along, and that's when..." She cut herself off, like she'd said too much.

8

"When what?"

Rose paused to consider her next words. "Well, she got sick not long after. I tried to visit, but your father was quite protective. So, we lost touch. And then..." she drifted off.

I waited for her to finish her train of thought, to give me something, *anything* extra about my mum. She didn't offer anything extra, so I pressed as much as I dared. "Then?"

"I'm sorry, Lena. Truly. For your loss."

Oh. That.

Nothing extra. Just the same old story that me and my brother hadn't been enough for my mum. Hadn't been enough to keep her happy. To keep her alive.

"I'm sorry I don't have more to tell you," Rose said gently. "Have you asked your father?"

Heat flashed through me and I scowled. He didn't deserve that title. "We don't talk."

Elly flashed me a look, but I couldn't really read it. Jealousy?

Hate, the voices seethed, followed by mocking laughter mixed with breathy moans.

I pressed my fingers to my temple and squeezed my eyes shut again to try to drown them out.

"Really, dear, are you alright?" Concern was etched into Rose's tone and face.

I nodded unconvincingly. "So, why are you here?"

"I only recently heard that you yourself had ended up in..." Rose glanced around the room. "... here. I wanted to reach out to see if there was something—anything—I could do to help."

I smirked. "Like get me out of here?" Gasps from my horde.

Rose's eyes lit up. "Well, yes. We would love to have you come and live with us. You're certainly not meant to be living in a place like this."

That was a jump from "get me out" to "come live with us." Besides, how would they?

9

"No offence," I said, "but why would you want to help me? We don't know each other." It had come out ruder than I intended. As always, making a mess of social interaction. Rude and entitled, just like the nurses said.

Leroy started tapping Rose on the shoulder.

She ignored it. "Like I mentioned, Lena—may I call you Lena? I felt terrible I couldn't help your mother, but maybe I can help you," Rose said, without giving me a chance to give permission to use my nickname. Which I would. I already had. Only the staff called me Alena.

And then she hit me with that age-old cliché, the one people tell you when they want you to feel less sad about being you. "You're very special, Lena. More special than you know."

I scoffed, rolled my eyes, and folded my arms. What was she going to be spouting next? Some religious propaganda, try to convert me or sell me something? Maybe they were making rounds of the psych units since no one in the real world would buy into their bull—

"Mum," Leroy tapped at Rose's shoulder. So that's how they were related. Elly must be her granddaughter. I certainly couldn't blame her for being unenthused about getting dragged along to visit a mental patient.

Rose ignored Leroy's tapping. I glanced at him. Maybe that's what she meant by me being "special."

I had to ask. "'Special,' how?" My question came out a mixture of sass and concern. *Please don't mean special like Leroy.*

"Oh," Rose said, her face brightening at the mere thought of telling me. "It's hard to put into words."

I scowled. Sure it was. The whole rehearsed act was "hard to put into words."

"Try me," I sneered.

"Mum!" Leroy cried out, tapping furiously against her fragile old lady shoulder.

Rose took a deep breath, inched away from his tapping, and turned to him. "Yes, Leroy?"

And then he uttered two words that anyone plagued by delusions of grandeur, grasping for their sanity, both longed and dreaded to hear.

"She's God."

CHAPTER
TWO

"I'M *WHAT*?" My mouth dropped open, and my face muscles yanked my cheeks into a disbelieving grin. Excited chatter sounded in my mind.

Rose became flustered and patted Leroy's knee, glancing back and forth between us. "Oh dear. Leroy, perhaps you should go wait outside. Elly—"

"Nooo!" Leroy wailed. "I want to stay with Mary!"

That name again.

"Who the hell is Mary?" My eyebrows were just as confused as I was. They squeezed together, distorting my whole comical face. These people were more bonkers than me.

"You're Mary, Mary is God," Leroy sang, bouncing on his heels back and forth into his seat.

"Leroy—" Rose turned to him, trying in vain to stop his movement by holding him still. "Quiet, please, you're frightening her."

My face probably looked like I was in desperate need of a bathroom, or a doctor. "Scaring me? Oh, no, I'm not scared."

This would make a great story to tell Aidan and Nia. More evidence that the world was crazy and this whole notion of psychiatry was just a Band-Aid for society. I'd been one of the unlucky ones to get caught in the middle.

Rose held Leroy's arm and shoulder in an old-lady death grip and directed him toward Elly. "Elly, please will you take Leroy—"

"No!" Leroy cried. He pulled against Rose's grasp, but there was nowhere for him to escape to with the table in the way.

"Yes, Leroy. Elly, I'll meet you outside," Rose said with a sharper tone.

Elly bounded up, energetic now that she got to leave this place. She held out her hand for Leroy and I was in half a mind to grab it myself so she could take me instead. Heck, I'd even go with Leroy, if it got me out of here.

"Come on, Leroy," Elly said.

He stood up slowly and took her hand. He inched past Rose, head drooped and shoulders slumped. He whispered a "bye, Mary," as he was led past me and out the door. I couldn't help but lean away a little as they passed. Leroy didn't seem to notice, but I was sure Rose would. The door clicked closed behind them and I stared at it a while longer, now acutely aware I was alone with this woman.

"Sorry about all that," Rose apologised, her tone returned to her sweet, innocent-old-lady act. "He gets a little excited."

"I can tell," I said, still intrigued by the weird man's ramblings. "Who's Mary?"

Rose huffed and glanced at the door before continuing, annoyed that Leroy had brought the name up at all. "That might be a bit much for today. I really just wanted to get to know you, and for you to get to know us."

I had little to no interest in getting to know this random bunch of people who showed up to the hospital—the literal psych ward—uninvited, but I needed the goss for the story for Nia and Aidan. Plus, she'd known my mum. "Cool, we can start with you telling me who Mary is, then more about my mum."

Rose leaned forward, pleadingly. "I don't know anything more, unfortunately. And I'd really rather we start a little slower."

Rose did know more about my mum. I'd bet my life on it. But this Mary thing was clearly a weakness for her, so she'd be easier to break. I leaned forward, mirroring her behaviour, despite myself. "You know avoiding the question is just going to make me want to know even more." Pressure rose against my chest for talking back to an older lady. Respect your elders, they say. But she'd hunted me down here, not the other way around.

"Well, let's start off with what you like to do in your spare time?"

Yeah, never mind that she was my elder. "Really? Okay, fine." I stood up, making out to leave.

"Wait!" Rose called, reaching for me.

I paused and dropped my hip to the side, like the nurses did when they wanted me to quit talking to them so they could leave.

Rose slumped her shoulders. "Alright. Firstly, tell me—do you believe in God?"

I scoffed. There was no God here, not in this place, not in my life. "That's not the deal. You tell me about Mary first."

Rose shifted uncomfortably in her chair. "Mary is the patron of our religious order."

I sat back down, and Rose continued. "Leroy just got a little excited today. He doesn't always know when he shouldn't say things in public."

Maybe she should have taught him better. Or, you know, not take him out in public.

"Why does he think I'm Mary?" I asked.

Rose's eyes darted to me, before glancing away. "There's a teaching that Mary reincarnates to live among us."

My cheeks tightened as I tried to hold back another grin.

"And so Leroy thinks I'm Mary? Isn't that a bit blasphemous or something?"

Rose pressed her lips together and was quiet for a moment. That moment was all I needed for it to dawn on me.

"Wait, you don't believe this, too?"

Rose softened her eyes. "I know this will be a lot to take in. I didn't mean to have to tell you quite so soon."

Leroy's words replayed in my mind. "He said Mary is *God*."

Rose's face warmed, relaxing into her beliefs. "Traditional Christianity only got things partially right. Jesus was the son of God, yes, but it was on his mother's side. God incarnated as Mary, Jesus' mother."

My mouth dropped open, those ghost fingers pulling a partial smirk.

"I realise this will be difficult to process," Rose continued. She held her hands out, palms to the floor, like people do when they're approaching a wild animal. "Christianity has pushed their doctrine so strongly. And the notion that God is a man is so widely accepted that there's not really room for any other consideration. But I know it to be true."

Her knowing grin should've got her admitted. This lady was cuckoo.

"Ah, how's that?" Now I knew what it was like being on the other side of a psych evaluation.

Rose leaned in again, the corners of her mouth turned up in that same knowing smile. She lowered her voice to a whisper. "The truth of it is, I have met God."

I stifled a laugh.

"She guided me when I was just a girl. Her name was Elizabeth at that time, in that life."

Maybe that's who Elly was named after.

"Right. And what does this have to do with me?" I leaned on the armrest, the incessant chatter taking indecipherable guesses at what her answer would be.

Rose glanced at her hands and took a breath before looking me dead in the eye and continuing. "Elizabeth told me we would meet again. I waited my whole life. And when I met you, Lena, as a little baby, I knew it to be true."

I turned my face from her, assessing her with my side-eye. My skin started crawling. She was off her rocker, but I had to ask. "Know what to be true?"

She pressed her hands together, and held them out to me. "You, my dear Lena, are Elizabeth—God—reincarnated."

CHAPTER
THREE

I EXPLODED INTO LAUGHTER. Specks of spittle flew out from trying to hold back. "Sorry, I'm sorry," I managed to wheeze out.

"It's okay, I know it's a lot." Rose relaxed back and looked at me with pitying eyes. That same look all the staff gave me. Hate bubbled in me, and the voices cackled.

"It's not that it's a lot, it's that it's crazy," I snapped. "Does anyone know you're talking to me like this? I feel like the staff wouldn't be too keen on you being in here saying this."

Her pity turned to pleading. "You don't belong in here, Lena."

I rolled my eyes. "You're telling me. How about you convince the doctors of that? Though I don't think they're gonna buy your 'Lena is God' story. Actually, tell you what, there's about three Jesuses in here right now. Shall I call them in for a family reunion?"

She glanced at her hands. "I know it sounds impossible. It'll be easier to accept when your blessings start to show."

"My 'blessings'?" I repeated, emphasising the word. Hadn't

seen any of those in my life. If I tried step foot in a church, I was likely to burst into flames.

Burn, a voice piped up, clear enough to understand.

Thanks, I thought back at it, *super reassuring.* I cleared my throat, and Rose glanced up at me, probably thinking it was for her.

"It's okay," she said. "We can talk about them another time."

"No, no, we're on a roll," I jeered. She wasn't getting out of it that easily. "Tell me about these 'blessings.'"

Rose inhaled through her mouth, her next few words floating on her outbreath. "They could manifest in many ways. Visions of the future, experiences of your past lives, control of events—"

"Those are called delusions," I cut in. This was why religion and mental illness overlapped so much. Both groups were as crazy as each other.

"That's what the doctors would have you believe, yes," she said with renewed enthusiasm. "Because they don't understand, either. It's not their fault. They're doing what they think is best. But like I said, Lena, you don't belong in here."

I looked at her sideways. All the doctors' and nurses' favourite questions, checking in if I was hearing voices, what they were saying, if I felt like I was being controlled or controlling others, bla bla bla. But these people actually believed it. And believed that it was all some God-given gift, rather than crossed wires in my brain. If only that were true. I wouldn't need a cure. But that would be good, and good things didn't happen to me.

"Well, the meds make that stuff go away, so it must be sickness," I said bluntly.

Not, a voice perked up, and I grunted.

Yes, not entirely, thanks for the reminder, I thought back. Two decipherable words within a few minutes of each other—the voices were on a roll. So much for that last dose of meds.

My mind darkened while Rose's eyes brightened. "You've experienced it already?"

My turn to inhale through my mouth. "You didn't hear me. It's mental illness. And it's awful."

"The medications stop it because *you believe* that they can," Rose said. She emphasised the words "you" and "believe" like this was all my fault.

"Right." I rolled my eyes again. All the work everyone had done to convince me I was crazy, and this lady was trying to undo it all—*and* making me burn through my meds at the same time. That familiar rage bubbled in me again. "So you're saying I did this to myself. Is that why I'm stuck in this hellhole? Is that why I got to bounce around foster homes, get beaten and abused, lose the only family I have, get stuck with these voices that won't ever give me an ounce of quiet? Is that all because 'I believe'?" I bit, putting the last two words in air quotes.

Rose sat up at the mention of voices. "Voices? You hear prayer?"

"Prayer? What—" Laughter rattled in my mind. She'd twist anything I said into working for her narrative. Why would anyone possibly pray to me? I couldn't be God, I was a mess. I couldn't fix anything, not even my life. Not even myself.

True, a voice whispered. We agreed on something.

Rose tipped her head to the side with that same empathetic look, the one I was so used to getting when someone thought I was crazy. When I'd say I'd caused something to happen. Yet here was Rose, giving me that look for the exact opposite reason —because she was telling me that I really could control things with my mind, and this time I didn't believe her.

Right?

Aidan believed I was sick, and I trusted Aidan. But then, he hadn't been around my whole life. He hadn't experienced what I had. Nia had been through similar, but she wouldn't give me a straight answer if she believed me or not. All she would say was that she believed that I believed it was real, which was frustrating in itself, but she did it in a different way to the doctors.

And the doctors and nurses, well, they were convinced that it was all mental illness.

Then here come these strangers, telling me that I'm right, it's all true, that I could make things happen just by thinking them, that the voices were—what? Prayers?

No. No, I was so close to discharge, to finally living with Aidan, to having a normal life, which was all I wanted.

This had been… interesting… but it was time to stop feeding the monster. It was all fun and games until she started making me doubt my insanity and got me locked in here for longer. Plus, a headache was starting to form behind my left eye. I glanced back at Rose, her hopeful face sending a pang of guilt as I tried my next words.

"It's not me, sorry. I don't know who you're looking for, but it's not me."

The disappointment in her eyes increased my guilt, which then flicked back into anger. How dare she come here and put these ideas in my head, make me feel guilty for rejecting her beliefs. I was the sick person here; I was the victim.

"But actually, you know what?" Rage fuelled me. "This isn't fair for you to come here and say all this to me. To anyone. You have your religion, whatever, but don't try drag me or anyone else into it. There's probably loads of people here who would buy what you're selling, which I guess is why you're here: target the vulnerable."

Come in here and tell me I'm the incarnation of God, when I'm trying to get out *of the loony-bin, rather than further in, thank you very much.*

Rose shook her head earnestly, concern etched across her face. "I'm only here to see you, Lena. My entire purpose, and the entire purpose of our congregation, is to support and care for you."

"For God, you mean." I scoffed. It wasn't me they cared about. It was this fantasy of theirs, and it would all come crashing down when they realised I wasn't who they thought I was. I couldn't be.

"Well, yes." She turned her palms toward me and lifted her shoulders along with them, gesturing that it was obvious that God and I were one and the same.

God, God, voices chanted, above the usual mumbled chatter, daring me to believe her. I pressed my eyes shut, clenching my teeth against my inner bottom lip. My canines broke open a fresh cut from the multitude of new and old wounds across the inside of my mouth, and the taste of blood teased my tongue.

As if pressing my eyes shut would make the voices quiet. They'd managed to push through my meds, all because of this lady's visit and the fantasies she'd shared.

"Actually, I think I'm done for the day," I said, careful to not let blood escape as I spoke. "If you're not going to tell me anything more about my mum. Nice meeting you." *Not.*

I stood up and Rose bolted up with me, as quick as she could on her knobbly, swollen knees.

"Oh, Lena, I'm so sorry if I've said something—" she said as she reached for me, desperate for connection, to draw me into her delusion.

"No, I'm just tired," I lied, using my last iota of patience to not bite her head off. I shuffled toward the door.

"Lena," Rose said, and riffled through her handbag at her feet. She brought out a small, folded piece of paper and held it out to me. "I understand this is difficult to hear, but it's the truth. I'll give you some time to process. Just know you can call for anything."

I took the paper and opened it, my curiosity getting the better of me. I crumpled it back up and shoved the phone number in my jacket pocket.

"We aren't allowed phones in here," I spat, with no intention of specifying that there was a ward phone we could use. "So, no, I can't just call for anything. Not that it would make a difference

23

anyway, since if you do know more about my mum, you clearly aren't going to tell me."

She took a deep breath in, and looked at me helplessly. "I wish I had more to tell you."

Lies, my voices mocked.

"Sure." I rolled my eyes, and my anger flared again as her previous words dawned on me. "As for truth? Well, if what I believe becomes true, then I believe I'm not God. How about that? I'm not God anymore. Go find a different saviour, because it sure as hell ain't me."

I whipped back around to the door, ready to make a dramatic exit and leave her in my metaphorical dust.

"Lena?" Rose said, so gently I couldn't bring myself not to respond.

I glanced back at her, my hand on the door handle.

"Don't let them convince you you're not well." She pointed to her head. "The voices, they're a blessing, even if you can't see it yet."

I opened my mouth to argue back, to absolutely rip into her that these voices and delusions and being labelled clinically insane and pumped full of drugs and floating through life was most absolutely and definitely *not* a blessing. But I closed it again, and ripped open the door instead.

I stormed down the corridor, back toward Nia. How dare that woman—a stranger—bring that into my life. How dare she come here and fill my head with this... this *hope*. Hope that maybe I wasn't crazy.

The same haunting voice whispered again.

True.

CHAPTER
FOUR

I DROPPED into the chair next to Nia, my elbows on the art table and my head in my hands.

"So, who was it?" Nia asked.

I groaned. "Some religious nutjobs."

"Oof," she breathed. She, of anyone, knew my pain.

"Pretty sure she made me burn through my meds," I grumbled, and the voices cheered in response.

She put her hand on my shoulder and squeezed. I flinched at the unexpected physical contact, and she removed her hand.

"Sorry, L," she said. I wasn't sure if she meant for the meds or touch, but turned and signalled forgiveness, either way.

Rose walked past the art room window, heading for the exit, and I ducked down behind Nia so she wouldn't see me. She hobbled a bit, like her knees couldn't fully be trusted.

"This cow," I mumbled to Nia. "That's the lady who just visited me. I hope she falls on her face."

"What?" Nia asked, glancing at her.

Rose lurched forward, her foot catching on the floor. Her arms shot out to balance herself, and she managed to get her foot back out in front of her in time to stop herself from crashing to the ground.

A surge of adrenaline coursed through me.

Did I do that?

My wide eyes trained on Nia, who slowly turned back to me. I opened my mouth to ask, but Nia cut me off.

"Don't," she said, and held her index finger up. "I know what you're thinking. Don't say it out loud. Don't do that to yourself. You're almost out, don't ruin it now."

I shut my mouth firmly. She was right, of course she was. And she clearly knew me almost as well as I knew myself.

Be a good patient, do what the doctors tell you to do, say what they want you to say. That certainly did not include telling them that you can control things with your mind. Which was crazy, anyway. It was just a coincidence, it always was.

"Yep, nope, you got it. I'm cured," I said dryly. "Just a coincidence."

Nia kept her eyes locked on mine. "Just a crazy coincidence."

Unless it wasn't. Unless Rose was right.

"What did she say to you, anyway?" Nia asked, perplexed about why I would want a seemingly sweet old lady to fall flat on her face.

"You're not gonna believe it," I said. "It's crazy."

She flashed her eyes. "Isn't everything in here?"

"True." I chuckled. "Her and two others were from some group who think God is living among us." I held my hands up and floated them away from me, with a spooky sci-fi kind of voice for the last part of the sentence.

Nia looked at me, eyebrows now raised. "You're right, that is crazy. Yet we're the ones in here."

"I know, right!" I laughed. She glanced back down at her drawing. I waited for her to say something else. She didn't, so I did.

"They said I'm God."

26

Nia turned slowly toward me, a grin spreading across her face. She looked like she was going to burst into laughter, until she saw my face. Her own dropped.

"Lena, don't tell me you believe it."

"Pfft, no," I scoffed. "Of course not. It's crazy."

"It is crazy. It's not real."

"I know. She's delusional." *Maybe.*

"Yes." Nia locked her eyes on mine. "Don't you get sucked into it."

"I won't." *Probably.*

"Religion is dangerous," she said.

"I know!" I exclaimed, apologetically, and broke eye contact. Religion was... a focus of hers, when she was "running hot"— our term for what the doctors called a manic episode. Her family was religious to start with, but she took it to the extreme when she was unwell. A couple of episodes ago, she'd shaved off all her hair so she could communicate with God better. When she came to, she'd been devastated, and didn't want anyone to see her for days. Not even me. She'd tried to cut religion out entirely after that, but it always wormed its way back in—or snaked, if we're going to keep with religious metaphors.

"What did they want from you?" she pressed.

I shrugged. "They said nothing, just that they wanted to help me with whatever I needed."

"I don't trust that. Lena, you shouldn't trust that."

"I know! You saw—I sent her away. I don't want her here."

"Good," she said sharply.

We sat in silence, both staring at the table. Nia resumed colouring in, carefully tracing the printed lines.

I replayed the conversation with Rose. She was crazy, and I didn't want her false hope. Though it would be fantastic if it were all true. If I really wasn't crazy. That would show the doctors. And Rose had known my mum, while I knew barely anything about her. Aidan didn't talk about her that much, probably ashamed that she had mental illness, too. Which didn't bode well for me.

I felt for the little piece of paper in my pocket, and the hive buzzed with excitement.

No, I shouldn't tempt it. I sure didn't need any more crazy in my life. I uncurled my hand and withdrew it from my pocket. I picked up a pencil and drew an offensively unparallel line along the border of a geometric print.

Do! A voice shrieked.

I grunted and rubbed my eyes with one hand. My headache hadn't let up in the ten minutes or so since Rose's visit, and that scream hadn't helped.

"Voices?" Nia asked, her own voice gentle, and much more caring than those in my head.

I sucked a breath in through my teeth. "Yep. They're even worse than before."

"Go watch TV, maybe? Read for a bit?" she suggested. "Or the nurses' favourites: deep breathing, meditation, journaling." She acted each one out as she said it.

"Maybe," I said, knowing I would do none of those things. I couldn't read when the voices got bad. Even if I could, it wasn't like there was a fantastic selection of books here. They were basically all rejects from personal collections, or so-far-overdue library books that they would've been written off ages ago. The only one that was any good I'd read about five times already, and giggled every time I got to Chapter 39, since the entire chapter consisted of a single word beginning with "F." It was a signed copy by some guy named John Marrs, who probably self-printed and signed every copy, then ended up having to donate them to places like this sad little psych ward's community library, in the hopes that someone, *anyone*, would read them.

This little someone had, and the story itself was actually pretty good. It even made me feel better about my own life. Sure, my family was messed up, but we didn't have literal skeletons in our closet like that family. Though if my birthfather had gotten his way, we would've. I'd be it.

But, no, reading wouldn't help right now. The only thing that helped me these days was the medication. The absolute only thing that kept the delusions at bay and quietened those mother-Chapter-39ing voices, and those religious nuts had made me burn through my last dose.

"I've got a headache now, too." I pouted.

"Get some meds then," Nia said, wobbling her head like it was the obvious answer. Which it was.

I told her I'd be back, then made my way to the nurses' enclosure and knocked on the door. The door swung open and a nurse stared at me without speaking.

"Can I have something for a headache," I stated, more than asked.

"Have you been drinking enough water?" the nurse asked.

I clicked my tongue. As if basic pain meds were a hot commodity. "Yes," I started to hiss, but cut myself off. *Be a good psych patient.*

The nurse pushed past me, and the heavy office door shut with a clang that sent a fresh surge of pain behind my eye.

I glanced at the clock and died a little inside. It was only ten forty. It was going to be a hell of a wait until my next dose of pink miracle pills. Hanging out with Nia wasn't making it go any faster, but maybe a phone call to Aidan would. I could check he was still going to visit on the weekend, since the no cellphone rule meant I couldn't just text like a normal person.

The nurse returned with paracetamol, and after a quick swig with the infamous chlorine-water, I asked to call my brother.

The nurse agreed, and went to get the phone. I recited Aidan's number and the nurse patched it through to the communal telephone box. I scurried over as the landline started its high-pitched screech.

"Hello?" I said into the receiver.

"Lena?" A wave of warmth washed through me at hearing Aidan's voice.

"Hi, sorry," I said, only a little guilty that I'd interrupted him during work time. He said I could call any time, and I was his sister, so that wasn't just him being nice. "I just... wanted to check in. See if you were still coming on Saturday."

"Hey, of course," he said. "And you can call me whenever, you know that."

I nodded, knowing he couldn't see me, but doing it anyway. Maybe there was some subconscious sibling thing where he'd be able to sense me. I *had* always had a feeling I had a family out there, before we'd found each other again. Though, in my dreams I'd pictured it was a big, happy family, living on a farm somewhere, and it was all just an awful misunderstanding that I'd somehow been lost in the system, and really they'd been looking for me my whole life.

A group of voices screeched with amusement.

Dreams are free.

We sat in silence for a couple of seconds, Aidan giving me space to speak. I didn't.

"What's going on, sis?"

A soft laugh escaped me. I loved when he called me that. It gave me a place, a connection. I was about to tell him about the crazy visit I just had, but the words caught in my throat. What if that put him off wanting me to come live with him? He wouldn't want that weirdness around. He already had enough weirdness with me.

"Not much, just one of those days," I said instead.

"Yeah, I get that," he said. But he most certainly did not. "The voices are bad?"

"Yep," I said, popping the "p."

"What are they like?" he said after a pause.

I frowned. He normally steered away from asking about my psychosis.

"Sorry, you don't have to tell me," he blurted. "I mean, you've told me you can't really understand what they're saying. It's just... I read that they're meant to protect you. That they're created from trauma, or something."

I scoffed. *Protect me.* It sure didn't feel like that to live with them.

"Sorry," he muttered. "I shouldn't have asked."

"No," I exclaimed. "It's fine. Sorry, I didn't mean to laugh. I know that's what the doctors say, it just doesn't... it's kind of like a million people all trying to talk to me at once. Only, they're all talking over each other so I can't even really hear what they're saying."

Aidan murmured an affirmative, like he was interested, but still didn't quite get it.

I tried again. "It's like when you're trying to have a conversation with someone and they just keep mumbling, even though you say 'what?' and tell them to talk louder, or clearer, but they just keep on mumbling and you get more and more annoyed and then you give up and either shout or walk away."

"Oh," he said.

Now I was on a roll. "Only, I can't walk away. They're in my head. All. The. Time." I enunciated each word. "The pills help. They drown them out enough that it's just like annoying background noise. But every now and then, one will scream a random word, like someone's turned earphones up to full blast, just for that one word. I don't even know what the word is, sometimes. Sounds foreign, or just like, a partial word. *Super* annoying."

"Do you recognise any of them?" Aidan asked. "The voices?"

"Nope," I popped the "p" again. "Sometimes it's my own voice, but mostly, nah, don't know who they are."

"Oh," he said again. "I read that sometimes people hear the voice of someone they know."

"Yeah," I agreed. "Everyone hears different things. Some

31

people even have them just hurling abuse, all day, every day. Constantly being told they're not good enough or that they're a loser or whatever."

Like mine. I couldn't hear their exact words, sure, but I knew they were saying those same things under their breath. Why wouldn't they?

"Whoa," Aidan said quietly.

"Yep, some 'protection,' huh?"

My voices warbled, as if in protest.

"Yeah," he said, then went quiet.

A chill flushed through me, followed by a hot flash. My cheeks burned with instant regret. I'd said too much.

"What's new with you?" I asked peppily, now desperate to distract from my outburst.

"Not a whole lot," he said with renewed energy, clearly also very relieved to get off the topic of his sister being a complete psychopath. "Just been at work. There's a new checkout system that's been such a pain to learn. But I won't bore you with that," he laughed apologetically.

"No, no," I exclaimed. "Please do." Anything was better than here. Anything to distract from my too-much-information rant.

I heard the shrug on his end—maybe he could hear mine, too —before he started describing the issues he and his workmates had been having with the system. And he was right, it was boring as anything, but it was soothing to hear him speak. I closed my eyes and leaned against the carpeted interior of the telephone box, mumbling affirmatives in appropriate places in his story so he'd know I was still listening.

There was a murmur and shuffling noise behind him, and he cut himself off partway through a sentence. "Hey, I gotta go," he said apologetically.

"All good," I said, though a wave of longing flushed through me.

"Keep your chin up, eh sis? Not long now. Tuesday's the discharge meeting, right?"

"You got it," I said, smiling, and tried the words. "Love you."

I braced myself, always afraid they wouldn't be reciprocated. Especially now, thanks to my outburst.

My heart sang as they were.

"Love you too, sis."

CHAPTER
FIVE

LUNCH the next day was a delicious combination of reconstituted "meat" and fluffy, overcooked noodles, covered in what was meant to be a bolognese sauce. Nia and I had been a little late to lunch, thanks to the very important and timely need to continue drawing in the art room. Fortunately, that meant that most other people had already eaten, and the dining room wasn't quite so loud. It did mean that the already near unpalatable food was now also almost cold.

I poked at the so-called "meat." Nia spun her fork around and around, building up the courage to shovel noodles into her mouth. Some patients had theories that staff hid medication in their food, but I doubted it. It'd be a waste of medication. Meals like this made you question how hungry you really were.

A nursing assistant came to the door and called to me. "Elly is here to see you."

Nia squinted. "Who's Elly?"

"She's one of the people from yesterday," I said, widening my eyes. The one who hated me. Why would she come see me? Maybe she was going to rip into me for speaking to Rose like I had.

She clicked with her mouth and rolled her eyes. "Lena, you said you sent them away."

"I did, I swear." But I'd thought about phoning Rose... was this what they meant by "God works in mysterious ways"?

"See, this is what I'm saying." Nia thumped her index finger on the table twice. "Religion is no good. They don't take the hint. Get the nurse to tell them to go away."

"Yeah, true." I turned to the girl staff member in the doorway. "Can you tell her I'm not up for a visit, please?"

"Too nice," muttered Nia.

"She said she'd be quick, she just wanted to give you something," the girl replied.

Give me something? Give me what? My curiosity got the better of me. "Give me something" may mean a slap to the face, but I had to know. These people were the most interesting thing that had happened in this place for a long time, and it wasn't like it was going to get any weirder than "God has reincarnated as a seventeen-year-old girl and that's you. Oh, and you have a whole church dedicated to worshipping you."

At least, I figured it wouldn't.

I grimaced at Nia and squeezed my shoulders up into my neck apologetically. She audibly sighed when I stood up. Clearly the whole "don't tempt more crazy into your life" was for people with self-control.

I followed the nursing assistant to the side room, where Elly was already waiting. She stood up from the same seat Rose had been in yesterday, smiling genuinely at me this time. Maybe I had been imagining her attitude before. Or perhaps it was really the dress she hated—she was wearing a casual shirt and pants today, and appeared far more comfortable.

"Hey." Elly lifted her chin in a casual greeting, confidence oozing from her. She was completely different to yesterday— relaxed, casual—more herself. And in that moment, I wanted to be her. Even with the brainwashed, religious cult thing, she

36

would get to walk out of here free, leaving me behind, a prisoner in body and mind.

I returned a quiet greeting, intimidated by her, despite myself. "Hi. The nurse said you had something to give me?"

"Yeah." She glanced at the door I'd left open. "Can you get the door?"

I frowned, briefly considering whether I should shut off my only escape. She didn't seem like she was going to slap me after all, so I obliged. I turned back to see her lift something from her bag: a diary with a rotating combination. She flicked the latch and lifted the cover, showing me a phone and cable nestled in a hollow of cut-out pages. She closed the diary and held the hidden contraband out toward me, placing a small wall charger on top.

Elly lowered her voice. "I thought it was pretty unfair you weren't allowed phones in here, so I thought I'd bring one, in case you wanted it. It's new, but I set it up for you. It's already got credit and my number on it, and Rose's, in case you ever want to talk, or message, or whatever. I don't know if you want to risk the charger or not... I couldn't fit it inside, too, sorry."

My eyes fixed on the diary, as if I could see through it to the phone inside.

"Seriously?" I asked. "For me?"

She lifted it an inch, indicating again for me to take it. "If you want it."

I already had a phone. A crappy, old, cheap phone, with a cracked screen and terrible battery life. Despite being the proud owner of the hunk of junk, my rights to ownership had been stomped on and my phone currently resided, dead, in the safe in the nursing station. And living without a phone these days was worse than living without the sun.

"I want it," I whispered back. I reached out to receive this treasure, appreciating the extra weight of the diary. I hugged it to my chest. "Thank you."

"All good," she said, like this life-changing gift was nothing. "The code is 371. Anyway, that was all. I didn't want to take up too much of your time."

Oh, no, couldn't do that. Couldn't take up my very precious time.

"Honestly, you've earned a bit of time for this."

Elly laughed, then looked at me more seriously. "You know, we weren't kidding yesterday, about helping you get out of here."

My face dropped, along with my excitement about the phone. It was a trade. They'd only given me the phone so I'd join their religious cult and be their false god.

I wanted more than anything to get out of there. But it was only a few days until I was going to get to go live with Aidan, and live a normal life, as a normal girl. Nia had been right. I shouldn't have agreed to see Elly.

"I can't come live with you," I said as confidently as I could muster, even though my fleeting happiness was shattered from having to give up the phone. I forced my muscles to release their pressure on the diary against my chest, and held it out to Elly. "I'm going to live with my brother soon."

She held her hand out, rejecting my offer. "That's for you. I don't expect anything back for it."

I kept the diary hovering between us as I processed her words, trying to read any hidden agenda in her face.

Lies, voices whispered, so I knew it wasn't. If those voices didn't want me to believe her, it must be true. No strings, the phone was mine.

I pulled it back toward me, a little embarrassed I'd jumped to that conclusion. "Thanks," I muttered again, shyly.

"Don't sweat it," Elly said. "That's cool about your brother."

My mouth drew into a smile. It was cool. It was great, for me. Not so great for Elly and co, yet she did sound genuine.

"Anyway," Elly said. "I'll let you get back to whatever you were doing."

My definitely cold spaghetti bolognese.

"Sure, yeah," I said. "Thanks again for... you know."

Elly winked. "Any time. See you round, eh?"

"See ya," I muttered, still clutching the diary.

She stepped past me to the door, giving one last smile as she exited. I stood for a moment, processing, then shoved the charger into my pocket and rushed off to tell Nia about my gift.

CHAPTER
SIX

IT HAD BEEN A LONG YEAR, this week. And it wasn't even officially the weekend yet—there were still thirty-one minutes of Friday left. Thirty-one minutes and eleven hours left of the drone of a million prayers and the usual "what ifs": what if Aidan decided not to come? What if they didn't let him in? What if he got hurt on the way here, or he decided he didn't want to know me anymore?

None of those things had ever happened, but what if?

I slipped from the bed, the rough carpet spiking into my feet, all the little bacteria making their way into my skin and under it and into my blood stream and... this place was so gross. I balanced so I'd only have to take two steps to reach the wall-mounted piece of plywood that they called a desk. I grabbed my "diary" and backtracked, leaning backward into my steps. I launched myself back onto the bed so I could touch as little space on the carpet as possible. I probably should've chucked a blanket down by now, but that's the sort of genius thinking that only happened at twenty minutes to midnight.

I angled the lock to catch the light that shone obnoxiously through the window in my door. Scratch that, the peephole in my door. Three… seven, and… one. The latch flicked open easily. It was so flimsy that it would be easy to force open, if anyone felt like invading my privacy that much. Based on the mere existence of a peephole in my door, that sounded entirely plausible. But it was all I had for now, and a reasonable protection for this tiny, contraband treasure.

Life was so much better with a phone. Being able to play music would be even better—we could have it playing in the art room while Nia did her colouring. But we would for sure get busted. Then there was the wee issue of charging it, as well. All the power points were in public spaces, assumingly so we couldn't fry ourselves by fiddling with any in our room. I had yet to work out how to plug and charge the phone without drawing attention.

I bunched together my sheet and the other blankets that I'd kicked to the bottom of the bed, and pulled them up over my head. The sheets scratched at my skin, but sacrifices had to be made for the modern wonder of Technology. I flipped open the diary and blindly fumbled for the phone's power button. I pressed the screen against my leg while it booted up. It was on the lowest brightness setting, but it seemed to forget that while it was starting up. I tentatively tipped the phone to check it was ready for use.

Allie had indeed saved her phone number, and name, which is how I found out her name was spelled Allie instead of Elly. So, she wasn't named after Elizabeth after all. Maybe her name was Alison. Anyway. I'd flicked her a message the day before, thanking her again for the phone. She'd been good about it, saying it wasn't a problem and wishing me a good day, rather than trying to start up a conversation.

But lying in bed, only voices and what ifs for company, I was alone and bored. What was the harm in messaging her again, anyway? Her and Rose were being good now, leaving me be, not

42

trying to shove the whole "you're-our-saviour-and-you-need-to-come-with-us" thing down my throat. Lest I smite them.

LENA

Hey, you awake?

My thumb hovered over the button for a second, then clicked send. She probably wouldn't be awake at this time of night anyway. Almost midnight. The good little Christian—no, not Christian... what were they called?—churchy girl would be tucked up in her nice warm bed, after having a hot chocolate and cookies and saying her prayers like a good—

ALLIE

Just. What's up?

Well, how about that, I got her just in time. Now that she replied, I didn't really know what to say.

LENA

Nm just bored

Cool. Anything but that. Way to have a personality.

ALLIE

Ha, I'll bet.

Wanna play 20 questions?

Allie for sure wouldn't want to be friends once she got to know me. No one did, apart from Nia. At times I thought even Aidan only liked me because he had to. But twenty questions... it was a good way to break the ice.

LENA

Sure. Me first. What's your religion called?

> Followers of Mary. What do you want to be
> when you're older?

Whoa, right to the hard questions. I'd never really thought about having a career. I'd be happy waiting tables or pushing shopping trolleys if it meant I got out of here.

I switched out and hit up Google for the Followers of Mary. The Society of Mary popped up first, also known as Marianists, but that wasn't right. They must've paid premium to show up first, trying to get some more suckers to join, or maybe they were just more widespread. Wiki up next. That had a whole list of them, all these different religions following Mary, the Blessed Virgin, Holy Mother of Jesus Christ, amen. Most were run by old white dudes despite Jesus being Middle Eastern, much to the ignorance of most of his white followers, it seemed. Followers of Mary were about the sixth one down, and there were just a few paragraphs about them.

> *The Followers of Mary, established in 1632 in Rome, are a religious group with a unique and distinct belief system that centers around the figure of Mary, the mother of Jesus. This religious movement was founded by Sister Lucia Maddalena, a devoted follower of Mary.*
>
> *The Followers of Mary assert that Mary, as the mother of Jesus, was herself God incarnate and that she continues to incarnate in different forms to live among humanity. This divine incarnation is believed to be a source of guidance, wisdom, and spiritual connection for the Marians. Central to their worship is the veneration of Mary as the living God, and their practices include prayer, meditation, and communal gatherings where they seek spiritual enlightenment and communion with the divine.*
>
> *The Followers of Mary have historically had a notable rivalry with the Disciples of the Living Savior (Arabic: Talāmīḏ al-Mukhallaṣ al-Ḥay), a religious group founded in 1573. This opposing faction believes in the divinity of Jesus, asserting that he not only was God but continues to walk*

the earth in a divine form, which has led to theological disagreements and occasional conflicts between the two groups.

Well, there it was. They were real. And they'd been around for yonks. I'd never heard of them before they walked into my life, but then again, I hadn't heard of any of the others on that page, either. So many religions. So much fighting and war for it, when the majority of it all came back to the same thing—worship of a single divine being. Except for the pagan religions, of course, which by all accounts might actually be right and those new religions wrong. Or everyone was wrong, there was no afterlife, and we were all just going to rot down to nothing when we died. Or, I was God.

LENA

Nooo idea. What's your full name?

The minutes ticked by and no reply. It was past midnight. Good little Allie must have drifted off to sleep. My eyes burned from the harsh light. It was turned right down but... oh, it was because I hadn't been blinking. Who was the creep now? I rested the phone on my chest, checking now and again. It was a shame Allie was so mixed up in all this religious stuff, she really was quite cool.

Based on Nia's reaction the other day, I absolutely was not going to tell Aidan about the visit from Rose and co. Didn't need to give him any excuse to say I couldn't come live with him. Besides, Rose wasn't going to tell me anything more about my mum, so what was the point? Even if the whole "I am God" thing turned out to be true... *Nope! Don't buy into it, Lena. You're not the one they're waiting for. Even if you can make that lady almost fall on her face.*

CHAPTER
SEVEN

MY RAGGED, crumbly curtains started to show light through, so it must have been getting closer to morning meds time. For most people, light in the morning would mean it was the start of another wonderful day. Time to get up and shower and prepare to be a functioning human being. For me? Meds, then more sitting around.

At least the morning meds were required, rather than me asking for them. The phone had been helping distract me when the voices got really bad, but I'd still given in a few times and sought extra meds. Proving to everyone that I couldn't handle my emotions without them and so wasn't ready for discharge. Which, if we're being honest here in my head, I wasn't, no thanks to this fantastic, awful declaration that I was the master of the universe.

It would explain why the world was so messed up.

Not wanting to seem too eager, I hung out in my room and waited for the nurses to get around to my meds. Only, it took forever. Aidan would be there before they'd got to me, at that rate.

The door creaked open and my usual nurse peeked in, her blonde hair pulled back in a neat ponytail.

"Good morning, Alena," she said, too brightly.

"Morning!" I sang back as cheerily as I could muster, with a forced smile. At least the smile was a little genuine—it was meds time! If only they would work well enough to shut the voices up forever.

She handed me the little white cup and another paper cup of water. The medicine would work. It had to work. Whatever I believed was what would happen, right?

The nurse eyed me dubiously. "Are you sure you're up for a visit today? We can always reschedule if you're not feeling well."

I shook my head, panic creeping in. "No, I'm fine. Really."

After another long look, she said, "Alright, your brother will be here soon."

"Okay, thanks." I downed the meds and put my mouth on display, then headed off toward Nia's room. The nurse stayed hovering in the hallway, watching me. That was new.

On the way to her room, I spotted Nia in the courtyard. It'd be nice to get some fresh air, and even a bit of sun, though it was overcast. Never mind all the spit, coffee spills and rubbish all over the ground, and the tall, barred fence that made it feel like you were in prison.

Hey, we basically were in prison. I mean, most of us were here against our will, even if we said the treatment was helping us. We'd all learned to play the game, do what the doctors told us to do, say what the doctors wanted us to say, be good little psych patients until they finally let us out those locked double doors.

Nia was sitting on one of the wooden benches next to a new girl who'd rejected my attempts to be nice the other day. I'd learned her name was Amy, after Nia had managed to pull her from her shell. Nia was better at that stuff than me. Better at relating, and caring. People just seemed to relax around her. The voices shrilled, informing me I had the opposite effect, as if I hadn't clicked onto that myself.

The grass that separated the concrete from the fence was still wet from morning dew. A boy kicked a pebble around the concrete pad, his hands shoved in his pockets. The people in here were just like me, all of us broken in our own way. Hey, even a few of us were God!

Nia and Amy moved over, making room for me next to my friend. Concern was etched into Nia's delicate features. "You alright?"

I sank onto the bench beside her, staring at the concrete path. "Yep!" I lied. *When was I ever alright?*

"When's Aidan getting here?"

"Eleven. It takes a couple of hours from his."

"That's gonna be so far when you get out of here," Nia said sadly. Would she even want to hang out when we were both free? "But I'm happy for you. It's almost here!" she squealed, and put her arm around my shoulder.

"Yeah." I held the hand she draped over my shoulder, and swayed with her. "A few more days until we find out when."

Nia and Amy returned to their meaningless chatter, and I joined in to waste the time away. The sun broke through the clouds and evaporated the dew on the grass. I kept checking the doorway, waiting and hoping Aidan was going to walk through, despite it being way too early.

The shadows changed direction on the path. I felt eyes on me and my body started to jump up before I even confirmed whose eyes they were. It was the same nurse from this morning, watching me again from the corridor. Creep-o.

Then Aidan appeared behind her. My male-version doppel-ganger, without a doubt my brother. I ran to him and jumped into his arms.

"Hey, sis."

Oh, how my heart beamed.

"Hey, bro," I said coolly, the massive grin on my face, and the fact I'd just sprinted across the courtyard in public and jumped into his arms, deceiving my cool, calm and collected tone.

"Hi, Nia," Aidan called out, and Nia waved back. He turned back to me and spoke more quietly. "I've got burgers, but only enough for us. You wanna stay out here or go eat?"

I rolled my lips in on each other and made my eyes wide, before grabbing his hand and dragging him inside. He pointed me to the meeting room on the right, with the door pulled to. We went in, the room already filled with the delicious smell of diabetes in a wrapper. I shut the door to lock the smells in and the people out.

The burger was just as delicious as it smelled, despite being a bit cold. Anything was delicious after the food in here. We chatted about random stuff between and during mouthfuls, laughing heartily, turning our burgers into see-food, no shame between us. TV shows, news, opinions on the weather and people, stories about Aidan's work and flatmates. It felt so *normal.*

"... and so my flatmate Ryan—you'll meet him—he ends up just ripping the smoke alarm off the roof and just stomping it, but it still wouldn't shut up! Till we got the battery out." Aidan sighed as I recovered from laughing. He took a sip from his drink. "You still want to come stay, right?"

"Oh my God, yes! Are you kidding?" My eyes were wide and my hands flailed like a lunatic.

He grinned. "Little bit."

I threw a french fry at him. He didn't bother dodging it.

"My review's on Tuesday, so I should know then when I can come. If it works for you, anyway."

"Yeah, course! Anytime, you know that."

I beamed, but then the brightness in his eyes faded and a

shadow crossed his face. He broke eye contact and dropped his face toward the floor.

"I... um..."

Oh, no. Here it was. Turns out I couldn't stay with him, or not for long, or he was moving, or there was some condition attached.

He cleared his throat. "James left me a message again."

Fire hit my skin and an army ran into battle in my mind. How did he even have the nerve, after what he'd done? The fire must've been evident in my face, because Aidan continued when he finally looked up.

"I thought you should know," he said quietly.

"What did he say?" I asked, squeezing my hands together, fingers interlocked. My knuckles ached as they pressed into each other.

"He wanted to explain—"

I scoffed. "Explain? Explain why he tried to *kill* me? That should be good."

"I know, there's no excuse. But don't you want to know?"

I did. I wanted to know, almost more than anything. But it wouldn't change the past, and I hated him for it. For ruining my life. For stealing all those years with my family away from me. For stealing the surname "Williams" from me, and estranging me from my brother. For condemning me to this life instead.

I shook my head as my eyes blurred from tears. I tried to shake fast enough to stop them building, but I couldn't. I wiped them away with the back of my hand instead.

"Well, what did he say?" I asked.

"I haven't answered him. I'm kinda not ready yet."

My protector Aidan was vulnerable, too. Of course it would have hurt him as well. Maybe even more, to find out your own father had lied to you for your entire life. Well, not *more* than what I'd been through, but different, and just as bad.

"Okay," I said, believing he would know that the single word also meant, "I understand, I trust you, take as long as you need."

"Yeah. Just thought you should know," he repeated.

"Thanks," I said. We sat silently for a while, the happiness sucked from the room by the black void that was our father. If I ever saw that man again, he would have to hope to me I wasn't God.

CHAPTER
EIGHT

TUESDAY. D-Day. Dooms Day... is that what that stood for? Dooms Day, Decision Day, either of those worked for me. I readjusted my grip on my interlocked fingers, grimacing at the clamminess. The air in the lounge was more stale than usual, though maybe that was just me, since the roof seemed lower, too. I didn't even have the good couch to sit on while I patiently waited for someone else to determine what was going to happen in my life.

Patience, patience. Like a good little psych patient, who did exactly what the doctor said, took her meds religiously, blocked out all the voices and strange happenings since they were just symptoms of a mis-wired brain. A good little psych patient who certainly never snuck contraband or bought into religious nutjobs who claimed she was God.

I stared blankly at the TV, trying to concentrate on it, but I was well and truly in my mind. Ha, that was a change from being out of my mind.

The girl on the good couch glared at me and I shrunk down as I realised I'd laughed out loud at my own joke. I looked behind me through the glass wall to check if any staff were watching me, ready to report back to the doctors about any little thing I did. They were milling about in their enclosure, pretending to be busier than they were. All paperwork, no time to spend with patients. They probably liked it that way.

This really was a test of patience. They'd said I'd be reviewed today, but no exact time when. Just wait around, possibly all day, going over and over the possibilities. It would drive even a sane person crazy. Maybe that was the game—it was some sick and weird business model where they'd recruit not-yet-crazy people into the hospital, tell them they were mad, then slowly drive them insane with all the waiting and meds and boredom. I mean, how do you convince someone you're not crazy?

Six months and ten days I'd been here, and that was this time around. They'd hooked me into this wacky "we'll drive you crazy" scheme nice and young, forever tainting my medical record to be "psych patient." Oh, you're feeling anxious about exams? That's because you're unwell. Back to the hospital you go! You're sad your mum died? Better admit you before you become an axe murderer. You broke your arm? No, no, that's just the psychosis talking.

This grand scheme would definitely be mixed in with the pharmaceutical companies, with how many drugs they pumped into us. God knows what it was doing to our systems—I'd seen some long-term antipsychotic users and I would much rather be snuffed out nice and early than end up like that, bent over from muscle spasms, barely able to speak, droopy eyes and forever bloated and constipated.

But I would tell the doctors that I would take the meds—of course I would, they made me better, just like they said. Besides, Aidan would make sure I took the meds, and I would get followed up diligently by the community mental health services, so nothing at all to worry about.

Now to convince them of that. To persuade them to discharge

me this week. Or, if not this week, then let me go home to Aidan for the weekend and discharge me next week. Just please, God, get me out of here.

Get me out of here. The words echoed in my mind. But no, no, nothing to worry about—hearing your own voice was just your internal monologue. A sharp pain screamed from my left thumbnail and I glanced down to see I'd picked the edge of it until it bled. I stuck my thumb in my mouth and sucked. The metallic taste was like my sleeping pills—how messed up was that? Pills that remind you of drinking blood. There's another checkmark for the "we'll drive you crazy" theory.

The blonde nurse with the ponytail peeked into the room, her eyes meeting mine. She'd barely called my name before I bounded off the couch. The room swam and I slowed to right myself, hoping she hadn't noticed. Either she hadn't noticed or didn't care, because she just turned around and headed for the meeting room. I picked up pace when the room came back into focus.

The nurse held the meeting room door open for me, then followed me inside. The doctors were already seated and didn't bother standing to greet me. They both wore their practised smiles; Dr Johnson with his balding head and thick glasses, and Dr Lee with her dark hair pulled back into a bun so tight it was like she was trying to give herself a facelift. I took my seat, as was expected, good little psych patient. The nurse closed the door and seated herself closest to it. *Never let a psych patient get between you and your exit, huh nursey?*

"Alena, how are you today?" Dr Johnson asked.

I plastered on my smile. "Good, thank y—"

"Good," he cut in, not giving a toss how I really felt. "And how have the voices been? Any better?"

My hope sank. They'd already decided what was going to happen to me. This meeting wouldn't make the outcome any better, it could only make it worse. I held my cheerful mask.

Bright, happy Lena, the meds were doing so well, thank you so much mister doctor.

"Heaps better. The meds really helped, you were right," I lied.

"Great. It's very important that you keep taking the medications, even when you leave," Dr Johnson said.

Hope swelled in my chest, and my enthusiasm became genuine. *When I leave?* "Yes, of course I will, definitely. I'm really looking forward to go—"

"And how about controlling things with your mind?"

I laughed. "No, I know that's so silly. I can't believe I ever thought that, act—"

"Good, that's good," Dr Johnson cut in again, clearly liking the sound of his own voice more than mine.

Dr Lee glanced down at her hands. There was a shift in the room, like a storm was brewing outside.

"So," Dr Johnson continued. "Why is it you're needing so many PRN medications, Alena?" He fixed his eyes on mine, baring into my soul, trying to bubble my crazy to the top, or maybe plant some of his own crazy in there.

The hope in my chest dropped away, a pain growing near my heart from this rollercoaster of emotions. "I... I'm not," I stammered.

"Your medication chart shows that you were using almost all of the available medication last week," Dr Johnson pressed.

Damn. I knew that would look bad. Why couldn't I have more self-control? I dropped my eyes, trying to hide the tears that were threatening to flow.

"I've been... that was last week. I've been trying to cut down, to get ready for discharge. It's just really boring in here." I fiddled with my fingers before remembering that looking away was a sign of lying. I made direct eye contact with Dr Johnson, even though the tears were brimming.

"So you're taking extra PRN because you're bored, not

because you're hearing voices?" He peered at me over the rim of his glasses, eyebrows arched.

I dropped my head to the side. "Yes, I know I shouldn't, so I stopped having so much." *With every ounce of self-control I had.*

Dr Lee was looking at her hands again. Dr Johnson spoke. "You know you can tell us the truth, right Alena? We only want what's best for you."

Lies. I couldn't tell them anything, except what they wanted to hear. How would they ever know what was best for me? They didn't even use the name I wanted.

"Yes, of course. Everyone's been so helpful," I said as confidently as I could. I released my hands that had been clasped together, and blood started to return. I wedged them between my thighs to hide the whiteness.

Dr Lee glanced up.

"That's good to hear, Alena," Dr Johnson continued. "I'm glad you feel that way. We think it's best that you stay here a while longer, until we can get your medication right, and find you an appropriate place to live."

The sharp pain in my chest hit so hard that I gasped and had to lean on my knees. The wind was knocked out of me. That was what it was like to have a heart attack. I was going to die in there.

No. It was panic trying to take hold.

Get it together, Lena.

Breathe. Breathe.

"Alena?" Dr Johnson's voice had a pitch to it that actually sounded a bit like concern. Or pity.

I raised my eyes directly to his, and as calmly as I could, said, "But I'm going to stay with my brother." *Believe it, Lena. Make it happen.*

Dr Johnson shook his head sadly, his face trying to reflect that too, and instead just showing pity. How dare he feel sorry for me, for something that was his doing.

"A flatting situation is not ideal. Your brother means well, but we have a responsibility to make sure you're looked after. And think, it's a lot of responsibility for your brother to take on, too, when he's so young himself."

I'm a burden, he meant. He thought I didn't know that? That I didn't feel that every second of every day? But I needed out of here, I needed a normal life. And Aidan was family, and he was safe, and he was willing.

"I'm better now. I'll be good," I said, my voice cracking.

"I know you think that, Alena." More false sympathy.

I crushed my inner lip between my teeth. The room started to sway. If I had a God power, now was the time to use it. I stared at him, my brow furrowed.

Let me go, I said in my mind, sending it to his. *Let me go!*

He sat back stiffly. *Oh my God, had that worked?*

"Now, the other problem is," he said. "We're concerned you haven't been taking your medication."

Not what I expected, and certainly not what I'd commanded.

"What?" I snapped. "You literally check my mouth when I take them."

"Yes," Dr Johnson said, flashing a look at the nurse. "But because of your continued symptoms—"

"I said I don't hear voices anymore."

"I know that's what you said." Dr Johnson's lips met in a thin line. Pity. Again. "But we're worried you're not being entirely truthful—"

"I am!" I lied again.

"—so we are going to start you on an injection."

I felt the blood drain from my face. Drain further, seep out of me, gush out of me for all I cared. Give me a quick and painless death, not the torture of getting injected, having that poison forced inside me, living in me, burning my muscles and my blood, leeching what personality and life I had left, taking the only thing that was truly mine: me.

No, please, not an injection.

Say it out loud, Lena, you have to stop this.

"You'll get the first one today," Dr Johnson said, "and the next in a week."

His voice was fuzzy, muffled. He tipped his head toward the nurse. I turned to her, all in slow motion, as if underwater. She stood and exited the room. The door opened and nearly fell off its hinges. No, it swung back. No, it was still; it was the room that was swaying. Or I was swaying. I gripped the edge of the couch, bending my fingernails back. Blood flooded my mouth. A crowd roared in my mind, ready for a show.

My lungs filled with air—more air than they should. They burned. I pushed the air out, and my lungs yanked it right back in. I pushed again, this time using my hand against my chest. The blood returned to my face, only now it was hot, returning from hell to burn and take me with it. Salt water covered my lips, and another tangy taste. I wiped the back of my hand across my face, tears and snot smearing onto my cheek.

Someone was calling my name. I leaned forward. I had to get out. Hands grabbed me. I shook them off and almost fell, even though I was already doubled over. *Legs, take me.*

I stumbled from the room, breaths coming short and quick, never exchanging enough air for what I needed to live. I was going to die, just like I thought, I was going to die in here. But not in years, and not from the injection. I was going to die right here and now.

Hands on me again. I tried to shake them off, but they held fast, bending my bones. They lifted me, and I could see outside. I stumbled toward the false freedom of the courtyard, and the hands let me. Cold air hit my face, teased my lungs.

Then there was Nia, right in front of me. I fell onto her, and she caught me.

"It's okay, it's okay," she soothed. We turned and walked, her supporting me, my face buried in her shoulder, covering her neck and sleeve in tears and snot. But still, she supported me.

"Come, sit," she repeated, until her support fell away and I registered what she was saying. The grass spiked my legs and arms, but I could breathe more. I rested my head in Nia's lap, she stroked my hair, and I cried and cried.

CHAPTER
NINE

WE SAT in silence until my breath came under control, besides the occasional hitch. Nia's sweatpants were saturated from my tears. My eyes burned, both from the tears and the air, as I stared straight ahead, the deep green of the flax bushes that edged the building helping to trick me into thinking I wasn't entirely a caged rat.

"I have to get out of here," I said, not breaking eye contact with the flax.

"I know," Nia whispered, still stroking my hair.

I turned to her face above me. "I'm serious. I can't let them inject me."

She pressed her lips together. I turned away in disgust. It was the same look as what Dr Johnson had given me—pity.

"Are you gonna call Aidan?" Nia asked.

Yes. Of course. I had to tell him what was happening. Maybe he could stop it, since he was meant to be my caregiver now. Or my next of kin, whatever the term was. He was meant to get a say in my treatment. I sat up, and the world spun a little.

"Careful, go slow," Nia said, then stood up and held a hand out. "Here."

She helped me up slowly, giving my blood time to go where it needed to. I brushed the grass off my legs and the seat of my pants, and Nia helped me with my back. She did her pants, and we made our way back to the concrete pad and across the court-yard toward the door.

The blonde nurse came up from the corridor, a male nurse assistant in tow. And a cardboard container in her hand. That too-familiar feeling of blood leaving my head hit me again.

"Alena," she called. "It's time for your injection."

"I want to call my brother," I said, my voice breaking.

"You can call him after."

"No, now." I stood straight, but my voice deceived me by cracking again.

"That's not how this works," the nurse said. I was sure her slight smile was smug.

"Why not?" Nia piped up. It made me stand straighter still. My wee protector. I wasn't alone.

The nurse sighed. She glanced at Nia briefly, then back at me. "Because. Are you going to do this the easy way, or the hard way?"

"I want to call Aidan," I said again, firmly now, with no break.

The nurse sighed again. "Guess it's the hard way." She glanced at the nurse assistant, and they both entered the safety of the nursing station. Most of the staff were in there, including the doctors, milling about, laughing. Laughing at me, no doubt. Sick, they enjoyed this. Playing with people's lives, like we were their own personal playthings. They'd run in there to hide and laugh at us crazy patients, as if we were the dangerous ones. Really, they were the predators.

I marched up and knocked on the nursing station door four times, trying to make eye contact with someone in there. A couple of them glanced at me, then looked away again, back at the other staff. That division of power. They knew exactly what I wanted. It wasn't hard to give it to me, but they wanted to show me that I was under their rule. I kicked the bottom of the door and turned back to Nia.

"They're not gonna let me," I said. "I'm gonna just phone him."

Nia frowned. "But they might see you."

"I don't even care right now." I marched past her toward my room. "I need to talk to him. He'll stop this."

The nursing station door opened behind me. I glanced over my shoulder as four or five staff exited, the blonde nurse in front, container still in hand. I turned to face them but kept backing away. Nia joined my side, then stood in front.

"Stay away from me," I snarled. Snarled is the right word—I was ready to bite.

"Alena, don't make this worse than it has to be," Blondy said. They advanced on me like a pack of wolves. Their five, with three big guys, versus our two little seventeen-year-old girls. Fair fight. How dare they come at me like that, threatening like that. They caused more trauma than any illness itself.

"Last chance," my own personal demon said. "Come with me, or we'll have to make you."

I told her to go Chapter 39 herself. She flicked her head toward me, and her pack descended. Sweet Nia stretched her arms out, trying to block access to me, but the guys swatted her away like a fly. Like the pests they thought we were.

I flailed out, whipping my arms in a frenzy to stop from being caught, trying to run backwards at the same time, aware there was nowhere to go.

"Get off me!" I screamed.

Nia repeated it.

"You can't do this!" I cried.

Nia echoed me.

They grabbed me, squeezing my arms so tight I was sure they'd snap a bone. I cried out in pain, but they didn't loosen their grip. I kicked out and connected with something. Their grip tightened and they started yelling, too. More people swarmed me, and something wrapped around my legs, crushing my ankles. I screamed, again from pain. I begged them to stop. There was so much screaming, now. Where was Nia? My hair hung in my face, sticking to it from my tears. Oh, God, that crushing pain. How could bones hurt that much? Please, God, stop, make them stop.

My voice reverberated through my mind. *Make them stop.*

The world flipped, but the pressure remained. No, I flipped. They were carrying me. I struggled, I screamed, but I couldn't shake them free. My top caught against my captor and twisted, bunching and cutting into me. It cut at my underarms, my neck. A coldness hit my belly and I realised it was exposed. How much other skin was showing? I cried deeper, begged for them to leave me alone.

We passed through a door and I clawed out, desperately trying to grab the doorframe. I got it for just a moment before my fingers were prised off and I was forced through to nothingness, except a fluorescent light screaming down into my eyes from above.

They were talking, but I couldn't register what was said. Then they were tipping me again, righting my helpless body. My feet touched the floor for just a moment before they were pulled backwards and I was going over, too far over. They threw me sideways and a bed rushed at my face. I braced for impact, pulling my face back and to the side just too late to stop my nose crunching into the mattress. My chest and body were pushed into the mattress and pressure, still pressure, on each of my limbs, pressing down into the bed. My bones ached, my ankles screamed. I screamed and begged and sobbed with them.

Then my pants were pulled down and I had the horrifying realisation that it was men on me, they were all in it together, the girls here too. This was all a ploy to hold me down and do what they wanted and no one would believe me because I was crazy.

A searing pain hit my buttock and shot outwards in every direction as what must have been a needle plunged down and ripped open my skin. The force with which it came down made the pain even worse, the pressure sending the needle deeper and intensifying the sting. The poison was cold and burned at the same time as it forced its way into my body, killing everything in its path.

The needle was ripped out, repeating its sting as it pulled on my skin and brought that poison out with it, burning through every layer of flesh. I felt what must have been a plaster get stuck over it, then my pants got pulled up awkwardly and the pressure on my body released.

Muffled talking again. Indecipherable in my now hazy reality. The fight drained out of me as a wave of defeat washed over my life. There was no escape from this place. From the needles, the drugs, the haze that would steal away all my sense of self. A tear slid down and over the bridge of my nose, dripping onto the pillow beneath me.

The doctors had won. Lena was gone.

CHAPTER
TEN

I LAY motionless on the bed, staring at nothing. Time passed in a haze, minutes blurring into hours blurring into seconds. I felt nothing, thought nothing. Just existed, along with the beehive drone in my head.

"Time for dinner, Alena," someone called. They were in the room. I didn't move, didn't speak. What was the point? The food all tasted the same, a mush of nothing that filled the void where my appetite should be. A frustrated sigh, then a click as the door shut again.

A familiar desk came into focus. I was in my room. I curled into a ball on my bed, clutching my arms to my chest. My buttock ached and bruises were forming on my arms and ankles.

More time passed. The light from the window faded into dusk, then darkness. Still I lay motionless, as unchanging as stone. I was no one, felt nothing, wanted nothing.

A nurse breezed into the room. "Alena, time for your medication." She rattled the pills in the small paper cup. I didn't react. I stared at the blank wall in front of me, my gaze empty and lifeless.

"Alena," the nurse said again in a sing-song voice. I ignored her. "Alena? Can you hear me?" Frustration entered her tone. She marched over and snapped her fingers in front of my face. I blinked, the only indication I was even conscious.

The nurse tapped her foot impatiently. "Come on, Alena. You know the rules."

Rules. There were always so many rules here, controlling my every move. Telling me where to be, what to eat, when to sleep. Stripping away my dignity and free will piece by piece. I continued to ignore her. I just stared at that same spot on the white wall in front of me. What little control I had left—they had stripped the rest from me.

The nurse's tone grew more frustrated. "Alena, don't do this again. Just take the medication and I'll leave you alone." *Until the next time.*

"Get out," I said through gritted teeth. Rage cleared my mind, making me acutely aware of her unwelcome presence.

"You need to take—"

"Get out before I scream."

She hesitated, then backed toward the door. "I'll have to come back with a team again if you don't take it."

Good. Do it then. Hold me down and jab me with your poison. If you want to do it, you're gonna do it. You like doing it, I bet. Sadists, all of you.

"Fine, have it your way," she said, before turning to leave. "But this is just going to make it worse for you."

The door clicked shut behind her, leaving me alone with my now racing thoughts. They would be back, to violate me again. Maybe I should fight, see if I couldn't hurt one of them like they were hurting me. Give them a taste of their own medicine.

I shuddered. Who even was I? That was not something I wanted or wished upon anyone, but for that moment I truly did want to hurt them like they hurt me, so they'd know what they were doing. An eye for an eye. But that made the whole world blind. And it wasn't me—what were they turning me into here? Not just taking my freedom, my dignity, but my entire identity.

I shuddered as I thought back to the first time I'd ever been restrained for medication. The time that should've taught me that fighting was futile. But that was for pills, not for an injection like this. That time, I had been so young, too tiny to give any real fight back.

My foster mother had held me down on the ground, trying to get control of my flailing arms and legs as I tried to wriggle free. Even though I was tiny, she couldn't do it all by herself. Controlling four flailing limbs while simultaneously trying to stuff a pill in my mouth and make me swallow was too much for just one person. My foster father had stepped in, his rough hands huge against my skinny arms and jaw, the force and pain he'd inflicted enough to make me give in, to allow the pill into my mouth, just to make him stop.

I swallowed it, too, but that wasn't good enough. I'd angered him, and he'd gripped my nose closed, nearly breaking it with the pressure. He'd held his other hand over my mouth, trying to make me swallow, or something more sinister. I couldn't breathe, even after I'd swallowed. I'd started struggling again, which he must've processed as me fighting to not take the pill, and he'd just gripped tighter.

I remember the pressure rising in my head, behind my eyes, and then, even then, the voices swelled in my mind, welcoming me home. Welcoming me to death.

Then he'd let go, and I'd sucked air into my burning lungs, and sobbed and cried as the voices mourned the loss of their grip on my soul.

I hated those pills, ever since then, but got far more crafty in hiding my not taking them. The little white and pink ones were good, though. They dulled the world and my voices in a way the other ones didn't. With them, it was like I could float through life, almost without a care in the world, if I took enough. The other ones, the antipsychotics, they made me lose a piece of myself—the one piece I actually liked, that gave the world its colour. But that was the one I had to have, lest they inject it directly into my blood. Their poison, that stole the vibrance from the world, along with any sense of hope or joy. But hey, at least then I was under their control.

I had to get out of here. And the doctors weren't going to let me. They wanted to keep me here for God knew how long. To keep me and inject me over and over. The next injection was in a week. That was, if they didn't bring another one now and do it all over. But the long-term medication, the doctor had said I needed a second one in a week. I had to get out before that. The sooner the better.

Or maybe Aidan could convince them that I shouldn't have the injection, and that I should go and live with him...

But no, they had decided, and their word stuck. When it was something bad, anyway. Clearly their word didn't count for anything when it came to things I wanted, like living with Aidan. They'd never actually promised it, just that they'd look into it. It had just sounded so promising, since Aidan wanted me.

He actually wanted me.

Would he still, after all this? After he heard I refused my treatment? Surely he'd understand. He didn't know what it was like in here, but surely he could understand not wanting to get injected. Anyone could. And he'd realise that I couldn't stay here any longer. Not to wait for another injection, not when living with him had been my only light at the end of a very long, cold, and damp tunnel. I'd escape and go to him, and we could live together after all. I might have to hide for a while, but he would help me.

I groaned internally. It wasn't like it was easy to escape. They literally locked all the exit doors and you had to have a swipe card to get out. I could try to steal a card or push past someone, but they'd know straight away that I was trying to escape, and I

70

wouldn't get far. They'd probably end up transferring me to the high security unit after that, too.

I closed my eyes, imagining the layout of the unit. My room was in the middle of a row of four, with a mirror image on the other side of the hallway. There were double doors between here and the nursing station, but they always stayed open. There was basically no cover, apart from the reading nook by the courtyard, and the short, angled walls that each bedroom door opened onto. The courtyard had a couple of doors this side of the nursing station, but they were locked before it got dark. Maybe I could try to jam them somehow so it wouldn't lock, so I could get out at night and climb the fence.

I scoffed out loud. *Climb the four-metre-high fence that was just straight bars, okay Lena. Funny.*

But others had before. I'd heard about it. They usually got a leg-up from someone, and then either went straight over or up onto the roof to get out the front. That would be a pretty big drop to get off the roof, though. Actually, it was a pretty big drop either way, but I'd rather chance it with the fence. At least that was down onto grass.

So, I needed help with this. Nia would help me, if she could, if she was strong enough to be able to help me up. And actually, the other people who'd escaped did it while the yard was open through the day. They'd timed it right, in between getting checked on, and when staff weren't around.

And when they'd failed, they'd been locked up in the high security unit for weeks. "High care," the staff called that part of the ward, even though it was anything *but* caring. Those poor people would've been dosed on heaps more meds until they were broken down and compliant again.

But the risk was worth it. Freedom was worth it. Getting away from this place, this life, was worth any price. And I had to, before they forced that poison into me again.

I took a deep breath, steadying my nerves. One week. I had

less than a week to figure out how to get over the fence. I had one week to prepare, to time the rounds and find the perfect moment to make a run for it. In one week, I'd be free.

When the door clicked open again, I didn't react. Not until a familiar voice called my name.

"Lena? I brought you—oh, God, what did they do to you?"

I gasped and sat up. Nia put a bowl of something on my desk then rushed over and threw herself onto me in a bear hug.

"I'm so sorry," she said, squeezing my aching body. "I tried to stop them."

I know, I tried to say. And then I cried. I couldn't hold it. My anger gave way to grief, to sadness and sorrow, all for myself and what had happened. How quickly my world had shifted from everything going on the up, to it all being ripped away from me with a simple command from the doctors. I pulled my head into Nia's arm and she tucked herself around me in response. There I lay, I don't know for how long, my sobs eventually subsiding, though the tears continued to fall.

"I have to get out of here," I finally said, quietly.

"I know," Nia said.

I looked at her. "No, I mean I'm going to escape."

Her eyebrows drew together in concern or confusion.

"Over the fence," I continued.

Nia sighed and looked at me sadly. "Lena—"

"You know what they did, Nia!" I shouted, without really meaning to. I was in it now. "Don't try stop me!"

She shook her head vigorously, drawing back in surprise at me raising my voice to her. "No, I didn't mean that—"

"I have to get out." I cut her off again.

"I know," she said reassuringly. "But the fence?"

"Others have." I sniffed and glanced down at the filthy, stained carpet. "I don't know what else. I can't get through the doors without getting noticed."

Nia sighed again and turned away, thinking. "I just don't want you getting hurt."

I smiled internally, but it didn't transfer to my face. Then panic swept over me. "You won't tell anyone, right?"

"I won't tell." She squeezed my arm. It tightened against a bruise and I winced, but appreciated the sentiment.

CHAPTER
ELEVEN

IT WAS the next day before I could face anyone else. The nurse had come back with the team the night before, as promised, with a final option of pills or injection. I took the pills.

I was still feeling the effects of the struggle from the day before, unless they'd also been slipping extra meds in my night and morning doses. My head was floaty, my body dizzy—or was it the other way around? I stumbled a little making it to the dining room, every muscle and joint aching, but no one seemed to care. Just the same old in this place, dealing in making everyone zombies.

The soup Nia had brought last night was barely enough to sustain me. I think it had actually made it worse. I hadn't been hungry until I had it, then was even more hungry after, despite at the same time not really having an appetite.

I requested a massive bowl of porridge, but only got a standard size, meaning I'd have to go back twice. I winced at every step I took, and at the pressure on my buttock and thighs as I sat down. I rearranged as best I could, and ended up perched half off the chair. Even bringing the spoon to my mouth was a struggle.

Nia brought my second bowl of porridge to me, being the good friend that she was. Maybe she still felt guilty she couldn't stop them the day before.

"Alena," a nurse called from the doorway. I ignored her and glanced at Nia through my eyelashes, my head down. Let her come and speak to me like a human being instead of calling me like a dog. "Your brother is on the phone."

I dropped the spoon into my bowl and threw the chair back, grimacing through the pain. I headed for the phone booth and was well prepared to push past the witch, but she moved out of the doorway. I leaned on the carpet wall of the phone booth, winced, and stood up straight instead, waiting for the scream of the phone when they connected us. I yanked the receiver up with barely a blip.

"Hello?" I said.

"Lena?" There was instant concern in Aidan's voice. "Are you okay?"

I thought my speech was clear, but my world started to swim, so maybe not. I murmured agreeance to his question, despite being far from okay. Still, the pills made everything matter less.

"You don't sound it." He waited for me to say something else. I didn't. "How'd it go yesterday? Did they say when you can come home?" Aidan continued. "I called last night but they said you were sleeping."

It all came flashing back. I pressed my eyes shut as the emotions welled up past the pills.

"I can't—" I started, my voice catching in my throat as I sucked in a sob.

"Can't what?" Concern was evident in his voice.

"They're not gonna let me live with you." I bit my lip to try to stop it from quivering. I failed.

"What? Why not?"

I shrugged—at least, I intended to. I don't know if my body actually did. My teeth pressed down until the taste of blood filled my mouth, a welcome distraction from the poisonous thoughts.

"Did they say why?" Aidan tried again, unable to see my non-existent shrug.

"No," I said sullenly.

"I don't get it, it was all set."

Could he be acting right now? He might have had something to do with me not going to live with him. Maybe he didn't really want me after all and this was all a big plot so that he could save face. I wanted to ask, but I didn't want the answer. My mind continued to replay the day, and my buttock ached in response.

"They injected me," I said flatly.

I heard Aidan take a sharp breath. Then the emotions caught up to the thoughts and words and started to overtake me again. My face burned with shame at my situation. I was so damaged.

"Oh, God, Lena." The concern in his voice made my breaths catch even harder. They hurt in my throat as I tried—and failed —to control them. Always a failure, couldn't even control my own breathing.

"Lena, listen to me," Aidan said firmly. "We'll sort this out, okay?"

He almost convinced me, he sounded so sure. But he meant he'd sort it through the system, through the doctors. He meant he'd talk to them. I couldn't trust that anymore. The staff here could do whatever they wanted. Who would stop them? Not Aidan. Not me or the other patients or staff. No one ever stopped them before.

And I suddenly realised I couldn't tell him my plan to escape, either. He'd try to stop me, worried that it would make things worse for me. All I did instead was whisper a little "okay" in agreement. Placate him enough so he didn't worry. I just had to get out and to him and then everything would be okay. Once I was out, and there at home with him, then we could make a new plan, together. But for now, I'd have to make it out on my own.

Well, me and Nia. Or maybe… Rose wouldn't have any kind of pull in the system either, but I would need a way to get to Aidan's without him getting suspicious. Maybe Rose and Allie could help with that.

I cut my phone call with Aidan short. I didn't like lying to him any more than I had to, and there was a weight on me that whole conversation. It could've just been my literal weight on every achy bone, but it felt like a metaphorical one as well.

Nia was still waiting for me in the dining room. After we ate, I took her hand and we went outside to sit on the tiny lawn again, the blades of grass cutting into my arms as I lay down, staring at the fence and roof. The fence wasn't that high—I could do it, with some help.

"No," Nia whispered. "Not the fence."

I dropped my head to the side and looked at her, narrowing my eyes at her ability to read my mind. I pushed my bottom lip out into a little pout.

She nudged me playfully. "I don't want you getting hurt."

I raised one shoulder. "It's probably worth the risk."

"No, Lena," Nia reiterated.

"What then? Can't steal a swipe card," I said. "Too risky. Even if I did get hold of one, they'd know straight away." We'd considered that before, back when escape was just a fantasy to pass the time. Now it was a necessity.

And I couldn't get caught. I couldn't go back to high care. That little box, those stark hallways, nothing to do, and the most unwell people I have ever met, just wailing all night. The staff treated you even less as a human there than they did out here.

Nia bumped her foot against mine. "We'll figure something out. You and me, right?"

I smiled, but needed a plan. Something more than "we'll figure it out."

I flipped onto my side and rested my cheek on my hand to

78

look at her better. "Are you sure you don't want to come with?" I asked, hoping she would change her mind, but knowing she wouldn't. She had a family to go back to, stability, and a discharge plan. Hers wouldn't get uprooted like mine.

She shook her head slowly and looked at me with understanding. "But I know why you need to."

I leaned back against the grass. I closed my eyes, mentally walking the corridors to see what could work. Imagination wasn't good enough.

"Let's go scope the place," I said to Nia, scrambling up. I took her hand and helped her up. We wandered across the concrete, walking slowly to help with my aches. The tiny step up into the corridor was enough to send pain through my thigh and back. Actually, every step did that.

Nia grabbed my arm, her fingers curled. They spiked into me and hurt. I winced and looked at her. Her eyes were wide. She relaxed her fingers out of the death curl, but tightened her grip and pulled me with her to the little alcove just next to the courtyard door, out of sight from the nursing station. She turned me and positioned herself right in front of me, her face close to mine.

"The fire exit," she said, her eyes still wide.

I tried to peer past her, thinking something or someone was there that she was afraid of. She gripped both my upper arms and held me steady.

"The fire exit doors," she said again, the corners of her mouth creeping upward, willing my brain to click into alignment with hers.

"What about them?" I had to ask. They were locked too, especially since they led straight to the carpark. Maybe she meant to break the glass?

"They unlock when there's a fire alarm," she said.

"What?" I scoffed. "No."

Surely not. Surely it wasn't that easy. With all these locked doors everywhere, including fire doors all the way through the building, and they had doors straight to the outside that opened automatically and would let all us crazies out?

"Yes," Nia said, her grin wider now, her hands still pinned on my arms.

"How would I not know that?" I asked.

Nia shrugged and dropped her grasp. "Maybe because we've never tried it. But I'm sure they do. They always have staff out watching those doors when there's a fire alarm. I bet that's why."

My shoulders dropped along with my hope. "So, you don't know for sure, you're just guessing?"

"Well, it's not like I've tried it myself. But what if?"

It couldn't be that easy.

"Lena," Nia continued. "This could work."

"How are we going to set off the fire alarm without getting caught?" I asked.

Nia scowled. "Of all the things, that's what you're gonna doubt? That's easy."

I stood up straighter, a spark of excitement catching in my chest, but still not showing on my face. Could it be that easy?

"We could do this," Nia said, her eyes sparkling.

Our eyes searched each other's. She really believed it.

"Okay, let's try it," I said. "When?"

Nia thought for a moment. "Probably at night is best, when there's not as many staff. Wear something dark."

I took her hands. "I've just gotta figure out how I'm gonna get to Aidan's, then. I thought—" I paused. Nia mightn't agree to me contacting Allie and Rose again. She didn't know I'd been texting Allie.

"Thought what?"

I sighed and dropped eye contact. "I thought I might ask those church people."

Nia breathed in, audibly. "If you think you need to. It's your life. You know what I think."

I looked her in the eyes again. Her mouth had drawn into a partial smile. Trying to be supportive. Succeeding, actually, very much so, despite not fully agreeing with me. I pulled her into a hug.

CHAPTER
TWELVE

NIA and I sat on my bed cross-legged, knees to knees, with a blanket over to better hide the phone in case staff came looking. We'd figured out a bit more of a clear plan, and it was sounding more and more doable. The main things it hinged on were those fire doors unlocking when there was a fire alarm, and me being able to get to Aidan somehow. I had zero money to my name, so if Allie couldn't get me a bus ticket or some other way to Aidan's, I'd have to beg, busk with my non-existent skills, steal, or walk the hundred and fifty-odd kilometres to Palmerston. I pictured myself attempting to dance on a street corner to earn money for the bus. It wasn't pretty. People would probably report me to the police for being sick in the head, just for trying, and I'd end up right back here anyway.

I glanced at the phone, the blanket draped across my knees giving only the tiniest gap to see what my thumbs were typing. Nia's eyes were fixed on the door, ready to alert me if a staff member came by so I could tuck the phone into my sock and prepare for our apologies. We weren't allowed to be in each other's rooms—hey, what *were* we allowed to do?—but all they'd do was growl at us for something like that.

> Hey... I've got a favour to ask... do you reckon you could get me a bus ticket to yours?

Aidan's was a two-and-a-half-hour bus ride from the closest bus depot, on the same route as toward the Followers of Mary. It didn't feel right lying to Allie. She'd been so supportive. But I didn't really want them knowing where Aidan lived in case they followed me there, and I figured they might not help me unless I was going to them. Plus, that way I might manage to get a bit of a refund from the bus service so I could have some extra cash.

Allie would forgive me. And if she didn't, well, I didn't know her that well anyway, so no big loss.

"Are you sure about this? What if they call the hospital?" Nia asked.

I scoffed. "They totally won't. She's the one who brought me the phone, remember? They'll be stoked I'm coming to them." Until I don't. And then they'd hate me. Oh well, Allie was part of a cult anyway, so did I even really want her in my life?

"If you say so," Nia said hesitantly. "It seems kinda risky getting them involved."

"Well what other ideas do you have?" I snapped, and Nia looked hurt. "Sorry. I just don't have many options. I don't even know what the doctors plan on doing with me, if I'm not going to Aidan's. It could be another foster home, or a group home." I shivered. "Or maybe they were just going to leave me here till I turn eighteen, then ship me off to an adult unit."

Can't trust me to live in society on my own. Too "mental" for that.

Nia glanced down at her hands on the blanket as she picked at her fingernails.

A silent message flashed onto the phone. I jumped to open it.

ALLIE

> I think so. For when?

I looked at Nia. "She asked when."

Nia's eyes widened. "Are you going to go tonight?"

There was a bus running every morning at six thirty from Wellington Central bus depot. That was the least risky, in terms of getting caught. If I could get out overnight, and make a lump in my bed that looked like a sleeping me, then they might not even realise I was gone until the next shift came on at seven thirty. I'd be well gone by then, halfway to Aidan's. They wouldn't care enough to follow me all that way, I bet. Probably just think "good riddance" and fill my bed with another poor young soul, ready and waiting to get drugged and abused.

I raised my shoulders slowly, then dropped them back down. "I mean, the sooner the better, really."

Nia nodded. "I know. I get it." She put her hand on my arm.

I dropped the phone into my lap and brought my hands out from under the blanket. I pulled her into a hug, wrapping my arms around her back and squeezing her as tight as I could, with our knees touching like they were. She squeezed back, and I knew this wouldn't be the end of our story. I loosened my grip first, and we sat back to look at each other.

"You'll text me when you're out, yeah?" I asked, already knowing the answer.

"'Course," Nia replied. "It was an honour conspiring with you, Lena Martell."

CHAPTER
THIRTEEN

THAT NIGHT, I took my regular meds like a good psych patient, though I'd asked for fewer sedatives with the excuse that I was trying to wean myself off them. I must have been convincing enough because the younger nurse just smiled sweetly and agreed. She was probably relieved she didn't have a fight on her hands for the regular meds.

I took them early so I could try to burn through their effect, and stayed up chatting with Nia in the dining room. The lights were brighter in there, which helped keep the sleepiness at bay.

By the time the nurses came to usher us off to our rooms for the night, both of our faces were sore from laughing, our eyes burning from holding back tears. Tonight, everything would change. Tonight, I would finally be free.

I checked I had everything I needed in my room: my shoes out next to my bed, easy to find in the dark; an extra pillow and blankets on my bed, looking as innocent as can be. Just a teenage girl wanting to get as snuggly as I could, with their threadbare sheets they called blankets. I switched the lights off but stayed up, pacing around the room, doing stretches and running on the spot to try to keep myself awake.

They'd sent us to bed at ten o'clock, so it was just a couple more hours I had to stop myself from falling asleep. The bus station was about an hour and a half walk from the hospital, so really I only needed to leave before five, but I didn't want to risk getting lost and missing the bus, or falling asleep here and missing the entire night.

I kept an eye on the time on my phone, which made it tick by even slower. At twenty to eleven I got into bed, just in case they decided to check early on their hourly rounds. I pressed my nails into my arm, trying to use the pain to fight any drowsiness, while making it look like I was sleeping soundly. Fortunately, the adrenaline pumping through my veins helped ward off sleep, my excitement and worry about the plan keeping my adrenaline going.

The nurses flashed their torch into my room at eleven twenty. The change of shift check. Late, as per usual with the evening staff. What was an extra twenty minutes when you were just checking if people were alive?

It was after midnight—when the lights were all dimmed, when everyone would have gone home, when the nurses would have settled into their shift—that's when I was going to make my run for it. Some of the night nurses did checks like clockwork, "on the hour every hour" to check I was still there, still alive, not plotting self-harm or some great escape. Others were a bit looser with the timing and intensity of checks, more like once every couple of hours to check we were still in bed, less concerned about whether we were still breathing. Here was hoping one of those nurses would be on tonight. Besides that, I knew they'd just be in the nursing station, watching movies on their phones, or sleeping, like they usually did.

I got up again in between checks, returning to my mini exercises to keep myself awake, wondering if Nia was doing the same. I didn't really have a whole lot of a backup plan if she fell asleep, besides waking her. She promised she wouldn't, but she agreed to leave her door unlocked anyway, just in case, to make me feel better. If she had fallen asleep, then at least we had a few spare hours up our sleeve. I could go wake her, then we could try again the next hour, as long as we didn't get busted in the meantime. That would mean back to the drawing board.

To be fair, it was unlikely the night nurses cared enough to "bust" us, unless we made it super obvious. But they might report anything suspicious to the doctors and day nurses, who didn't need much of an excuse to make my life worse.

I got back in bed before the midnight check. The light flashed over me for the second time, and I made myself count to three hundred before checking my phone, not wanting to risk the nurse walking back past my room to check on other people. Six past midnight.

All was quiet in the hallway, so I slipped out of my bed, already dressed in my dark pants and top. I put on my black jacket and shoes, then padded my extra pillow and blankets under my sheets to form the shape of a sleeping me.

I checked my charger was in my jacket pocket, put my phone in the other side, then peeked out my bedroom door's window. The corridor was empty. I opened my bedroom door as gently as I could. There was a tiny click, but that wouldn't be audible from down in the nursing station. I peeked out again, before stepping out and closing the door as quietly as I had opened it.

I slunk over to Nia's door and gave a quiet, single knock. She appeared in the window and opened her door quietly, too. We grinned at each other, our eyes mixed with excitement and sadness. I reached for her hand, and we both squeezed. She held up the lighter she had gotten from another patient. I drew her into a hug, not wanting to let go, but knowing I had to.

She gestured for me to get going, and I mouthed "thank you." The words were wholly inadequate. I slunk all the way down the end of the corridor to the fire exit. I tucked myself behind the curtain, sure that no one would see unless they came down here.

I heard Nia open the bathroom door. Then I waited.

It seemed an age to wait, and I started to worry it wouldn't work. Then a stark screeching sounded, and I heard the lock pop on the door beside me. I exhaled with relief, pulled the handle and pushed the door.

It didn't open.

CHAPTER
FOURTEEN

NO, *no, no.*

Nia had been wrong. The doors didn't unlock.

The voices roared in triumph. Now I'd be found here, and they'd drag me away and put me into high care and inject me again and—

A flick of rational thought flashed through my mind. I had heard the lock pop on the door.

I tried the handle again, releasing it fully before pulling right down. I pushed my weight against the glass.

The door swung open, and I fell forward. I stretched my hand out to catch myself. It connected with concrete. *Concrete.* Cold and damp and *real.* A fresh breeze hit me, stopping my breath for a moment.

The door had opened. I was free.

I crawled through the narrow opening, then turned to guide the door back into place, hoping that the breeze didn't flow down the corridor and alert the nurses.

I crouched there for a moment after it clicked shut, sure that it would whip open in a second and I would be caught and thrown into the high security unit to stop me from ever escaping again. Then I realised I was insane for waiting around to find out.

I turned and almost fell forward again as I launched myself away from the building and across the grass. I sprinted, still so sure I was going to hear yelling behind me or that someone was going to step out in front of me and it would all be over.

I ran toward the carpark, careful to stay on the grass so the sound of pavement wouldn't attract attention. The carpark stretched out in front of me, the gravel illuminated by the glow from the overhead light that was meant for staff safety, and now threatened mine. The silence, devoid of any crickets or traffic noise, made my steps thunderous.

My eyes, wide from panic and minimal lighting, searched for the shortest route to the hospital exit. I traced a line from the carpark, up to where the driveway disappeared behind a fence. I kept along the grass verge toward the fence line, quieting my steps as best I could. I hugged the fence and darted through its shadow cast by the carpark light, my heart racing like a wild animal that had just escaped its cage. I dashed through some bushes, their branches scratching at the exposed skin on my hands. I burst out of the bushes and onto a footpath running parallel to the driveway. There, just ahead, were the carpark barrier arms. Beyond them, the street.

I slowed to a fast walk. I had to play it cool now. Security would be watching the exits, for sure. I took a deep breath and rolled my shoulders back, straightening out my posture to look as confident as I could. I glanced up and saw the cameras perched on metal poles, positioned for watching cars and pedestrians enter and leave the grounds. I dropped my gaze back in front of me, not wanting to draw attention by looking at the cameras. I walked briskly, now aware that even just walking alone at this time of night would raise concern from onlookers. I was a single female walking outside at midnight, with nothing to defend myself.

The hive buzzed with excitement and I shook my head to try to dispel them, without luck. I wasn't entirely alone after all, though the voices were more hindrance than help.

I rounded the footpath and was on the street. In public. *Free*.

I glanced back, but couldn't see anyone following me. Once out of the view of the cameras, I took to running again, though my legs were starting to shake.

I got to the main road, lit by the few cars on it, the streetlights, and ahead, shop lights. I pulled my hood up and tucked my hands into my jacket, hoping not to draw attention from passing cars, other people, or police. The staff might come looking for me, too, if they knew I was gone. I had to get off the main road.

I pulled my phone out and retyped the address for the bus station, trying not to seem conspicuous. "Act normal," as they say, and everyone whistles and glances around and looks anything but normal.

The map plotted a course for walking, and I zoomed in to check which side streets I could take. It would add time to the trip, but was worth it if I didn't get picked up and dragged back to hell. My best bet was heading over the road and down a series of side streets before having to cross what appeared to be another main road.

I waited for a big enough gap between cars, so they wouldn't care I wasn't using a designated crossing, then bolted to the other side. I veered left on the footpath, with the first turn about a hundred metres ahead. I tucked my chin back down to my chest, hands in pockets again, and walked briskly, trying to look like I was cold and in a little hurry, but not like I'd just robbed a liquor store.

A car passed me, and I turned away a little to avoid their headlights shining on my face too much. I mentally pleaded them not to stop and help this girl on her own out here at night, and they didn't. Times like this it was great that humanity didn't care about each other.

I rounded the street to my right and straight away could see my next goal. I continued at my "walking home" pace, sweat starting to coat my skin, despite the cool night air. I unzipped my jacket, growing more confident that the staff wouldn't find me. That was, if they were even looking yet.

Meanwhile, Nia was sure to get in trouble for setting off the smoke alarm. We weren't sure what would happen. Maybe she would have her leave revoked or something. She was amazing for putting herself out like that, for me. I smiled as tears welled up. She was the best friend I had ever had. No one had watched out for me like her.

Except for Aidan. My breath hitched. I was out. I had escaped. All those years trapped inside, and now I was free to have a normal life with Aidan.

A jolt shot through me. What if Aidan had changed his mind and he didn't want me? Surely he knew I couldn't stay there anymore. Surely he would support me. I said "surely" but I wasn't sure. Aidan played by the rules. All I could do was hope. And if he didn't... well, then what? I hadn't really thought that through. I didn't have anywhere else to go. I'd probably have to go to a soup kitchen or something. Maybe even live on the street. I hadn't done that in years, and I didn't even know my way around this neighbourhood so well. Perhaps I could make my way to my old stomping ground, if Aidan chose the government over me.

But he wouldn't, would he?

I rounded the next turn and settled even more. Just being away from that place was all I needed. And if Aidan rejected me, well, what was new. Everyone else in my life had already. Hell, my own father even disowned me. I'd made it this far without them.

Somewhere in the distance, a dog barked. I froze, breath

94

caught in my throat, and peered into the gloom. Nothing but shadows stirred. I was alone.

I glanced down at my phone, its dim light casting a faint glow on my pale face. The battery percentage hovered at eighty, and I couldn't help but feel a pang of anxiety. What if it died before I reached Aidan, and I couldn't charge it? What if I was left stranded, alone and vulnerable?

I took a deep, steadying breath and wiped the sweat from my brow.

Maybe if Aidan did reject me, the Followers of Mary would help. I'd go be the saviour for their backwoods cult. We could all drink the Kool-Aid together.

They had already helped. Allie had got me this bus ticket to go to her and the other Marians. No questions, no challenging my decision, no being torn between what was best for me and what the law and rules were. She'd put me first, and I'd betrayed her. Or at least, I was going to. The guilt wasn't going to stop me from making it to Aidan. It was worth the betrayal. It had to be. I would've lost her friendship, though the Followers of Mary would probably take me back. Their "God." How could they deny me?

Maybe I could've just told her the truth. She probably would've helped me anyway.

But it was too late now. Sort of. I didn't want to take the risk.

CHAPTER
FIFTEEN

AFTER NEARLY TWO hours of walking, the bus station finally came into view. Its exterior lights cast harsh shadows across the pavement, creating an eerie atmosphere that sent a shiver down my spine. As I drew closer, I realised that the building itself was closed, the windows dark and uninviting. My planned shelter was gone—I still had hours to wait until my bus arrived at six thirty, and the last thing I wanted was to be caught out in the open.

I made it, which was kind of more than I expected. Everything had gone to plan, which wasn't the standard for my life. Something had to go wrong. At least one thing. And I sure didn't want that to be getting picked up by the hospital staff or police and taken back to that hellhole.

Desperate for a place to hide, I scanned the area and spotted a shadowy corner near the edge of the station, tucked away from prying eyes. I made my way over, my body stiff and sore from the long walk and prior assault. I curled up on the chilled ground, trying to find some semblance of comfort. I pulled out my phone —now at sixty-two percent battery—and set an alarm for twenty to six. Not so long before the bus that I'd fall back asleep, but long enough that there wouldn't be that many people around yet. Plus, sunrise was only at twenty past six, so it would still be dark enough that people shouldn't be able to see me in my hiding spot.

I pulled my hood and jacket tighter around my face and waist, trying to conserve my heat for the hours-long wait. That'd be the next thing to go wrong—I'd curl up with hypothermia and either not even make it onto the bus, or just die right there in a concreted corner of a public bus station.

I could really use some pills right now. My teeth plucked at the cuts in my mouth instead. The voices whispered, welcoming me to the fold, now that I would have to let the medication wear off.

The cold seeped into my bones as I drifted in and out of a fitful sleep, each restless moment punctuated by the sound of my own shallow breathing. The world around me was still shrouded in black when I finally woke, but I could make out the faintest hint of movement through the darkness, as the trees lining the carpark bounced in the breeze. I glanced at my phone —five twenty.

I was still the only one around. It was much too early for people to be there. The depot only opened at six, so even the workers probably wouldn't be there until quarter to six, or maybe five thirty if they were really eager.

I stayed huddled in my little corner. Dressed in all black, I'd look a bit dodgy hanging around the depot so early. Didn't want to raise any extra concern. If anyone was looking for me, if they'd discovered my escape from the ward and knew where I was headed, then my name could give me away the moment I checked in.

I should've asked Allie to put the ticket under a different name, then I wouldn't have that risk. Stupid me. But it was only a risk if they knew I had a bus ticket. Would they have pressed Nia for that info? Probably. Would she have given me away? Doubtful. Even if they threatened her with high care, her parents wouldn't stand for that. She was protected, more so than me. They could do what they wanted with me, really. Have their fun, do experiments if they wished. It was going to be my word against theirs, and who would ever believe a psychotic teenager over a group of nurses and doctors?

Rhetorical question, of course. No one would.

Except maybe the Marians. Because I wasn't just a teenager to them, and I wasn't psychotic. I was their Lord and saviour. How good if that were true. I could go back and smite all those nurses and doctors for all they'd put me through.

This line of thinking gave me renewed satisfaction and warmth, and helped pass the time. The bus station opened at six, but I didn't want to be there right on time. I needed a balance between not being late, but also being late enough that there'd be less chance the police could get there in time if my name did sound any warning bells.

I watched from my hidden corner as people began to trickle into the bus station, their footsteps echoing in the morning air like whispers of ghosts. Part of me wanted to join them, to hurry putting distance between myself and this place, but I needed to be cautious. So, I waited.

The bus pulled in, its engine rumbling, and a pang of terror washed over me. I was going to miss it. I checked my phone, which only read ten past six, but maybe it was wrong. I launched out of my shadowy hiding spot, every bruise and muscle screaming in protest. The adrenaline shot confused my legs and made them feel like jelly. My luck would have me on my face and everyone looking at me. I tried to compose myself, but still hurried over to the depot entrance.

The clock there read ten past six as well, with the bus north still listed as departing at six thirty. It must've just been early, waiting there, since this was the first departure point. I rounded the bus and saw there were a few people already queued up, but the bus driver stepped out of the bus and said something to them, making them turn away. Yes, I still had time, he was just getting the bus ready. Yet again, something going my way. This couldn't last.

I trudged over to the counter to redeem my ticket, and hopefully a partial refund so I'd have some spending money. I was third in line, helping to blend into the masses. I had my hood off so I wouldn't draw as much attention, though kept my hair draped down either side of my face to try obscure it a little. I tried standing taller and more confidently to make myself seem older.

"Destination?" the man behind the counter asked when it was my turn to step up. His eyes were heavy with weariness, but still flicked over me, judgingly. I swallowed hard, trying to keep my voice steady.

"Um, Wellsford," I said, trying to process how to get my point about the refund across without giving away too much. I'd already stuffed up by using my actual name for the ticket, and I didn't want to tell everyone exactly where I was going. If I could get a refund, I'd pretend I was going further than Palmerston, so if anyone went looking, it would still be in the wrong place. "But I don't actually need to go the whole way today. Can I get a refund, at all, if I don't go the whole way?"

"Sure," he said, his tone indifferent.

I breathed in, relieved I'd have some cash with me. I didn't have a backup plan, and was starting to get hungry. Should've squirreled away some food for the journey. Again, stupid me.

"Have you got your card there?" the ticket man asked.

I squinted in confusion. A card? But it was prepaid. Blood drained from my face. *Oh, no.* This was the sort of situation where you booked the ticket, but still had to give the card over when you actually collected it, for added security or whatever. I was gonna have to make a run for it, try to scam my way onto the bus, or else I would miss it and be stranded here, so close to the hospital, waiting to get found and dragged back there and put in high care and medicated and this whole thing was such a mess. Of course it had to turn into a mess. It was my life. My life was a mess and nothing ever went to plan.

The voices roared in amused agreement.

"My card?" I squeaked.

"For the refund," the man said bluntly. My face screamed confusion, so he continued, putting me out of my misery. "The refund will be returned to the same card the ticket was purchased on."

I breathed in deeply. "Oh," I breathed out, relieved. If that was all it was, I'd take it. I'd be broke, go hungry. Thank God I could still get out of this town. "Never mind, then, I'll just take the ticket. Thanks."

"Suit yourself," the man shrugged, and processed my ticket.

If the money went back onto Allie or Rose's card, they'd know something was wrong. Since I wasn't gonna be getting any cash, it wasn't worth it. Might as well have just asked them directly for a ticket to Aidan's. Which, to be fair, they probably would've given me. But I'd rather they didn't know where I lived. I'd make contact with them on my terms.

I pulled my hand out of my pocket to retrieve the flimsy paper ticket he slid across the counter. I clutched it to my chest, not letting the faint breeze have any chance of blowing it from my grasp. I hurried over to the bus, relieved that the driver was already letting people on and I could shelter inside, away from potential hospital staff, police, and other prying eyes.

The driver barely even glanced at my ticket, just nodded me on. All that and I probably could've just got a stub out of the bin or on the ground, and made it onto the bus anyway. Without my identity being tied to it, no less.

I whispered my thanks and went to step onto the bus, just as I heard a deep male voice cry out from behind me.

"Excuse me! Hey, miss, wait!"

My blood ran cold and my legs near froze on the spot. Of the flight or fight responses, I was lucky enough to have the most useless of all—freeze. Disassociate and wait for death. My forward momentum from being halfway through a step tricked my body into carrying on, and I gripped the handrail to assist my shaky legs into propelling me onto the bus.

I dared not look behind. They were here for me, I knew it. I knew my luck couldn't last. I threw myself down the aisle, the few people already seated watching me with their beady, uncaring eyes, as panic gripped me. Everyone had taken a seat in a different row, because it would be weird to sit directly next to someone on a near empty bus. Who wants social contact, right? Yuck.

I crouched as I stumbled my way to the back of the bus, hoping the person chasing me wouldn't see which seat I was in. Hoping the bus driver wouldn't let them on, just send them away—they didn't have a ticket, they shall not pass.

God, please, of all my luck, don't let them on.

I slipped down to the floor in the second to last row and wedged myself under the seat, along with all the rejected old chewing gum and whatever other dirt and slime was there. I braced my feet as best I could, one each against the foot of the seat in front and behind. If I wedged myself well enough, they wouldn't be able to pull me out. Not with the awkward layout of the bus aisle. If I could resist long enough, the bus driver might kick them off, or just have to drive anyway. I could play the poor, innocent victim—that I was, really—and maybe the other passengers would vouch for me and stop me from being taken. That, or I could call upon Aidan or the Marians or my Godpowers to smite them all.

My heart hammered in my chest and ears, making it harder to hear what was happening. Then, footsteps. Slow footsteps, like someone was walking down the aisle, searching for something. Searching for me.

"Did you see where that girl went?" the deep voice asked a passenger.

Please don't tell him, I mentally begged, clenching my teeth to stop from whimpering.

But the world was against me. The feet came into view, walking with more purpose, knowing exactly where they were going. They stopped by my chair, and I braced, waiting for large, rough hands to wrap around my ankles and drag me back to hell.

Instead, the deep voice wavered, almost as if the speaker was nervous. "Uh, excuse me, miss?"

I stayed curled up, all my muscles engaged to keep me firm in my place. Maybe it was a trick, a trap.

Danger... kill... the voices wailed and sniggered, and I was able to decipher enough of their words to confirm I wasn't safe.

The feet stayed where they were for a moment of awkward silence, then aligned to be right next to my chair. From the way I was wedged, everything above the speaker's knee was cut from my view. The man crouched, and brought his face lower, trying to meet my eye. I curled further into myself, and closed my eyes.

"I, um... I think you dropped this." His voice had softened, trying to lure me into a false sense of safety. I held my brace.

But there was no pressure on my legs. No one trying to rip me from the filthy hiding place on the floor of the public bus.

I opened one eye by just a sliver. It was enough to see the man was holding something out toward me. I snapped my eye shut again, and held my position. I wouldn't fall for that trick.

Lie! Not... the cheering squad were with me on that. The man wanted me to reach out, accept whatever he was holding, so he could grab my wrist and yank me out from under the chair and back to the high security unit to lock me away for God knew how long.

He crouched there a moment longer. I could feel his presence. Then he sighed, and stood. "I'll leave it just here for you." His footsteps receded along the aisle, and off the bus.

At least, that's what he wanted me to think.

Lie, a voice repeated. He was still on the bus, waiting for me to come out, so it wouldn't be such a big scene.

But two could play at that game. If I waited there long enough, the bus driver would either have to kick him off, or take him with us.

Or, as a third option, maybe everyone would have to exit the bus to transfer to another one, so they could all go on their merry way while I was left here to fend for myself. A fresh wave of panic began rising in my chest, just before the bus roared to life, its doors closed, and we began to move.

I was trapped with him. But at least we were moving. I would wait here until my stop, then make a run for it.

CHAPTER
SIXTEEN

I JOLTED AWAKE, and became acutely aware of my vulnerability. My feet were still pressed up against each of the chair poles, but I could've easily been ripped from my hiding spot while my guard was down. My legs ached in that numb way they do from having the blood supply reduced, and my shoulders felt like they were developing pressure sores.

I had no idea how long I'd been asleep, or where we were. I could've missed my stop already and been halfway to the Marians. I fumbled for my pocket and retrieved my phone. I pulled up the mapping app and it highlighted my location. I zoomed out, and exhaled in relief to see we hadn't passed Palmerston. I punched in the bus stop location, which calculated the estimated arrival time as twenty-three minutes away.

And a text from Allie.

Hey! Safe travels :)

I stared at the message until my screen switched off, then opened it and stared at it some more. This poor girl. She'd been so kind, and I was throwing it in her face.

But I had to look out for me first. No one else was going to.

I hugged the phone to my chest and dared to stretch my legs

out, one at a time. I listened for movements in case the man spotted me, so that I could wedge myself back there before he came for me.

Twenty-three minutes to decide how to outmanoeuvre him and get away at my bus stop. Less time than that, now. Maybe I could try to blend into the rest of the crowd. But he'd be watching for me like a hawk, probably ready to grab me as I went past his bus seat. I could put my jacket on loosely, so that when he grabbed for me, I could slip out of it and run. It might give me just enough time to hide.

But they might've figured out where I was going, even with my ticket listed as travelling halfway up the country to the Marians. They might have other people waiting for me at the bus stop, so running would be futile.

If that was the case, well, I'd have to fight my way out. Try to appeal to the concerns of members of the public, and maybe they would help me.

If I did manage to get away, I'd need to know where I was going.

I punched Aidan's address into my mapping system and listed the local bus depot as the starting location. It was about a forty-minute walk. My feet ached from my overnight hike and being pressed against the seat posts for two hours, but I was so close to being there. I'd be able to shower, and wash, and put my feet up, maybe even have a sleep in a decent bed, for the first time in years.

The twists and turns the bus made down streets became sharper and shorter as we narrowed in on the bus depot. Eventually, we pulled to a stop.

Passengers stood up from their seats and shuffled into the aisle in preparation to depart. If I were to blend into the masses, I had to move out quickly. I wiggled out from under the seat, every muscle complaining from being forced into the same position for so long. I brushed at my sleeves and pants briefly, grimacing at the dust and grime I'd attracted. Then I spotted a small piece of white paper on the seat.

It hadn't been there when I got on the bus. I was sure of it, despite my being in a rush to escape my pursuer. What had he said? "I'll leave it here for you"? I picked it up, unfolded it, and felt a sinking in the pit of my stomach. On the paper was the note and phone number Rose had left me.

It must have fallen out of my pocket at the ticket counter, and that man had come and found me to return it. But if that were the case, then... I wasn't being chased. He wasn't from the hospital, come to drag me back, kicking and screaming. He was just a member of the public, trying to do a nice thing, and I'd responded by running and literally hiding from him.

Heat flashed into my cheeks as I realised how incredibly weird my behaviour was. If the other people on the bus hadn't thought I was odd to start with, they certainly would've thought it after that.

I scanned the mass of passengers, searching for a threatening looking man, to prove that I had been right to hide.

There was none.

I scrunched up the paper and shoved it back into my pocket. I pulled my hood up, wanting to hide my shame as much as wanting to hide my face in case anyone really was looking for me. I joined the queue in the aisle, constantly scanning the passengers in the bus and those in the crowd outside for any sign of threat.

There was no one suspicious, but that didn't stop me continuing to scan while I stepped off the bus and made a beeline away from the depot and toward Aidan's.

Distancing myself from the bus depot calmed me, as much as it could, in a way that I was both distancing myself from any potential abductors, and from the shame of acting like a complete psycho when someone was just trying to help. What would that man even think of me? He'd probably go home and tell his family about this weird kid on the bus, how we're all such tweakers these days, probably on drugs.

What did it matter? I was free. I made it to Palmerston. I was almost at Aidan's, then nothing else in the *world* would matter.

My phone's map had me mostly walking along main roads, but I used the side streets again, even though it would take way longer. I kept a pace that I thought was close enough to a casual walk, rather than someone who was scoping out properties for some thieving. I took my hood off to avoid the cat-burglar look, but let my hair drape down next to my face.

The walk ended up being closer to an hour and a half, by the time I got to Aidan's street. This was all getting so real. How would he react? What would he say? Would he just embrace me, happy I'd finally come to live with him?

With how everything had gone, maybe this would be my downfall. Perhaps the hospital staff did know I was gone, and knew exactly where I was going, and were lying in wait for me, ready to drag me back to the hospital just when I thought I was safe.

I paused before the corner. That could absolutely be what was happening. I crept up to the corner and peeked around, a familiar taste in my mouth before I realised I was biting my cheek. Aidan's house was way further down the street; further than I'd be able to see from here. But I checked out the cars I could see, and none were police cars, nor looked like they were parked with people in them.

I had to risk it. I'd come this far. If I saw anyone coming for me, I'd make a run for it. My phone battery was still at forty percent, so I had enough of a chance to use it to find somewhere else to go.

Not that I had anywhere else to go. Aidan was it. My only family, and my only plan.

Apart from the Marians. They'd be peeved I'd ripped them

off, but they'd have to forgive me. God forgives, right? So, they'd have to, too.

Anyway, Plan A. I straightened my posture to avoid that lurking look, and walked as confidently as I could down the sidewalk toward Aidan's. My eyes darted around, vigilant for any movement, and hidden people in cars or behind cars, or peeking out from behind bushes or fences. My body was tense, my heart racing, and I fought to keep my composure and not make a run for it to Aidan's. As if I would be safe there, that the outside world wouldn't exist—if they were here, they'd drag me out, no matter what doors I tried to hide behind.

His house seemed to get further away the longer I walked, like that movie effect where they move the camera out while zooming in, and you're in this perpetual time warp where you can't ever get where you need to go. The countdown on my phone grounded me, informing when I was a hundred metres away, then fifty, then... finally, there I was. Standing outside Aidan's flat. I'd hyped myself up for nothing—there was no one waiting for me, preying on me. Not unless they were going to wait until the last possible moment to rip my freedom from me. The cruelty of that was... entirely plausible.

I glanced in both directions to check for traffic, then crossed the road. I stepped off the public footpath and onto Aidan's, waiting for police to rip round the corner, guns drawn, or hospital staff to tackle me. But step after step, no one came. And then I was at the base of his steps, leading onto his front porch. I walked up, my legs shaking, heart still racing. I hesitated, then knocked on the door.

Nothing.

I knocked again. Still no response, no movement inside, nothing. I walked over to a window and peered inside. There was no one moving around, and I probably looked like I was about to break into the place. I went and sat on the steps and checked my phone.

It was past ten in the morning—Aidan would be at work.

I hadn't even thought of that. Stupid me.

I considered phoning him. But I still didn't know how he'd react to me being there, and if I interrupted his work and annoyed him and he had to come home early, that would make it more likely he would send me back. He'd said I could call anytime, but he hadn't said I could show up uninvited.

No, I couldn't be a pain. I'd wait for him to come home, despite the gnawing at my stomach. I really should've packed something to eat. But I'd been through worse, and he'd probably be home about five. That was standard work hours, nine till five, just like that song.

I glanced around and considered curling up on his porch, so I could watch for people coming for me. That would just make me more exposed, though. I got up and walked confidently around the side of his house, hoping I didn't look like I was breaking in.

The backyard was unkempt, with grass in need of a mow, and a tin barrel in the corner, like what homeless people might gather around. There were garden chairs placed around it, including a chair that was on its side. Aidan and his mates probably hung round it for bonfires. Bonfires and beers, just like normal people.

There was a concrete path leading from a standalone pole washing line, up to the back porch. The porch was tiny, not much more than a metre-by-metre concrete slab, but it'd do. I ambled over to it and sat down, leaning against the house. I scrolled through videos on my phone for a bit, but it drained the battery too quick, so I switched the phone onto battery saving mode, then curled up and shut my eyes.

CHAPTER
SEVENTEEN

THE SLAM of a hospital door woke me, just as I was being locked away forever. My eyes snapped open, blinking against the harsh light that had since crept past the trees in the backyard, and was shining directly onto my now crisp face.

For a moment I couldn't remember where I was. Then it came back to me: Aidan's place. I was safe here, for now. The slam had been a house door, not a hospital one.

My heart pounded as the remnants of the nightmare faded. I could still feel the grip of rough hands dragging me across the floor, hear the clang of the high care door slamming shut.

With a shiver, I pushed the memory away. I was tired of living in fear, always waiting for them to come for me. I was angry at myself for having these nightmares, angry at the hospital staff for putting the thoughts in my head, angry at myself again for not being able to control them. But why should I be able to control them? I was nothing special, the voices reminded me. I was at the whim of my mental illness, and the doctors could play with me how they liked. I pressed my eyes together, shunning those thoughts. There was a chance—there had to be—that I could live without medication. That I could decide my own life. And I had—I'd made it out of the hospital, even if it hadn't all gone smoothly so far.

I checked my phone. It was quarter to five, and I had two missed calls and five messages from Allie. I sighed and opened them. Yet again I was a disappointment. The messages were brief, asking how I was getting on, where I was up to in the trip, then growing increasingly concerned, was I okay, they were worried they hadn't heard from me, hopefully my phone was working okay, confirming the time to meet that evening.

Even when I deliberately betrayed her, she was still nice. Though, she didn't yet know I'd betrayed her. She wouldn't deliberately betray someone like this. I just used her for my own needs, to hell with what she wanted. Typical Lena.

I heard movement inside the house. Aidan was home. I leapt up, straightened my hair and clothes, and held up my fist to knock on the back door. I hesitated. It was weird that I was out the back of his property, without permission. Like I'd been lurking there... which I had, but that was the point.

I crept around to the front door, realising it would be even creepier for Aidan to see me lurking outside his house. I glanced around for neighbours, also realising how dodgy I would look since I was crouched over and literally creeping along the side of a house, all in black. I straightened my posture when I got out the front, hiking all the way down to the sidewalk so it might seem like I had just come up the street.

I composed myself and walked as confidently as I could toward the front door. My pulse was racing, a combination of sneaking around, realising I looked like a creeper, and that I was finally about to see Aidan. The excitement on his face, that I was out, I was free to live with him.

I flattened my hair again with my hand, checked the corners of my eyes for sleep with my fingertips, then took a deep breath, and knocked on the front door.

I waited for a moment. There was nothing. I held my fist up to knock again, but then heard it. Movement inside.

Here he was, my brother. Coming to open the door. He would smile, he would laugh, he would be so happy to see his little sister, finally free to live a normal life with him. We would laugh together, and hug, and he'd invite me inside, and we would talk and talk and make dinner together and play board games just like a normal family.

Footsteps approached the door. The door handle turned, the door pulled open, and there stood...

Not Aidan.

CHAPTER
EIGHTEEN

"HI?" the young man in the doorway asked to my deer-in-the-headlights face. Correction: the incredibly attractive young man in the doorway.

Even my mouth was open, caught between bewilderment that this was indeed not my brother, but then also that he was stunning, and not too much older than I was, by the looks. I checked the number on the house; it was number seventeen, just like it was meant to be.

"I... I'm looking for Aidan?" I croaked. "Sorry," I added for good measure. Rule number one of being an introvert: always apologise when you haven't done anything wrong.

The model leaned on the side of the door, one hand up above his head, just like they do in those swoon-worthy video posts. Butterflies fluttered in my belly in response.

"He's still at work," he said. "Do you wanna come in and wait?"

I blinked a few times in surprise. He didn't even know who I was, but was happy to invite me inside... was that a little flirty twinkle in his eye, to go along with his peacocking pose and husky smooth voice?

He didn't have to ask twice. "Sure," I said.

He stepped aside, opening the door a little more, but not enough to let me easily walk in. I stepped into the dimly lit flat, having to turn to my side to pass him closely. This guy had moves.

The place was small and compact, with an open-plan living room and kitchen that looked like it hadn't seen a good cleaning in a while. The furniture was old and worn, but seemed sturdy and comfortable. A faded blue couch sat in the middle of the living room, facing a television against the wall I had crept along, with a small coffee table in between. A couple of mismatched chairs sat on either end of the coffee table. Piles of papers, empty cans, chip packets, and used dishes were scattered on various surfaces, confirming that this was definitely a flatting situation.

"I'm Ryan, by the way," Ryan said from behind me. That was good, Ryan was Aidan's flatmate's name, though Aidan hadn't told me he was so cute.

I spun to look at him, and saw he had his hand out low. "Lena," I said, blushing, then glanced toward the carpet.

"Lena?" He turned his head. "Dan's sister? Aren't you..."

My face dropped. What had he heard? What had Aidan told him about me? Probably my entire life story. Ryan probably thought I was a freak. Or, worse, some psycho who just busted out of mental prison and was now a risk to the world. "From the loony bin," I almost finished for him.

"Does Dan know you're here?" Ryan changed his approach.

"No, I wanted to surprise him."

Ryan nodded slowly. "Right on. I might give him a text, eh. I'll bet he'll want to come home early to see you."

I shrugged. "I don't want to be a pain," I said quietly. Read: please don't message him.

He dropped his head back. "Lena, come on. You're his sister, you're not gonna be a pain. Take a seat. I'll—"

Ryan pointed to the couch. His face dropped and he rushed over to the coffee table. "Sorry about the mess," Ryan said as he swiped up the cans, empty chip packets and dishes. He awkwardly balanced it all between his arm and chest, clearly having never waited tables.

He gestured to the couch. "Take a seat, if you want. I'll grab us a drink."

I slipped my shoes off by the doorway, then took a seat on the couch.

Ryan rushed over to the fridge. "Coke or beer?"

"Beer?" I said. I didn't really get the fuss about beer, but it was the cool thing to choose. I took off my jacket and lay it over the arm of the couch, swapping my phone to my pants pocket.

Ryan returned with two cans of beer. He popped one and handed it to me, before popping his own and clinking his can against mine. He took a sip, and I copied. The bubbly yeasty taste was gross on my tongue and tickled the fresh cuts on my bottom lip, but the coolness was good. I realised I was parched, and had a longer drink.

"So what's the occasion?"

I tilted my head. "What do you mean?"

Ryan gestured to the room. "What's brought you to our humble abode?"

"Oh. Aidan said I could come stay here for a while. It was meant to be later this week or next, but I thought I'd surprise him and come early."

Ryan made a "hmmph" noise, frowned and nodded at the same time, processing. It seemed like it was the first time he was hearing about that plan. But he was Aidan's flatmate, so he'd have to be on board with having someone else stay in the house, wouldn't he? My heart sank.

"Aidan didn't tell you?" I asked meekly.

Ryan shook his head. "Nope, first I'm hearing it."

My heart sank further.

"But that's all good," Ryan continued, and dropped his hand on my leg, just above my knee. "It's good to have you here, good to finally meet you!"

He didn't remove his hand, and I was suddenly uncomfortable being here alone with him. Why was that? Because he was drinking? This was normal, he was cool, he was Aidan's flatmate. *Don't stuff this up, just be cool. If he kisses you, just go along with it, don't make this awkward.*

The voices hummed, reminding me that no one would ever kiss me.

"Good to meet you too," I said, almost holding my breath as I looked at his hand. I took another drink, trying to build that liquid courage. I was stiff, I could feel it. He must have sensed it, too, because he took his hand away. He made it seem so natural, like it was just something he was gonna do for him, not because of how uptight I was being.

"I better text Dan," he said, pulling his phone out of his pocket.

I didn't object this time. I felt too awkward to say anything, really. I couldn't even play it cool for a few minutes. The mere gesture of human touch made me shut down. What a weirdo. I started to feel a little weird from drinking beer on an empty stomach, and the voices cheered on my terrible decision making and awkward human interaction.

Ryan was texting on his phone, then it started vibrating. He swiped on it and lifted it to his ear.

"Hey," he said into the phone. He glanced sideways at me then got up and walked over toward the door, trying to make it look casual, but it was so I couldn't hear the other side of the conversation.

"Really?" Ryan said, then looked at me sideways again, before turning away and curling into the phone a bit. "Damn. I just figured—yep, okay."

I watched Ryan from the corner of my eye, my face angled

more at the coffee table to not seem like I was prying. There was nothing quite like knowing people were talking about you, right in front of you. Still, talking about you like you're not even in the room while you're sat right in front of them was worse, just like the doctors and nurses would do to me.

Ryan came over to me and held out his phone. "He wants to talk to you."

I crunched my bottom lip between my teeth and took the phone. There was something in the way Ryan had curled over the phone and hunched away from me. This wasn't good news. Aidan wasn't excited I was there. He was going to send me back. I lifted the phone to my ear.

CHAPTER
NINETEEN

"HELLO?" I said nervously.

"Lena?" Aidan's voice was full of concern. My sweet brother. "What are you doing there?"

"I... I wanted to surprise you," I stammered, no longer sure of my plan to live happily ever after with Aidan. He was about to reject me, to send me back, to have the police sent to this house and drag me, kicking and screaming, back to the hospital. Because I was not going without a fight.

"Surprise me... Lena, the hospital told me you'd run away."

Of course they would have called him. He was listed as my next of kin. I hadn't even thought of that.

"I've been freaking out." He paused, and his voice softened more. "I'm glad you're safe."

That was his main concern? Tears welled in my eyes. I turned away from Ryan to hide my face. I pulled my bottom lip under my top teeth to stop it from quivering, trying to trick myself into being fine.

"Sorry," I whispered. "I didn't mean to worry you." My voice cracked on the last two words, unable to hold back. Aidan cared. He cared a lot. And I had doubted him so easily.

"It's okay, just… stay there, okay? I'll be home soon."

I nodded, forgetting he couldn't see that, so I gave a little affirmative grunt as well.

"Okay," he reaffirmed. "I'll see you soon. Can I talk to Ryan again?"

I kept my head low to hide my eyes and probably flushed cheeks, and held the phone out at arm's length toward Ryan. He took it, and our fingers touched briefly, which grounded me a bit more. I had to pull myself together, I was acting like a baby.

Ryan spoke briefly to Aidan again, no more than a few agreeable "yep"s and such, before hanging up. He stood there awkwardly for a moment, then wandered off to a different room. Makes sense he'd want to get as far from this freak show as he could. Aidan would've told him I'd run away from the hospital, that I was meant to be in a mental ward, medicated, not out running around in society, and certainly not here, in Ryan's house, where he was completely alone with me. With the mental case.

A door squeaked behind me, then footsteps approached, and Ryan appeared in my peripheral view. He leaned in toward the coffee table, holding something—a box—and put it down on the table. It took a moment for me to register that it was a box of tissues.

I bit my lip again, emotions running hot. Why was it I got more emotional and cried when people were nice to me, more-so than when they were awful? That was the sort of thing I should be unpacking with my currently non-existent therapist. The familiar metallic taste hit my tongue.

Ryan disappeared again and I heard the fridge open. He came back and placed a can of coke on the table in front of me, before dropping onto the couch beside me.

"So," he said casually. "You've had a day."

A smile pushed through my self-loathing, followed shortly after by a single scoff laugh. I sat back a little and looked at him through my scraggly hanging hair. He was leaning into the corner of the couch, one foot on the floor, and the other crossed on top of his knee. He was grinning, but not in a laughing-at-me way.

"I have had a day," I agreed, testing the waters.

"What's it like to escape from a psych ward?" he asked, still grinning.

I gave a nonchalant shrug and brushed my straggly hair behind my ear. "Easier than I thought. Should've done it ages ago."

"Right on, right on. Freaked Dan out a bit, didn't you?"

My smile faded. "Yeah. I didn't mean to. I didn't even click that the hospital would call him."

Ryan inhaled sharply. "Yep, there's that. Can't get far these days without the Man watching."

I raised my eyebrows and smirked cheekily at him. "That's the sort of talk that'll get you locked up in a mental hospital."

He flashed his eyes, grimaced, and held his hands up. "I won't tell if you don't."

I leaned over and stretched my hand out toward him before I even knew what I was doing. The voices shrieked at me, but it was too late now. I had to commit, and do it with confidence, else I'd seem even more of a freak. "You've got yourself a deal," I said as confidently as I could.

He grinned, thank God, and reached his own hand out to shake mine. His skin was rough, but warm and comforting. He held my hand longer than I thought he would, his hazel eyes locked on mine. This was what normal was. That butterflies-in-your-stomach feeling, but without a nurse or orderly watching your every move. There was no one else here, no one but us. This conversation was entirely our secret, our own private moment.

I released my grip a little more and Ryan took the signal, releasing his grip too. I leaned back, still looking at him, still smiling. His gaze travelled over me in a way that made warmth pool in my belly. He now knew one of the darkest, most embarrassing things about me, and he was still talking to me, still laughing with me, not at me.

The murmuring in my mind mocked me, that I could possibly think this was normal, that I was normal. I twisted my neck to shun them, not that it did anything.

Ryan asked about my life in the hospital, my escape, and I told him. He sat there, riveted. Intrigued by my life—by boring old me. He wasn't afraid of me. The opposite—he was actually genuinely interested in me. Maybe even more now than he was before. He empathised with me about the staff, marvelled at the things I'd had to go through, and laughed with me about the crazy things that happened in there.

His laugh was hypnotic. It was so real, so full of life. And I had made it happen with my stories.

"Get this," I said, swept up in the enjoyment of someone genuinely interested in my life, and wanting to hear that sweet laugh again. "These religious people came to visit me the other day. Never met them before. Said they were the 'Followers of Mary.'" I did air quotes along with their name.

Ryan was glued to me, eyes wide, grinning, ready for the next part of the story, hyped for where it would go. He nodded in encouragement for me to continue.

The voices rose, warning me not to say it. But I was too far in, now.

"They claimed," I said, pausing for effect, "that I'm the incarnation of God."

Ryan's mouth dropped further open as his grin grew wider, then burst into laughter. That sweet, sweet sound. "The what?!"

The voices tried telling me he was laughing at me, not with me. But they were wrong. They couldn't take this moment away from me.

I laughed too, a natural, real laugh. It felt so good. "I know, right!"

"God! You're God! Why would they even think that? They should be locked up in there, not you!"

"I know, right!" I repeated, still chuckling.

"I'm gonna look them up." He pulled his phone out of his pocket.

"I did! They're there, they have a Wiki and everything." I leaned over to see his screen as he searched, becoming aware again of his scent and warmth, waking more butterflies in my tummy. I wondered if he would try to kiss me this time, not sure if I wanted it or not. But he was engrossed with his phone.

"Well, I'll be damned, there it is. 'The Followers of Mary, established in 1632... assert that Mary, as the mother of Jesus, was herself God.'" Ryan's tone changed in disbelief, getting higher pitched. He changed it again, enunciating each word as the description continued.

"'She continues to incarnate in different forms to live among humanity.'" Ryan looked at me. "So why the heck did they think you're God?"

I lifted my hands and shoulders emphatically. "Beats me."

"Nah, nah, they must have something. Like do they think you have powers or something?"

"They reckon the—" I cut myself off, about to mention the voices but realising that was way too weird. "Apparently what I believe, comes true."

"Yeah, I'm sure that's why you chose to be locked up in a nut house for however many years."

"Exactly!" I went to tap him on the shoulder playfully, but it hit more on his chest. He looked at my hand, then at me. He sat up, and I grew uncomfortable again. I wanted to say sorry, I didn't mean to hit him there.

"Let's see if it's true," he said.

Huh? I wasn't expecting that. I sat back.

"Let's see if you've got powers!" he said.

I shook my head. "I don't have powers."

"Have you tried?"

"Have you?" I teased back, trying to lighten this line of discussion back to how it was.

"I'm not the one getting accused of being God, Your Highness. Your Almighty, whatever. Come on, let's see if you've got powers. We'll start easy." He looked around, then grabbed an empty can and put it on the coffee table right in front of me. "Move that can."

I eyed him, puzzled.

"Come on, move it." He pointed at the can, grinning.

"Seriously?" I asked.

"Seriously! You've got to believe it though, right? So, believe. You can move things with your mind. You are the creator and master of the universe. You can move the can."

I rolled my eyes and looked at the can. Stared at it, like I could use telekinesis to move it. Like if I stared it down hard enough it would rattle, like how it happens in the movies.

Ryan was quiet. I kept up the show. Like he said, imagine if I really could. If the Followers of Mary were telling the truth. If I was God incarnate. As if I would choose to be locked up in that hellhole. Hell. Ha, what a choice of word. My life was hell, really. Hell on earth. So, what, I'd done this to myself? But then with their logic, maybe that was because I didn't know what I was. And when I kept imagining bad things happening to me, they would. And now if I imagined—

The can moved.

CHAPTER
TWENTY

JUST A MILLIMETRE, but it moved. A tiny metal screech had sounded with it.

I looked at Ryan, my eyes wide. The colour left him as he looked back at me, his eyebrows drawing together.

"What the—" he started.

"You saw that, too?" I whispered.

"You blew on it," he said flatly.

"What? No! Did you?"

He shook his head slowly.

Did that mean… was it really… was I?

I scoffed and fell back into the couch. "You are so full of it," I said. He was having me on. A good prank, for sure. He had me going for a second there.

But his face remained white.

"You can cut the act," I said.

He mouthed words, indecipherable.

"Ryan, really," I said.

He turned back toward the can, unresponsive to me. He was really trying to sell this.

A key jiggled in the front door, and I whipped around, then

jumped up. Ryan was still staring at the can on the table. He could have his little prank to himself. Aidan was home. My brother and I were finally together.

I sidestepped around the edge of the coffee table as Aidan came through the front door, his backpack hanging off one shoulder and his jacket draped over his other arm. I yelled his name. He glanced up to see me rushing over to him, and just managed to kick the door closed and get his arms partway up before I launched onto him. I threw my arms around his neck, standing on my tiptoes, and gave the biggest sisterly hug. I would've been hanging off his neck if he were any taller.

"Hey, sis," he said warmly. He dropped his jacket off his arm then wrapped his arms around me. He gave me a squeeze and lifted me off the ground for a second. It was good. We were good.

He released his grip to indicate it was time to part, so I let go as well and stood back. He looked at me, then past me to the living area, and his face dropped.

"Seriously, Ryan?" he said grumpily. "She's seventeen."

He'd seen the beer cans, now about half a dozen strewn across the coffee table.

"I was just drinking coke," I reassured him.

Aidan glared at me and dropped his head to the side. "Mmh-mm," he mumbled.

Ryan hadn't turned around. Instead, he now had his hand to his mouth.

"Oi, Ryan," Aidan said, and went over and pushed the back of Ryan's head. "Don't just ignore me."

Ryan slowly turned around, still white faced. "I don't…" he trailed off.

"Dick," Aidan said, then turned to me. "Have you eaten?"

I shook my head and my tummy grumbled on cue.

Aidan pushed Ryan's head again. "You didn't even feed her. Come on," he said to me.

I followed him to the kitchen and he made me a peanut butter sandwich.

"Sorry it's not much," he said as he was making it. "I didn't exactly expect we would have company." He looked at me sideways.

I smiled innocently back. "I know, it's all good. Thank you." I took the plate from him and bit into the sandwich, then devoured it. The bread was a little stale, actually more stale than the hospital's, but it was freedom bread, so it was better. Plus, it was made with love.

"How are you doing?" Aidan asked. What a laden question. Did he mean with what just went on with Ryan? Or in general? Or the whole running-away-from-hospital thing? Likely all of it.

"Fine. Good," I said, my mouth full. "Thank you."

Less is more, sometimes. Less description of how I had come to be in his kitchen, for one. Normality was so close, I just had to convince Aidan I was okay, and then maybe he would let me stay, like we planned. I'd find a job, I'd help pay rent, and cook, and clean. I'd be the best sister, and I'd never have to go back to that place. I'd be free.

Aidan stood across from me in the kitchen, both of us leaning against countertops. He folded his arms. We stood in silence for a bit, while I finished the last of my sandwich.

He sighed, shrugged, then finally asked, "What happened?"

I shrugged, too. "They weren't gonna let me come live with you. So, I took control of my life."

A unified cheer sounded through my mind.

He scoffed. "Took control of—Lena, you can't just run away from hospital. You're legally required to be there."

Rage flared inside me at Aidan's insistence on the government and hospital staff orchestrating this puppet show that was my life. They'd had control for too long already.

"Who are they to tell me how to live my life?" I yelled.

"Professionals, Lena!" Aidan raised his voice back, trying to

129

rationalise his brainwashing. "People who can help you better than I can!"

I scoffed again. "Help me? You think they help me? It is literally hell in that place—torture!" There was no way he'd understand. No one would. Not unless they'd lived it.

"I know it feels like that, but they're just trying to help—"

"Help? Help what? Because it's certainly not me."

Aidan exhaled in defeat, then softened his voice. "So what do we do here?"

My head and body shook with frustration mixed with fear. "You can just tell them I'm okay, that it's okay for me to live here with you."

Aidan raised his eyebrows. "And you think they'll be okay with that?"

No. "Maybe."

"And what about your meds?" he asked.

I shook my head and shrugged. "I don't need them."

"You don't need them," he repeated. "Is that you or the doctors talking?"

My mind raced for how to sell the lie. "They gave me an injection so I don't have to take regular meds." Lie. "The rest of it was just to help calm me down. I don't need it if I'm with you." Lie. The injection wouldn't build up in my system until the third dose. And no way was I getting that far with it. And the PRN meds... well, there was a slight chance I would withdraw from them. But hey, I'd just have to hide it. I had to prove I was okay without them, that I could be normal. Normal—that meant less yelling. I straightened up and composed myself.

"Really, I'll be okay. You'll see. I just need sleep," I lied again.

Without a word, Aidan walked back toward the front door, and rummaged in his backpack. He lifted out a small paper bag and brought it back with him. He tossed it to me. I turned it over. Dread enveloped me as I read the printed word: "pharmacy."

How did he get these? Why did he get them? Then realisation washed over me. He must have called the hospital to get a prescription. They'd know I was here.

"What have you done?" I hissed.

"What have I done? What are you doing? You're sick, Lena, and you refuse to admit it. I try to help you, to be supportive, but I can't support you in this. You're running away from hospital, you could've got yourself hurt, or killed! How did you even get here?"

I flared my eyes at him. "Took a bus." *Like a normal person.*

"And how'd you afford that?"

I kept my mouth shut tight. No way was I telling him about the Marians now. He already thought I was crazy, and a cult following wouldn't help with that. Meanwhile, his flatmate's having a laugh at my expense about it. No way, I wouldn't be telling any more people about the Marians, or their claims.

"You don't know how this world works, Lena. It's not safe." He was trying to veil control as care.

"You're just like them," I seethed.

"Just like—" He rolled his eyes. "Just like the doctors? The doctors who care and want to help you get well? Then, yes, I guess I am. And no surprise, you're lying to me as well."

I had to lie to protect myself. To take control of my life. The spectators in my mind cheered me on.

"I'm taking you back," Aidan said, his tone devoid of warmth.

I stared at him, a lump forming in my throat. I'd rather die than go back to that place. The needles, the stark walls, the forced poison medication that drained my being—it was a special kind of hell, and nothing could convince me to return.

"No, you're not," I said, just as coldly.

"I am. Or I'll have them come get you."

My rage silenced me. He needed to shut up.

Aidan opened his mouth to speak again, but nothing came

out. His face twisted in anger and he marched over to the cupboard. He pulled out a glass and filled it with water at the sink. He marched over to me and took the paper bag back, shoving the water into my hand instead. He ripped the bag open and pulled out the pill bottles, reading the label and opening one clumsily.

"I don't need meds, Aidan," I said, my anger settling calm into my voice.

"Yes, you do, and you will take it," Aidan snapped.

Ryan stood up from the couch and turned to us. "I don't think…" Ryan started, but trailed off.

"You stay out of this," Aidan snapped. He tipped a pill onto his hand then shoved it toward me. "Take it," he said, glaring into my eyes.

I exhaled. "No."

"Take it!" he yelled, forcing it into my face.

I slapped his hand away, knocking the pill to the floor.

Aidan watched it bounce across the tiles, then turned to face me. Rage and hate burned in his eyes. How quickly he had turned on me. But why should I expect anything less? Everyone in this world turned on me at some point. Tried to control me. I had hoped for better with Aidan, but this was my life I was talking about. Nothing worked out how I wanted.

"Lena," Aidan said quietly. Coldly. "Take the medication or I will phone them right now and they'll get the police to take you back."

I narrowed my eyes and stared into his. "No."

His eyes softened for a moment, like he regretted giving the ultimatum that he'd now have to follow through with, then rage burned again and he stepped back. "Fine, have it your way." He pulled out his phone and swiped through before pressing what must have been the call button.

"Dan, really—" Ryan started.

"You shut up!" Aidan yelled at him, then straightened to

make eye contact with me again. We stared at each other, my heart breaking, trying not to show it, but I could feel my face starting to crinkle. How had this gone so wrong? Maybe I should just take the pill, let him win this one small thing. It was Aidan, after all.

But no, he had chosen a side, and it wasn't mine. I wasn't safe here. I wasn't safe anywhere.

I pushed off the kitchen cabinet and launched myself toward the door. Past Aidan, past the pill, past Ryan. I didn't think to grab my shoes or jacket, I just had to get out. I yanked open the front door and dashed down the steps and onto the street, the cold pavement pressing into my socked feet.

CHAPTER
TWENTY-ONE

MY FEET POUNDED the pavement as my breath came in ragged gasps. The evening air was cool, seeping through my thin shirt. But I barely felt it. All I felt was the burning betrayal coursing through my veins.

Aidan. My own brother. The one person I thought I could trust. He sold me out, ready to ship me back to that godforsaken hospital like a defective toy. Tears blurred my vision as I blinked them back angrily. I wouldn't give him the satisfaction of making me cry.

I had to get away. As far away from him as I could. I dared to glance behind me, not wanting him to follow me.

The street was empty, which hurt even more. He didn't care that I was gone, running in an unfamiliar town. He was probably pleased I wasn't his problem anymore.

My feet ached and screamed and were cold and hot all at the same time. My socks were probably getting ripped to shreds, running in them like this. But that was a future Lena problem. For now, I had to get away and hide, before the police came to drag me back to the hospital.

I darted across someone's front lawn, cutting the corner of

the street. I made a few more turns and found a walkway that curved slightly, hiding me from public view. Only then did I slow, my lungs and throat burning from the cool air.

I followed the path to a small playground and park. I scanned the park before leaving the walkway.

The path curved round to stretch along to a small carpark at the end of a cul-de-sac. A second path jutted off to the small playground, with a couple of swings, some monkey bars, a wooden bridge, and a plastic tunnel and slide. The playground equipment sat vacant and lonely in the growing darkness, giving it an eerie vibe. Trees loomed over the grassed area, bordered by high fences on peoples' private properties. The cul-de-sac seemed quiet enough that it might be safe to hide there overnight.

Was I really going to spend the night outside? In only my shirt and pants, since I'd left my shoes and jacket at Aidan's? I could try slipping inside a garage or shed for the night, but at this time of day it was too risky. There had to be somewhere I could lay low until morning. Or somewhere I could feel safe, if only for a few hours. I wrapped my arms around myself, trying to ignore the chill seeping into my bones. All I wanted was one night of peace. Was that too much to ask?

The indecipherable murmur in my mind mocked me about my brother choosing the doctors over me. They teased in their wordless way, that I had nothing, no one.

But that wasn't entirely true. I had the Marians. Maybe, anyway. Allie would be so mad at me, Rose too. They would have expected me any time now. They might have already left to go and get me from the bus station. It wasn't like I could make it much worse than that, so what really did I have to lose? I'd already lost my brother, my one lifeline. I'd lost my hope, and shoes, and jacket, and—darn, my phone charger was in my jacket pocket. The police would be scouring the city soon, intent on dragging me back to the hospital. Panic rose in my throat at the thought.

I crawled into the short tunnel in the playground, curving my back against its wall and bracing my feet against the other side. I pulled out my phone—now at eighteen percent, and fortunately still alive, thanks to the battery saving mode. I should've charged it while I had the chance. I thought I had more time at Aidan's.

Shoulda, woulda, coulda.

I opened my messages and replied to Allie's last message, confirming they'd meet me at Wellsford at half past seven, and she'd see me soon. I scoffed. I would've been better off staying on the bus.

LENA

Hey. I messed up. Sorry :(

I got off the bus in Palmerston. Now I'm stuck :(

Sorry :(

How many "sorry"s were too many? Not a bad idea to humble myself. Be the victim, when it suited.

I stared at my phone, the dim light illuminating my face. My eyes burned, and a headache was forming behind them. I willed the little dots to show that Allie was typing. Two minutes ticked by, watching the clock.

I could really *use some pills right now.*

I should've taken the good ones from Aidan, instead of rejecting them all. They weren't all bad.

Doubt crept in. What if the Marians turned me away? Or worse, sent me right back to the hospital like Aidan had? I shook my head, banishing those thoughts. This would work. It had to. I just needed someone to believe in me, to see me as something more than a diagnosis.

Finally, the dots appeared. Then disappeared.

I breathed in. She was mad. She was too mad she didn't know what to say. Maybe they would abandon me, like I had tried to abandon them. Would serve me right. Then I'd live out here, on the street, probably have to pick food from dumpsters, or steal, or beg. Anything would be better than the hospital, even being homeless.

The voices mocked me, agreed with me, that I should be living on the street like the vermin I was.

My phone screen changed to an incoming call. *Allie.* I pressed the answer button.

"Hello?" I said meekly.

"Lena, wow," Allie breathed. "Are you okay?"

I dropped my head back against the rigid tunnel. The impact hurt a little, and sent fresh shockwaves to the headache building behind my eyes, but relief dampened the pain.

She wasn't mad. She sounded relieved. She was just happy I was okay, and now they would help me. Again. Even though I didn't deserve it. Tears pricked at my eyes. I half verbalised an affirmative mumble.

"Where are you now?" Allie asked. "We'll get someone to come get you."

I looked around for a sign for the name of the park. "I... um... I don't know. Hold on a sec." I took my phone from my ear and changed out to the mapping system. I zoomed in to my location, then put the phone back to my ear.

"I'm at Kinley Park," I said. "In Palmerston," I added for clarity.

Allie repeated what I said away from the phone, then spoke to me again. "Okay, we're gonna have someone to you soon. Are you safe? Do you wanna stay on the phone?"

As safe as I could be, scrunched up in this little kid's tunnel. I was relieved it wasn't later at night, or this place would have felt even more creepy.

"My battery's running out, so I better go, actually," I said. "How long do you think they'll be?"

Allie repeated my question off to someone at the side again. "About thirty to forty minutes. Is that okay?"

I took a deep breath in. It wasn't actually that long, while also being ages to sit here alone as darkness loomed. But then I'd be safe, with… someone from this religious cult who thought I was their saviour.

Okay. Yeah. Safe.

CHAPTER
TWENTY-TWO

MINUTES TICKED BY LIKE HOURS. I sat curled up in the tunnel, watching the road with a mixture of dread and longing. My mouth was dry, and headache well and truly formed, thanks to not having any water in almost twenty-four hours. Another thing I should've planned better for.

After what seemed an age, a fancy black sedan—one of the ones that would cost more than most peoples' salaries—pulled into the small carpark, angling across several parking spaces, since there was no one else there. A man in a suit got out of the driver's side, and opened the rear door. The other rear door opened as well, and an elderly couple heaved themselves out of the car.

They looked around like they were searching for someone. It had to be me. There was no way they'd be out here at this random park at this time of night. But that car was flash, more flash than I expected.

They were dressed respectfully, both in knit sweaters, the man in tan trousers and the woman in a grey skirt. Both had white hair, and gripped each other's hands. That show of affection toward each other was the clincher for me to approach them.

But their car and clothes were fancy and clean, and I was a mess. I'd been in these clothes coming up twenty-four hours, and had been through a fair amount in that time. I ran my hand through my hair in an attempt to tame it, and took a deep breath to steady my nerves. The voices mocked me again, about how these people would judge me.

I crawled out of the tunnel and took a couple of steps toward them, before the woman saw me. She grabbed at her husband's arm and her line of sight made him turn to me. Both their eyes widened and they hurried toward me.

"Lena? Are you Lena?" The woman's voice wavered, seemingly in disbelief. I nodded.

"Oh, Lena, it is so wonderful to meet you." The man reached out like he wanted to pull me into an embrace. I instinctively pulled back, and he withdrew his hand, placing it on his wife's shoulder instead. "My name is Reg, and this is Anne."

Anne clutched Reg's hand on her shoulder, her grey-blue eyes welling with tears. "Our Lady has blessed us with this day."

A shiver ran down my spine at the religious intensity, and the term "cult" flashed through my mind again. I forced a smile. "Hi," I said quietly.

Even if they were religious nuts, I wished I would have a love like that—one that would last the decades. But right now, I had no one.

"You must be starving," Anne said, then glanced over me and down at my socked feet. I turned them inward, waiting for her kind face to change to one of disgust, but it remained soft and caring. "Come, dear, you'll catch cold! Give her your cardigan, Reg."

Reg obeyed instantly, fumbling to remove his sweater with his aged, stiff joints.

"No!" I thrust my hands out. "No, please, don't. I'm okay for now, but it would be good to go… wherever."

Reg paused midway through lifting his sweater. Anne patted his arm then reached out to me.

"Yes, come, come," she said, gesturing for me to come with her as she turned. "I've got some cookies in the car, and we'll take you home for a nice hot meal."

I started salivating at the mere mention of non-hospital food.

"It's so wonderful to meet you, Lena," Anne continued as we walked toward their car. She turned to Reg. "There always seemed something a bit off about that other girl, and now we know why."

Reg murmured in agreement and I glanced at them both, thinking that would make a pretty good line in a horror movie just before they led a young girl to her sacrifice, but they didn't really seem the sacrificing type. And I was hungry.

I followed them in silence down the concrete path to their car. The suited man still stood beside it, and he opened the rear door.

"Lena, this is Hundley," Reg said, holding his hand out, palm up, toward the suited man. I watched for it, but Hundley didn't even flinch at my clothes or socked feet. Reg stood aside and held his arm out for me to pass him. I took my seat in the back as directed.

Reg rounded the car and opened the other rear door for Anne, who got in next to me and smiled warmly, scrunching up her wrinkly face and eyes. Reg got in the front, with Hundley in the driver's seat. If the car wasn't enough to show they had money, the chauffeur sure was.

I put on my seatbelt, then crossed my arms and hugged myself instinctively, providing that subconscious and false sliver of protection, suddenly feeling more exposed than I had outside. I let my hair drape over my face as I dropped my chin down, retreating into myself. *I should feel safe, shouldn't I? Feel cared for?*

The Marians had come as promised. I was no longer alone. What was wrong with me?

Everything was wrong with me, the voices reminded me. I was crazy, just escaped the loony bin, was planning to run away to a cult, and now had sucked these two lovely people into the mess that was my life. I squeezed my eyes tight, not wanting to make any attempts at silencing the voices too obvious and have Reg and Anne ask if I was okay.

We pulled out of the parking bay slowly, Hundley careful to give a smooth ride.

"We have waited so long to meet you, My Lady," Anne said from my side, leaning toward me. "It really is such an honour."

A chill rushed through me at the term. My Lady? So, they believed I was Mary reincarnated, too? Word was spreading fast, about something there was currently no evidence for. It was a nice dream, but that might be all it was. If I wasn't God, I hoped I wasn't around when they found out. Though it wasn't like I was claiming to be God. That was their belief. I was just asking for help, after it had been offered to me.

Offered to their God incarnate, really. Which wasn't necessarily me. So, yes, I was taking something that wasn't mine. I was taking advantage. And who knew how mad they would be or what they would do if they found out I was the wrong person.

I pulled further into myself and wished Nia was here.

I wondered how she was doing, whether she had gotten in trouble for helping me. Whether it would delay her discharge. I'd have to find a phone charger for when she finally got out and was allowed her phone back. If she'd given me the correct number. A pang of realisation shot through me, that she might've been faking the whole thing, and given me a fake number so she could be free of me once she was discharged.

Or even if it was by accident, that she'd accidentally given me the wrong number, or I'd typed it in wrong, and now I'd ruined my chance at staying in contact with the one friend I had in this world. She'd think I didn't care—that I chose not to make contact. Or she'd worry that something had happened to me. I didn't know which was worse. Either way, she'd always wonder. And that would be a terrible thing.

Or... or she wouldn't care at all, because she would have forgotten me. Maybe that was more likely, anyway, once she got back to her happy life. She might worry for a while, but then she'd move on, forget about me. Maybe it was better to think I didn't have her correct number, so she wouldn't have to make up an excuse to not talk to me.

No, not Nia. Would she? She was more likely to keep talking to me, even if she didn't want to, just so I didn't feel bad. But we were friends, surely she would want to... until her life got back on track. Then why would she want to stay in touch with the crazy girl. The crazy girl who escaped from the hospital and ended up running away from her only family to live with a cult who believed she was their God.

The voices settled into their mocking, and I accepted them.

145

CHAPTER
TWENTY-THREE

WE DROVE IN SILENCE, Reg and Anne clearly accepting that I didn't want to speak, taking their lead from their deity. Or maybe they were just being respectful of me, as a person, and I was giving too much clout to this religious thing. Either way, I appreciated the quiet. It was hard to converse with a party of one million in my head.

I munched on the cookies Anne offered, their dryness not helping my parched throat, and watched out the window as the town went to sleep. People travelling home, in cars and on the sidewalk, bikes going past, people taking down shop signs. The small-town shops soon gave way to farmland. Eventually we pulled off the road and into a driveway lined with towering trees. My pulse raced as I took in the arched entryway and lush fields, realising that Reg and Anne were, in fact, mind-blowingly rich. I had only seen such places in books and movies, a fantasy world far from the sterile walls of hospitals and group homes.

"Welcome to our home, My Lady," Anne said warmly. I glanced over and shivered at her grin. I faced forward again, still unnerved by the whole idolising of it all, but needing to be respectful. This was their home they were inviting me into, sweatpants and socked feet and all.

The car pulled to a stop. Hundley and Reg opened their doors, so I did the same.

"Let him get it, dear," Anne said. "It really is such an honour to serve you."

Serve me, like a queen. Or a god. That chill that was growing ever more familiar rushed down my spine, arms and legs. I left the door partly open and put my hands back on my lap, doing as I was instructed. Hundley opened my door and stepped back, sweeping his spare arm across to indicate for me to step out. I obliged. Reg was doing the same for Anne. Chivalry was certainly not dead here, but by the look of Reg, it didn't have long to go.

With Hundley leading, Anne and Reg joined my side before verbally inviting me inside. I followed behind them a couple of steps, my feet feeling every stray little stone and imperfection in the concrete. They ached from my walk, and I longed to be able to put them up somewhere.

I stepped onto the cool stone steps leading into the house, taking in the perfectly manicured flower bed on either side of the entryway, illuminated by garden and wall lights. It was a mixture of roses, bushes shaped into spheres, and colourful and wonderful smelling flowers that I couldn't name nearer the ground. The house itself was brick, that old-timely red and brown brick that had been weathered, but still kept its strength and charm. Huge windows faced the driveway on the first and what must be the second floor, likely bordering the house right the way around to give the best views of their land, and let in enough light.

Hundley opened the massive wooden front door, and it creaked only a little, despite its size. We stepped inside and my eyes grew even wider. Their lobby floor was marble tiles. A giant staircase loomed in front of us, the landing stretching to the right and left, like those fantastic grand old houses that you see in movies. The ones that always seem to feature in horror films.

The hive in my mind buzzed with excitement, ready and willing to watch this turn into a house of horrors. I exhaled loudly, trying to drown out their hum.

A giant chandelier hung from the ceiling, that was I don't even know how high. It looked like there were only two storeys, but the ceiling for each was higher than I've ever seen, besides in a mall. I breathed in the scent of roses and polish, my fingers twitching with the urge to reach out and touch the smooth stone pillars that supported the massive house structure.

"You like it, My Lady?" Anne asked.

I was too enthralled to be affected by that title again. I nodded absently as my concentration was drawn to the detail in the stonework, the towering ceiling, the glittering chandelier. This place was ridiculous.

"Shall I show you to your room?" Anne held her hand out toward the stairs.

I nodded slowly again. I followed Anne up the stairs, her holding the hand rail, me more than happy to match her snail's pace, so I could keep taking in all the sights. We went across the landing to the right, the grand ceiling still towering above until we turned down a corridor. The ceiling there was still high, at least twice my height, but a little closer to normality.

The hallway was lined with plush carpet and art that probably cost more than most people would make in a lifetime. I swallowed hard, following her down the hall. My mouth was dry and I realised it was open. It must have been for a while. Everything about this was surreal, as if I might wake up any moment back in my tiny, bland hospital room.

We passed a room with its door standing open. A quick glance inside displayed a huge corner-post bed, tidily made up, but with slippers next to it.

"That's our room," Anne said, and kept walking. "Yours is just next door. I do hope you like it."

Anne stopped on the other side of the next doorway, the door already open. She stood back and gestured for me to enter. I gasped, overwhelmed by the spaciousness and luxury within. Heavy drapes framed floor-to-ceiling windows looking out over rolling green fields. A cream leather couch was positioned along one wall, angled well enough that you could sit there and gaze out the window. A dresser sat between the two windows, with a mirror on top. And on the other wall, a giant corner-post bed, just like in Anne and Reg's room, looking absolutely plush. I mean giant. Like, the biggest bed that probably existed. I would get lost on there. And I couldn't wait.

"I'll let you get settled in, My Lady," Anne said. She indicated to a door on the same wall as the couch. "There's a bathroom just through there, and everything you might need in the meantime. Julia has set out some clothes in the dresser for you."

A lump formed in my throat. No one had ever served me or given me anything so extravagant. Part of me wanted to burst into tears of joy and gratitude. But there it was again, that whisper of doubt. This wasn't for me, I was a fraud, a fake, and they would soon find out.

"Thank you," I said quietly, unable to really form any other words.

"Of course, My Lady." Anne curtseyed. "We'll be downstairs whenever you're ready for dinner."

She closed the door carefully, and with that, I was alone. Alone again, with nothing but my voices and thoughts. But this was a different kind of alone. I wandered around the room, trailing my fingers over the silk bedspread and wooden furniture.

I opened the middle drawer of the dresser, expecting to find old lady clothes, hand-me-downs from Anne. Instead, I was met with the scent of fresh clothing. Inside was a light blue cardigan and a matching cream one, both incredibly soft to the touch. I wondered if they were cashmere. Three silky tops were next to them, a dark blue, white, and a beautiful maroon colour. I'd never even touched anything so beautiful as these items. Next to them were spotted fluffy blue pyjamas.

I hurried to open the other drawers to see what else there may be. A maroon coat was in the drawer below. I lifted it out to admire it, before trying it on. It fit almost perfectly, if not a little large. Its weight reflected the quality. Whoever this Julia person was, my, she had classy taste. I took it off and carefully folded it back into the drawer, aware that I didn't want to dirty it too much with my filthy top. The next drawer down housed classy black pants, and another pair of cream pants that I would absolutely not be able to wear—I couldn't be trusted to not get them dirty. The bottom drawer housed a pair of taupe short heeled boots and black laced shoes. Julia sure was giving me options.

The top row of the dresser was split into two drawers. In the left, there were a collection of bras in different sizes, including a couple of sports bras, socks, and a few styles and sizes of underwear.

I slid the right-hand side drawer open and my heart dropped. I vaguely registered a hairbrush and deodorant among other small items, but my attention focused sharply onto the brown paper bag tucked into the back corner.

On it, the most dreaded word I could think to see on a paper bag.

Pharmacy.

CHAPTER
TWENTY-FOUR

THE VOICES roared with laughter as my own thoughts swirled. Here it was, they did think I was crazy, too. Despite all the talk of me being their God or Mary or whatever, they still want to drug me. I picked the paper bag up to throw it, but it felt squishy. I looked inside and instead of pill bottles, I found a packet of sanitary pads and tampons. I hugged them to my chest as tears welled in my eyes. It was my turn to laugh at the voices —they were wrong. The Marians didn't think I was crazy; they truly believed I was God incarnate. Anne and Reg might not even know I had been in hospital.

I sifted through the other items, now able to focus more. There was a packet of hair ties, a lip balm, and a perfume.

I went back through the drawers and touched everything again, loving on them. The clothes were beautiful, and I hoped perhaps I might be able to keep some.

A girl could dream.

But the rest of this was so surreal, it might just be possible at this point. A pang shot through me. This couldn't be real. I had to be dreaming, trapped in another delusion.

But it felt real—the coolness of the wood on my hands, the

silky bedsheets, the thick curtains. I sank onto the bed, awe and dread competing for my attention. This wouldn't—couldn't—last. Nothing good in my life ever did. I'd do something to muck it up, or they'd find out I wasn't God—that I was a fraud.

So, I might as well enjoy it while I could.

I went to check out the bathroom, and it was just as amazing. I'm not sure why I would think any less. There was a free-standing bathtub next to another full height window, a separate shower, and two basins in front of a huge wall mirror. There was even a seat in the corner opposite the toilet, I guessed for getting dressed or waiting for the bath to heat, or whatever. Two glasses sat next to the basin, and I rushed to fill one, drinking back two full glasses before my thirst was somewhat satiated.

The full height window had blinds sitting at the top, available to pull down. Outside, there were no neighbours or anything that would even be able to see in. Fields stretched out for ages, with tiny lights of civilisation twinkling in the distance. Reg and Anne probably owned all of that land, to ensure their privacy. What were they doing being part of this Followers of Mary cult?

Whatever the case, this was for me to enjoy for the moment. I turned the bath on full. Water plunged into the deep, white bathtub. I picked up the bottles on the edge of the bath and inspected them. It wasn't long before steam started to rise. I checked with my hand it was hot enough, then put the plug in and dropped the entire contents of the bubble mixture next to the stream of water. A beautiful lavender scent filled the air as the bubbles started frothing.

I wandered around the room a little more. There were towels neatly rolled and placed into a wooden rack. I got one out and laid it on the seat. When I turned around, I spotted a white robe hanging on the back of the door. That'd do me. I went to touch it. It was soft, like it was made from the fluffiest and softest towel material ever invented. Two white spa slippers sat on the floor next to the door. Surely, those were all set there for me. And I surely intended to use them.

I went back to the main room door and locked it. Just as I did, my phone started ringing, sending a jolt of panic through me. I glanced around for nurses, waiting for them to come and take it off me, then realised where I was. I fumbled in my sweat-pants pocket and registered the name on the screen.

Rose.

I briefly considered hanging up or letting it ring through. Rose came on too strong, basically even using my mum as a card in her game with me. But, then, she had put me in touch with Allie, and Anne and Reg when I really did need the help. Maybe making her almost trip was punishment enough. I swiped to answer.

"Hi, Rose," I said into the phone.

"Lena, it's Rose."

A pause. "Rose, hi," I said again, frowning and smiling at the same time. *Old people.*

"I hope I didn't disturb you. I wanted to let you know that I will be there tomorrow morning."

"Oh, okay," I said. She sure was moving fast.

"Yes, I managed to get an early flight. I've booked flights back tomorrow about midday."

I'd only get one night in this luxury. The thought of leaving this place, of giving up the fantasy... I wasn't ready to wake from this dream. The voices piped up to mock me. I should know better than to hope for longer. Nothing good ever lasted, and Rose got to decide where I stood with the Marians. I'd traded the hospital overlords for religious ones. A fresh pang of headache started.

"Lena?" Rose prompted.

I swallowed hard. "Okay. Is that... to Auckland?"

"Yes. Then we have just over an hour's drive to Wellsford."

Wellsford. I'd pretended like I was going there when I got the bus ticket, but never had any real intention of going all that way.

155

I'd never been there. It was so far from anything or anywhere or anyone I knew. So far from Aidan. But being so far away… maybe that was what I needed. It would keep me from the hospital. Clearly Rose was on board with me not going back to the hospital. But maybe that was because she didn't know I had escaped, that I hadn't been released legally. Maybe if she knew, she'd change her mind, too. Or make me take meds.

How would she find out, if I didn't tell her? I'd just have to keep quiet, play along, get a handle on the voices and show I was okay. Their murmur was like stifled laughing, knowing I had little to no control over them, particularly without meds, but not wanting to tempt me to try.

"Okay," I said quietly.

"Get some rest. The McDowells will get you anything you need."

"The McDowells? Is that Anne and Reg?"

Rose exhaled sharply. "Anne and Reg, yes. I see you're on first name basis. I hope they've been good to you."

"Yes," I said quickly, hoping I hadn't just got them in trouble somehow. Surely not, she'd introduced herself and Allie and Leroy with their first names. "They've been so nice," I said for added effect.

"Good. They'll be so pleased to have you, I'm sure. Rest, now. I'll see you soon."

"Okay." I was being ungrateful. "Thank you, Rose. For everything."

"You're most welcome, Lena. Anything you need, really. I am so pleased you called."

I waited for her to hang up, but she didn't. I awkwardly added another "see you soon," to which Rose replied, and then I hung up.

I wandered over to the window and gazed out at the night sky, my view of stars limited by the glare of the room's light. Somewhere out there, Rose was coming for me. Coming to take me to a place I wasn't sure I belonged. But then again, did I really belong anywhere? I had jumped from place to place my whole life. The only place I really felt safe was with Aidan, and now even that was gone.

But for now, I had this place. The most luxurious place I might ever set foot in in my whole life. And I... *might be flooding it!* I rushed back through to the still-running bath. The water was only about half deep, but already looked incredibly inviting. I lowered the blinds, stripped off and sunk into the hot water with the faucet still running, my worries evaporating with the steam. I leaned my head back on the edge of the bath and closed my eyes. The murmur of the voices was still there, always there in the background, whispering and mocking my life and choices. I hummed to myself slightly louder than the voices and they didn't fight back. I dropped my hum to the same pitch as the static-like voices, and breathed in deeply.

Accept it, be at peace here. The hum and voices faded together, and for the first time in forever, I started to feel relaxed.

CHAPTER
TWENTY-FIVE

THE HOT WATER didn't do much good for my headache. Well, it did do good in the sense that it made it a whole lot worse. Dehydration, stress, and the incessant mumbling in my mind had finally driving the pounding inside my skull to the point where I was gritting my teeth and done with suffering, and decided to venture downstairs before dinner to ask Anne if she had anything that could help.

I'd chosen the dark blue top and black pants with the light blue cardigan, unable to bring myself to wear the white top or cream pants, figuring I'd get them dirty somehow, even in this well-kept house. I ventured back the way Anne had brought me, and passed their open bedroom door before pausing. Surely, they'd have something in there for the pain, and I wouldn't have to face people until dinner was ready.

I stepped inside and instantly felt a bit weird being in their room uninvited, so decided I better make it quick. Their room was a mirror image of mine, though they had a large dressing table in place of where the couch was in my room. Their ensuite backed onto the same wall as mine, the door not far from the dressing table. I made a beeline toward it, unable to stop myself noticing the dazzle of jewellery on display on the table, symbol-ising the life I wished I could have but knew I never would. No touchy-touchy, though. I'd manage to break something or lose it if I even looked at it too long. Their riches continued to astound me. I would never in my life reach this level of wealth. What had they even done to earn it? Less suffering than me, for sure.

I stepped around the partially open ensuite door and scanned the room before ducking into the cupboards below the vanity. I pulled shampoo, conditioner and moisturiser bottles out temporarily, hoping I'd come across a stash of meds, but nothing.

I put it all back and closed the cupboard doors. They had to have medication somewhere. They were old. Probably be dead without it.

I sighed and got up, gradually resigning to the fact that I'd have to troop all the way downstairs and make conversation and ask for something for the headache. Then, chances were, they were going to fuss over me, their Grace, their Lord and Saviour. Maybe an innocent old headache for me would signal the end of times.

I trudged back out to their room, hoping I was just amping myself up and the conversation wouldn't be that intense. My eyes landed on their bedside table and a cartoon lightbulb switched on above my head. That's where they'd keep their medication, for easy access. I tiptoed over to the table closest to me and the door. There was a sweet photo of Anne and Reg with what must be their kids and grandkids.

Big family. Happy family. At least as far as that photo showed. I'd bet those kids would be real loyal, up until the will got read out. I wondered if they'd been sucked into the Followers of Mary, too. If not, whether they knew about it, what they thought about it. What they would think about me. Espe-cially while I was here, prying through their parents' personal belongings.

Well, desperate times. I crouched down and pulled the drawer open, trying to support its weight so it didn't make too much sound. It dragged open awkwardly, on what must have been wooden slats instead of rollers. I was greeted by the most wonderful sight—a sea of pill bottles, packets and strips. This was the bedside drawer of an old person, for sure.

I shuffled through the boxes, the first few of which were for physical health conditions, then found a strip of paracetamol tablets.

"Yes," I said out loud, and popped a couple into my hand.

I dropped the packet back into the drawer and was about to close it—I swear. Then curiosity got the better of me and I had a longer hunt through the mini pharmacy. I should've taken those pills from Aidan, but I didn't. And now I was without. But maybe Anne had something that could help take the edge off, just while I got a handle on the voices in a more natural way.

The voices screamed in alarm. They'd been so close to being free, being unrestrained. Their protest fuelled my mission. I picked up each bottle, quickly scanning the labels. Most seemed to be for physical health issues, like blood pressure or vitamins, and a few I didn't recognise the name of so didn't want to mess with.

Then I found it. A small plastic bottle, filled almost to the brim with quetiapine. My salvation. I thought about just taking some to get me through, but from the label, it was almost expired. Being that full and almost expired, Anne definitely didn't use them. She wouldn't even miss them.

I pocketed the bottle and closed the drawer, supporting its weight as I pushed it, trying to reduce any noise.

I wasn't quiet enough. I stood and was about to adjust my pants when a female voice came from the doorway. My blood turned to ice, my whole body tensed.

"What are you doing?"

CHAPTER
TWENTY-SIX

I SPUN around to meet the gaze of a middle-aged woman standing in the doorway. Her features were sharp, her dark brown but greying hair pulled back tightly into a bun. She was wearing a dress and apron, her expression unreadable. I was like a specimen under her microscope, each and every one of my flaws magnified for her to dissect.

"I, uh…" *Am busted.* "I had a headache. I was just looking for some painkillers."

The woman's eyes narrowed, judging me, as if trying to see into my soul. Guilt was plastered across my face. She would've seen me pocket the quetiapine. She was going to tell Anne and Reg and they were going to kick me out and the Followers of Mary wouldn't want me anymore, a thief, a druggy, a messed up psychotic teenager. I was no saviour, they'd see it all now. What kind of saviour would steal from someone who was helping them? I wasn't worthy of being their God.

"I think I have some downstairs," the woman said warmly.

Was she messing with me? Or was that eye narrowing just her thinking face?

I held up the two white paracetamol tablets in my hand, and

did my best impression of a genuine smile, which turned out to be more of a grimace. "Found some!" I said cheerily.

"Oh, that's good," the woman said. "Do forgive me, my name is Julia. I was just coming to see if you were ready for dinner?"

She sounded so... relaxed. Like she wasn't actually worried about my snooping, this strange teenage girl in her house.

"I, um..." I stammered again. At that moment, I was not hungry at all, my stomach twisted into knots. "Yes, thank you."

"Great," Julia said. "I've got roast lamb ready, if you would like to join Mr and Mrs McDowell downstairs."

"I, uh..." *Can't speak properly.* "Sure." I tried a genuine smile again. "I'll just be a minute?"

"Certainly," Julia said warmly. "I'm glad to see the clothes fit."

I blinked, not really registering what she was saying, then remembered Julia was the one to set the clothes out for me in the dresser.

"Oh! Yes, thank you," I said enthusiastically. "I love them. Were they yours?"

Julie furrowed her brow a little. "No, Ms Martell. Mrs McDowell had me buy them for you. They're all yours."

I looked down at my sweater and touched it with a newfound appreciation. "You mean... to keep?"

Julia laughed gently. "Yes, to keep."

My eyes bugged wide, just like my mouth, as I tried to say thank you, but little croaks came out instead. Eventually I managed to mumble a "thanks," which definitely didn't do my appreciation justice.

"Not a problem, Ms Martell. Mrs McDowell says you are to have anything you want or need."

I just stared, unsure what to say. Perhaps she did loathe me for being in Anne's room, rifling through her things, but just wasn't allowed to speak out against me.

"We'll see you downstairs soon." Julia did a little bow, then turned toward the landing and left me standing in her employer's private bedroom.

I exhaled loudly and stared at the two little white pills in my hand.

"Thanks," I said out loud to them, and meant it. If I hadn't been searching for them, I wouldn't have found my pink pills. If I hadn't found the pain meds, it would've been harder to convince Julia I wasn't just snooping. I put my other hand in my pocket and caressed the small plastic bottle. It was more than just a bottle of pills; it was my lifeline to a moment's peace, to keep a lid on the relentless mocking of the voices. The soft inner of the pants pocket was a good home for something so precious.

When I got back to my room, I poured another glass of water from the ensuite tap, and downed the two white pills for my headache, along with two pink pills for my sanity, then prepared myself for some people-ing.

CHAPTER
TWENTY-SEVEN

THE EVENING PASSED in a bit of a blur, thanks to my wonderful pink saviours. The roast had been delicious, the conversation awkward but heartwarming at the same time, with all Anne and Reg's dreams for the future. My future. They'd told me all about their family, and the times they'd met the previous me, back when I was Elizabeth. I listened, quite open that I didn't remember any of it, but they were happy enough to reminisce without me contributing much.

My bed was just as wonderful to sleep in as I imagined, and the morning came too soon. I dressed slowly, my limbs heavy with despair. Today we left for the airport. I would be travelling far from this place, the luxury of this house, the welcomeness of Anne and Reg, into the unknown of a religious... what? Commune?

A gentle knock sounded at the door. I opened it and there stood Julia, holding my freshly washed and folded socks, underwear, sweatpants, and t-shirt. She glanced down at a small suitcase by her feet.

"Good morning," she said warmly, handing me the laundry.

"Here are your clothes. Would you like me to pack the rest of your belongings?"

"Oh, I can do it," I said awkwardly, having not even considered that she would offer. The staff in the hospital wouldn't even make your bed for you, even if there were only sheets thrown on it.

It was safer for me to pack my things myself—I'd wrapped the pills up in a pair of underwear, figuring no one would invade my privacy like that. Like I had invaded Anne's last night.

Julia obliged and wheeled the suitcase to me before venturing off to do other Julia things. I placed it on the bed, then carefully transferred all my belongings, all that I now owned in the entire world, from the wooden dresser into the small suitcase. I guessed I owned the suitcase now, too, though mentally prepared to give it back if needed.

I joined Reg and Anne downstairs for a cooked breakfast. It was luxurious, on their grand dining table, but also homely. I didn't want to leave.

I slipped another couple of pink pills before we left for the airport, same seating configuration in the car as the day before. Reg and Anne wanted to see me off as best they could.

The drive to Wellington airport was mostly silent. My nerves grew with each passing minute, my palms slick with sweat. So many people, so much expectation ahead, my own included— how different my life would be if this was all true, if I really was God.

I slunk further down into the seat the closer we got to Wellington. The car windows were tinted, but I didn't want to risk being seen and identified as an escapee, and get dragged back to the hospital kicking and screaming while poor Anne and Reg just looked on in disbelief that they had allowed such vermin into their house.

The pink pills were kicking in as we pulled into the airport VIP drop-off zone, but it didn't fully relieve my anxiety, nor the murmur in my mind. This was a mistake. I wanted to go back, to somewhere quiet and safe, to the McDowells. But I'd given myself over to Rose now; I had to do what she wanted. I didn't have anyone else.

"Rose should be arriving any moment," Anne said from beside me.

"I'll go and check," Hundley said, before unbuckling his seat belt and stepping out of the car. We sat there for about ten minutes, with reassuring words from Reg and Anne, about how wonderful it was to meet me, how they knew I'd do wonderful things, that if I ever needed anything, to simply call them—I was welcome to stop by at any time. All the things I wanted to hear. All the things that were meant for their deity, not me. All the things I knew I couldn't really ask of them, not without Rose's blessing.

Hundley returned and advised us that Rose's plane had landed and she would be coming out shortly. Anne suggested we go inside to wait, so Hundley opened my door, and Reg opened Anne's, just as had happened yesterday and this morning.

Hundley got my suitcase from the boot and wheeled it inside for me before going back to the car to wait. It was weird walking without anything to carry, especially since the suitcase was so small. I gripped my phone in my hand and crossed my arms so it felt like I was doing something, even though it wasn't useful. The pill bottle was tucked into a pair of underwear in my suitcase, so I kept a close eye on where it was wheeled.

The airport was a sensory assault—crowds jostling, suitcases rumbling, announcements blaring. I wished I was wearing my jacket instead of this cardigan, so I could've hidden my face better and blocked out the world with the hood. I was relieved to have the pink pills onboard. We took seats at the arrivals gate and waited for Rose. It was only about another ten minutes before she came through, which made for pretty good timing on everyone's part.

Anne and Reg embraced Rose like old friends, before Rose turned to me, said my name, and held her hands out. I wasn't sure what she was going to do to start with, whether she was going to invade my personal space and come in for a hug, or wanted to shake hands, since I'd never let her before, or whether she just wanted to stand and admire me. I tentatively put my hand out and she swept it up, pressing it between both of hers. "It's so wonderful to see you again," Rose whispered. She leaned in, staring into my eyes, as if she were searching my soul, all the while pressing my hand between her own. "Do you—"

I ripped my hand away, immediate regret that I'd given it over to begin with. My face screwed up in disgust at this weird woman fawning over me. I'd rather she leave me here with Reg and Anne.

But I'd only met Anne and Reg because of Rose; without her I may still be curled up in that playground tunnel. I tried to twist my face into something less offensive.

"How's Allie doing?" Anne asked Rose, thankfully pulling attention away from me. "This must be a big adjustment?"

"Oh, you know Allie," Rose said, and smiled sweetly at her. "She'll bounce back from anything. Such a strong young woman."

"Yes, yes," Anne said, returning the smile. "A shame what happened. But all's well that ends well."

Rose's face seemed to flash with annoyance, or something similar, and she turned back to me.

"Now, we don't have long before our return flight, so we better get through security. I thought we could wait in the lounge, what do you think? Are you looking forward to seeing your new home?"

My eyes bugged and I was grateful for the pink pills doing their job at dulling my anxiety and voices. I hadn't really considered it like that, that the Marian's place would be my new home. I supposed it would be, until they realised I wasn't their saviour.

I didn't want to be rude, so I just nodded.

We bade farewell to Anne and Reg, and I afforded them both a hug, something I certainly wasn't comfortable doing with Rose yet, but maybe I'd get there. There was something odd about Rose, compared to Anne and Reg. They seemed so doddery and old and harmless. So, what... was Rose the opposite? Not exactly the opposite, but she had hunted me down in a literal mental hospital. At least she didn't think I was crazy. Though, no promises there wouldn't be something else... a tasty cordial drink, perhaps.

CHAPTER
TWENTY-EIGHT

OUR SEATS WERE in business class. I'd never been on a plane before, but I don't imagine they were all so luxurious. There was a television in the partition between me and the seat in front of me, and I scrolled through all the options of television shows, movies, music and games, eventually settling on watching the live trip guide, where it zooms out and shows the plane on its projected journey over the country, telling you how long it's been, how fast and high the plane is travelling.

The flight was only about forty-five minutes, and it felt like just as soon as we were free to have our seatbelts off, we had to put them on again for landing. I took the lollies offered by the flight attendant, and Rose explained what they were for. I sucked on them and found it weird how my ears would pop, and wondered what was going on inside my ear drums.

I expected that Allie and Leroy would be waiting for us at the airport, but instead it was another man. Middle-aged, his hair was grey and his skin was weathered, but he seemed full of life and energy. Rose waved to him as we exited the arrivals gate. He waved back with a single hand held up stiffly, though he grinned and then raced over to us.

"Lena," he said warmly, sticking out his hand. "I'm Tim. It's wonderful to meet you."

I couldn't help but grin back and extend my own hand, he seemed so genuine and gentle. "Hi, Tim. Nice to meet you, too."

He took my hand just as gently as expected, and wrapped both of his around it, just as Rose had done. Maybe that was some form of subtle manipulation, or a cult thing.

"Please, let me take your bag," he insisted more than offered, taking it from my hand. "The truck's this way."

Rose smiled at me, and my own dropped a little. I fell into step behind them as they led me through the busy airport and out to the pick-up and drop-off zone. We stopped beside a white ute, skirted in mud and dust, like it had been out on country roads. Tim opened the back door and put my suitcase on the far seat, then stepped aside, probably to let Rose in, or at least to get her guidance as to who was going to sit in the back.

I didn't give them a chance. I crawled in beside my bag.

"Oh, no, Lena, you take the front seat," said Rose.

"No, really, I'm okay," I said back earnestly, fake-smiled at her, then pulled the door shut behind me.

Tim and Rose gave each other a look, as if Tim was waiting for her to say or do something, then Tim shrugged and opened the passenger door for Rose. Maybe chivalry was tied to religion.

The drive to the Followers of Mary's home was long and uneventful. Tim and Rose tried chatting to me about my life and interests, but as I mentioned earlier, I'm a bore-zo, so didn't have much to say. Tim took to telling me all about dairy and deer farming, and how to ensure the fruit and vege crops survived in different weather events and potential disease or predators. His family had owned the farm for over a hundred years, and his kids helped on it now—George, Peter and Lucy, I'd meet them— and his grandkids were even getting into it. They sold their produce, dairy products, meat and skins locally and shipped it nationally, too. I drifted in and out the longer the journey went on. Some of it was actually pretty interesting, mostly because of the way Tim talked about it with so much enthusiasm, but it was exhausting keeping up with his chatter and details.

We traversed away from the hustle of the city, through smaller towns, and out to the countryside, dotted with what were hardly town centres, with just a few shops and houses. The number of mailboxes and associated driveways and houses dwindled as we continued on into the countryside. The roads became narrower, with deep ditches on either side, and no shoulder for evasive manoeuvres in case someone else cut across the centre line, or you took the corner too fast.

Eventually, we turned off down a wide gravel drive. Thick, grey steel gates loomed in front of us, casting imposing shadows in the afternoon sun. High wire fences spread out on either side of the gates—to keep people out, or in?

I rubbed my hands on my pants, sweat already forming. It was really happening—I was following Rose, this weird lady who tracked me down in a hospital claiming I was God, into her home. No one knew where I was, and my phone was on the brink of death, without a charger. This far away from town, there may not even be reception if I did want to call anyone. I could jump out of the ute now and make a run for it, or be taken inside these gates and have no way out. I bit open a fresh cut in my cheek—even if I ran now, I wouldn't make it far. The country roads stretched on for ages before reaching civilisation.

Tim pulled up to the gate and reached into the centre console, before bringing out a small remote. He clicked a button on it and the gates groaned to life, shifting forward to open into the farm.

What if I was making a mistake, trusting these strangers? Allie seemed kind, but I knew nothing about her, really. And Leroy—he would be here, with his obsession about me being Mary, not even calling me by my actual name.

I thought of the hospital, with its sterile white halls and the haze of drugs dulling my senses. Anything would be better than that. And, as my life would have it, this religion was the only thing I had left. Aidan had made his choice, and I was alone. Maybe things would be different once I'd been out of the hospital for a while, and they could all see I was fine without meds.

Rose turned to me, twisting awkwardly in the front seat. "Welcome home, Lena."

It was meant to be welcoming, but this wasn't my home. I forced a weak smile in return. *Don't make a scene. Don't be any more a freak than you already know you are.*

Tim eased the truck up the long driveway, gravel crunching under the tyres. Fields stretched on until out of sight, lines of trees strategically grown to separate paddocks. In the distance were tiny brown animals, which must have been the deer Tim was talking about.

Way up ahead stood a large old house, surrounded by smaller cottages that appeared to spread out further into the fields toward the horizon. To the left, those same high fences stretched all around.

I dug my fingernails into my palm, holding back a rising tide of panic. *Breathe. It's a farm, there's bound to be fences.*

We drew closer to the main house, and people started to gather. I watched from my window as best I could, again wishing I could pull a hood over my head, so I could watch the world without them seeing me.

But these people would be gathered to see me. To welcome their Lord and saviour to their home. I wasn't going to be able to avoid it.

Allie appeared from the front door of the main house, and walked down the steps onto the driveway, arms crossed. At least there was someone I knew, someone who seemed somewhat normal. Other village people were peeking out their windows, looking up from their gardens, or walking toward the house and driveway, stopping and staring.

Staring at me.

The truck pulled to a stop in a wide gravel spot to the left of the house entryway. Allie, along with some other people I didn't recognise, some young and some old, stepped toward the truck. I waited for guidance from Tim and Rose.

Tim twisted in his seat and grinned at me. "Ready?"

Attempting to mirror his enthusiasm, I forced another smile. I wasn't at all ready.

Rose and Tim opened their own doors, and Tim bounded out. A gust of fresh air, smelling of grass and clover, filled the vehicle before he slammed his door shut and turned to mine. I grabbed the door handle at the same time as he did. I could either hold it shut, or...

I took a deep breath and stepped out into the sunshine and expectations.

CHAPTER
TWENTY-NINE

THE VILLAGE PEOPLE were crowded around in awe, some grinning, some with mouths open and hands over their hearts. It gave me the jeebies.

Allie stepped forward and wrapped me in a tight embrace. "Hi, Lena."

I froze, my body not knowing whether it should fight or run so instead following through with the most useless of reactions and darn near dissociating until the attack was over. Only it wasn't an attack, it was genuine care, however disconcerting.

Allie released her grip and stepped back, tipping her head at my expression. She glanced behind her, then turned back to speak to Rose.

"Is it okay if I show Lena her room?"

Rose paused. She looked at me, then at the crowd, and back to Allie, smiling sweetly. "That's a great idea, Allie." Rose stepped forward to address the crowd. "Thank you for coming, everyone. It is my pleasure to introduce Lena to you all. We've had quite a day, though, so formal introductions may have to wait until this evening."

People in the crowd smiled and waved—some even bowed—

before turning and chattering to one another as they wandered back to their chores.

A couple of women and men with their three kids remained behind. They stepped forward as the crowd departed.

"Hey, Dad," one of the women said in Tim's direction. Her brown hair, soft cheekbones and nose didn't really resemble Tim's sharp features, but once I knew the connection, it was obvious. Their eyes were similar, as was the way they held themselves.

Her two kids, seeming no more than six or seven years old, clung to their own father, staring at me, a stranger, an outsider, as if they saw right through the lies about me being God.

The others said their hellos, which were brief, seeing as they'd only been apart a few hours in the time it took Tim and Rose to drive, fly, and drive back that same day.

Tim's children—Peter and Lucy, I learned, George was still out working, and had Leroy with him, thank George—and their partners greeted me kindly and with far less intensity than Tim had on the drive. They encouraged their children to say hello as well, which they did shyly.

"Peter, Shona, Lucy and Greg live in the house with us," Rose explained. "We have a room set up for you already, Lena. I hope you won't mind having a roommate?"

I shuddered a little at the suggestion. Even at the hospital I had my own room. This entire place... they'd always be watching. I'd never get peace.

Allie nudged me with the back of her hand. "It's me," she whispered warmly.

Maybe it wouldn't be so bad after all. It'd be like being at college. Besides, not like I had much peace anyway—the pills were already wearing off, so the voices could taunt me more.

"Come on," Allie said, indicating toward the house. "I'll show you around."

My legs were glued to the spot, my muscles shaking as I

willed them to move. I managed a stumble forward and my legs caught me, remembering what their job was.

Allie led me toward the farmhouse. A collection of gumboots and shoes were piled by the front door, some belonging to the tiny feet of the kids who lived there. The entire place was built from beautiful deep brown wood, which creaked underfoot on many of the floorboards. The large double front door already stood open, exposing a huge entryway with a wooden staircase on the right, leading up to an open landing that stretched out left and right, with a hallway leading off each direction, and a series of matching wooden doors standing in a pattern along the front of the landing, likely bedrooms for the house's masses of residents.

The entryway and landing shared the same ceiling, towering above me in all its wooden glory. There was no fancy chandelier like at Reg and Anne's, but it had its own charm. It was clear it was built by the same people who lived in it, and shared memories across generations.

A large room stood off through a doorway to the right, filled with wooden tables and benches.

"That's the dining room," Allie said, gesturing to the room. "Come take a quick look, but we'll be back there this evening."

I followed her over and peered in at what was more a hall than a room. Allie pointed out the kitchen at the back, where women were milling about, preparing for the shared feast. There was a door toward the back of the hall leading outside, and another in the store room at the back of the kitchen, to allow for easy access to the fields and outside in general.

We turned around and Allie pointed out the other large room on the opposite side of the house, to the left of the entry.

"That's the living room. It's got a fireplace, couches—there's a little library off to the side of it, too," Allie explained.

We took a peek at the living room, but not all the way around to the library. There was a large window facing the driveway, with sunlight streaming onto a window seat next to it. It would be a pretty nice spot to sit and read a book. Maybe I could get a bit of reading done here, since it seemed like they were short on televisions and other electronic gaming, unless we hadn't got to those yet.

Allie led me toward the back of the entryway, where a row of doors matching those on the landing above lined the back wall and stretched out down hallways left and right, just like above. Allie pointed to the right end of the hall.

"Lucy and Greg stay down here. The kids still share, but they've got their own family room down that way. Peter and Shona have the same deal, but upstairs." Allie walked down the hallway to the left, pointing at the doors as she went. "This one's Rose's room, bathroom, and Tim's room is at the end."

We passed the library, now on our left, as we wandered past all the rooms. The library was quaint, with wooden bookcases on every wall and a couple of sitting chairs in the space that led through to the living room.

Allie turned to me, a big grin plastered across her face. "You and me are upstairs." She slipped past me and took me up the stairs. I followed like a lost puppy.

She pointed to the rooms again as we walked down the hallway to the left. "Leroy's room, spare room, bathroom, and this is our room." I was pleased to have at least a few rooms between us and Leroy, though had hoped he'd be on the ground floor. I'd feel even more secure if our door had a lock, so he wouldn't come in to bow and pray to Mary in the middle of the night.

Allie twisted the doorknob and the door creaked open. The room was huge, and bright, with windows on all three walls. Twin beds stood on the wall backing the bathroom, facing out toward one of the windows that looked out over the gardens and fields below. Each bed had a dresser, and a couch sat under one of the windows. I ran my hand over the quilt on the nearest bed.

"We've got the best view in the house," Allie said, beaming, then pointed to the couch. "And that is the best sunning spot, too. Gets sun pretty much all day."

It wasn't like the luxury of Reg and Anne's—I doubted I'd ever taste luxury like that again—but just like the whole house, it had a homely feel. A place of safety and family and relationship building. And Allie was willing to share all this with me.

"It's perfect," I exaggerated. It wasn't a king-sized bed and private ensuite, but it was a different kind of near perfect.

And now it was home.

CHAPTER
THIRTY

ALLIE HAD GONE to check if Rose wanted us to help with meal prep, and left me on my own to ponder for a short while before she returned saying Rose had insisted we rest. I'd slipped another couple of pills and buried the bottle back in my undies, and was laying on the bed staring up at the ceiling when Allie got back. She'd taken up residence on the couch by the window, soaking up the sun. We'd chatted a little about the daily routines and rules of the commune. It didn't sound overbearing. They were allowed to go out to the shops when they wanted, and the kids went to regular school. They grew and raised all their own food and sold it at the market and to wider retailers, just like Tim had said. Not so cult-ish after all.

We'd sat in silence for a while before I finally drew the courage to ask a question that had been burning on my mind.

"What does Rose want from me, do you think? With this whole God thing."

"What do you mean?" Allie asked.

I stayed staring at the ceiling, afraid I might cry or blush or something embarrassing if I faced her directly. "Well, like... if she really thinks I'm God, does she expect me to have superpowers? For me to fix the world, take it over, what?"

Allie laughed softly. "She'll want to help you figure your power out, sure. But we can go slow. I know it's a lot to take in. As for taking over the world—that didn't happen with any of the previous incarnations, so I don't see why it would be any different this time. We could help you to help make the world better, sure, but other than that..."

I paused before speaking again. "So, you don't think she's gonna expect me to get up tonight and do anything?"

Allie laughed again, the kind that wasn't laughing at me. "No, I don't think she expects you to do anything tonight except enjoy yourself and probably say hi to people. Nothing Godly. Just a person, having dinner with other people."

I stared at the ceiling some more. If that really was the case, if they didn't expect me to perform some miracle tonight, heal a paraplegic kid or make a blind man see, if they didn't expect me to make an inspiring speech and appoint disciples or whatever, it might be okay. If I wasn't God, it was a matter of time before they figured that out, and I disappointed them, too. But that didn't have to be tonight. That was a future Lena problem.

"How come you're being so nice to me?" I asked, knowing the answer: because she had to be.

"Why wouldn't I be?"

I shrugged. "You don't even know me. And I haven't exactly been nice to you," I said, not needing to elaborate on the point that I had planned to stand her and Rose up after they gifted me a phone and bus ticket.

Allie spoke as if she'd read my mind. "You did what you felt was best for you. I mean, yeah, you could've gone about it a different way," she teased. "But I'm not gonna take it personally."

I chewed my bottom lip.

"I'm choosing not to take it personally, you know? I'm not..."

She paused. "Like you... but whatever we put into the universe is what we're going to get back. So, I focus on the positive, and the good, and helping each other."

Easy to do when good things happen to you.

Allie continued after a pause. "Have you ever heard of manifesting reality?"

"Like when you believe something enough, you make it come true?" I asked.

"Yeah," she replied. "That's it exactly. Except you—or God—has that on a massive scale. Whatever you believe can and will actually come true." She shook her head. "You—or God—has the opportunity to help so many people. It's an incredible honour, and duty."

With beliefs like that, she would make a better God than I would. Nothing ever went how I wanted. I'd end up burning the world down, or causing the apocalypse or something. Guess I could start again in another life.

A shiver went through me as I pictured a blackened Earth, that was my doing. "What if I muck it up?"

She turned to me. "You won't muck it up. Just believe in yourself." Clearly, she hadn't met me. "Besides, you have me now."

If only I could stop thinking about the world burning.

CHAPTER
THIRTY-ONE

MY STOMACH RUMBLED and mouth watered as the dinner smells wafted to our upstairs room. Allie heard it and laughed.

"Shall we go downstairs?" she offered. "We might be able to sneak something before dinner."

I grinned back. Our first secret mission together. "Sure."

The dining hall was already beginning to crowd with families and individuals of all ages, laughing and talking as they gathered inside. Food was being laid out on the long wooden tables, and I wondered where everyone would sit, if the tables were taken up.

Movement outside the window caught my eye. There were people milling about, and lines of tables and chairs set up outside.

"Uh, how many people are coming to this thing?" I asked nervously.

"Everyone," Allie said quietly.

"How many people is 'everyone'?"

Allie looked to the ceiling, thinking. "I think we have about eighty people living here, now?"

"Eighty!?" I repeated, in awe.

"Around about that. And then some people who live nearby, as well."

Almost a hundred people, all gathering here for me. All living in this commune, together, dedicated to me.

No, dedicated to Mary. As nice as that would be, to be special in a good way, there was no guarantee that I was Mary.

I followed Allie over to one of the tables, laden with a range of breads and meats and salads. My mouth watered more, taking it all in. Allie snatched up a bread roll and indicated to me to do the same. I reached for it, then the sound of my name made me jump and retract my hand.

"Lena!" Rose exclaimed. "You're looking rested."

"Yes, thank you," I mumbled, faking a smile. My heart was racing, waiting to be scolded for digging into the food before dinner. Maybe it had to be blessed. Maybe *I* had to bless it.

"Come, come. There are people I'd like you to meet." Rose placed her arm around my shoulder and guided me toward the back of the room. A piece of me died as I was escorted away from the food and toward the ever-growing busyness of the hall. Rose led me to a group of people where she introduced me to an older couple, and their daughter and son-in-law, who had a young child themselves, before moving on to meet other people in the commune. Though normally shy with strangers, I couldn't help but smile back at their enthusiastic welcome.

The Marians, young and old, were so welcoming. Many stepped in to hug me, which I rigidly accepted. Their intentions were good, despite my discomfort.

We made our rounds, my stomach getting evermore wishful of the food that was being brought in from new arriving guests, and out from the kitchen. I managed a sideways glance at Allie, hoping to communicate a you-told-me-this-wouldn't-be-a-big-deal, and a please-save-me, in the same look. Allie took the hint, and suggested to Rose that it may be time to eat. Rose laughed, apologised, and agreed. She invited us to take a seat, and Allie led me outside and over to a table where Leroy was seated, much to my disappointment. I managed to position Allie between us, but his enthusiasm at sitting near me—near "Mary" —was still too much.

I greeted the others around us, including Shona and her two kids, and some other people, whom I had met briefly just prior, and already forgotten their names. The rest of the Marians took their seats at one of the many tables laid out in what seemed to be little to no ordered placement—the tables were all different sizes; some long and wide, others narrow, others round. It was as if people had brought their personal dining table from home.

Rose stood next to the house, facing the group. When everyone was seated, or near to it, with only a few people wandering about to get a drink or fuss over their children, Rose held up a circular metal plate. She lifted what looked like a ball on a stick, then smacked the ball onto the plate. A low rumble sounded out, and the Marians fell silent and turned to her.

"Welcome, everyone." Rose's voice was dulled by the ambient outside noise, the breeze pushing past people, leaves rustling in the trees, insects and birds singing. She strained to address the gathering, her old vocal chords wavering as they worked hard to produce speech loud enough for everyone to hear.

"As you will all know, we are gathered here today for the most wonderful of reasons. Not only do we welcome a newcomer to our humble following, but we welcome our one, true, and only Mary, returned to life through the wonderful Lena." Rose looked over at me and lifted her hand to gesture toward me. Every set of eyes followed hers, traced to me, set upon me. My own eyes widened, as did my mouth, as my cheeks flamed. I wanted to flee, but I was frozen yet again. Allie had said this wouldn't be weird.

Allie must've read my horror, and maybe recalled her promise, because she gripped my forearm under the table and whis-

191

pered, "sorry." It grounded me enough to hear what Rose said as my panic and brain fought for control of my body.

"Welcome, Lena." Rose's voice was filled with warmth. "We have waited with open hearts for the day you would find your way to us."

A ripple of agreement and understanding coursed through the crowd as Rose's words settled over them. Heads bowed in my direction, hands were raised and clasped together. Many placed their hands over their heart and mouthed words to me I couldn't decipher.

"Please, everyone, enjoy your meal, and thank you all for your contribution, and joining together to welcome Lena home," Rose finished, before stepping aside. People restarted their chatter, but remained seated, watching me. Waiting for me to go and get food first.

Allie rubbed my arm. "That was... a lot. Sorry. I really didn't think they'd be weird."

I tore my eyes from the surreal scene in front of me and blinked at her. "I don't... I'm not... what if I..." I couldn't finish a sentence, couldn't get the words out, to question their belief that I was this saviour, God reincarnate.

"Hey, hey," Allie soothed, putting her face in front of mine to lock my eyes with her brown ones. "Don't go there. Forget about all that. Just sit here with me."

I stared into her soft brown eyes, the same colour as mine, and linked my breathing to hers.

"Let's go get some food, eh?" Allie suggested. I followed her inside, almost in a trance. She kept me close, and thanked people on my behalf as we walked.

CHAPTER
THIRTY-TWO

THE REST of the dinner was, thankfully, less intense, besides Leroy basically staring at me the whole time. The woman across from me had reiterated how wonderful it was that I was there, asked me about my travels, and I answered in between mouthfuls, dipping my head to indicate I was trying to eat, while also aiming to not be rude. I was only eating thanks to their shared hospitality, after all. Allie let it go on for a short while, I guess because it wasn't God-related, but then came to my rescue.

"I think she's trying to eat, Ruth," she said.

"Of course, of course, sorry dear, yes, you eat!" Ruth exclaimed, appearing embarrassed.

I briefly considered reassuring her, then just smiled and returned to my food, bumping my knee against Allie's under the table in thanks.

After dinner, people hung around for more socialising.

Older residents and those with young children left the party first, while it was still mostly light. The gathering thinned out as the light faded, and several tiki torches were placed around pathways and lit. Lucy and another woman brought out candles for the tables. It was quite a magical feeling, being outside in the evening like that.

It had been a Very Long Day, though, and eventually I whispered to Allie asking if I could go to bed. She went over and had a word with Rose, then came back over with Rose to tell me it was fine, and she was going to bed, too.

Rose placed her hand on my upper arm. I flinched, even though she meant it to be comforting.

"Have you had a good night, Lena?" Rose asked.

"I'll see you up there," Allie said with a strained smile, kind of like a grimace, because she knew exactly that I did not want her to leave me there with Rose. I shot her a pleading look, one that I hoped screamed "don't do this," before she turned and rushed off.

"Uh, yes," I muttered back to Rose. "Thank you."

"Good," she continued, her hand still on my arm. "I do hope you know how pleased we all are to have you here."

I glanced around at the tables and remaining partygoers, then thought back to her speech. "Yeah, you made it pretty clear." It came out more snarky than I intended. "Thank you. For everything," I followed up with, trying to sound sincere.

"Not at all," she said. "We look after each other here. And you're one of us now. Come, I'll walk you to your room."

"No, that's okay, I know—"

"I insist," Rose cut in, kindly, but forcefully at the same time. I was supposedly her God, but she was still the ruler of this religion. She gestured with her other hand for me to move inside, giving me a nudge with the hand already on my arm. She let it fall off once I started walking where she wanted.

Leroy rushed over from where he'd been seated, watching the festivities. "Is Mary going to bed now, Mum?" he asked Rose, as if I wasn't really there, or couldn't speak for myself. I narrowed my eyes at him.

Rose noticed my glare, and spoke gently to him at first. "Yes, Leroy. I'll be down shortly."

"I'll come!" he chirped.

"No, you'll stay here," she said sharply. His face dropped in disappointment and hurt, both that he didn't get to follow me, and that he'd been spoken to like that. I couldn't help but smirk at his reaction.

"If there's anything you need," Rose continued saying to me as we walked toward the stairs, leaving Leroy pouting behind us. "You just ask. Myself, Allie, whomever you're most comfortable with."

"Okay," I said. "Thank you. Allie's been really good. She's told me a little about the place already. It's a lot to wrap my head around." It was true. I was still processing questions about this place and what my role was in all of it.

"Of course," said Rose. We started the slow climb up the stairs, slowed significantly due to this elderly woman insisting on walking me up them, despite her room being strategically placed on the ground floor. If she tumbled down those stairs I would partly blame myself—especially now having put that thought out into the world. *Great use of manifesting reality, well done, Lena.*

"Really, you don't have to walk me," I said.

Rose held her hand up. "It's no problem." *Famous last words.*

We made it to the top of the stairs—just—and Rose hobbled with me to our room. Allie had left the door ajar, but Rose pulled it shut quietly.

"Wait out here with me for a moment," Rose instructed. "Can you hear Allie inside?"

I turned my head to the side and listened, but couldn't hear anything. I put my ear next to the door and still couldn't hear anything, so I pressed it hard against the door. I heard murmurs from inside, but couldn't make out who was speaking, nor what they were saying. Logically, I knew it was Allie, but nothing more.

I stepped away from the door. "No, why?"

Rose considered this. "How about if you close your eyes, and picture Allie praying?"

I frowned, sighed, and did as she said. She was housing and feeding me, so I'd entertain her for the minute.

I pictured Allie best I could, and tried to clear my mind well enough that I could listen to every sound of the house. There was still lots of movement down in the kitchen, but otherwise it was mostly quiet. Still, I couldn't hear Allie. Just the usual hum and chatter of the millions of indecipherable conversations happening in my head.

I opened my eyes and shrugged. "Sorry," I said to Rose.

She exhaled with disappointment. "That's alright."

I turned to go into our room and she stopped me.

"Oh, Lena?"

I raised my eyebrows to her.

"When was the last time you took psychiatric medication?"

I folded my arms across my chest and blew the air out of my lungs through pursed lips, making my cheeks balloon outwards. I looked around like I was thinking. "Oh, I guess that would be... the day before yesterday?" I lied. She didn't need to know about my stash of pink pills.

Rose smiled at me, pleased with my answer. "Very well. I think it would be good for you to spend some time getting to know the farm, maybe for a few days. Allie will show you around."

I nodded slowly. "Sounds good."

"Very good. Goodnight, Lena. Sleep well."

I turned to go into the room. "You too." *You crazy old bat.*

I opened the door and walked into our room, closing it behind me. Allie was kneeling by her bed, praying. I snuck over to my dresser and took out my undies-wrapped pill bottle, and fluffy blue pyjamas that Julia had picked and Anne had bought for me, then headed to the bathroom. I popped my pills and changed, and by the time I got back, Allie was done praying, and in bed herself.

"Okay to turn the light off?" I asked.

"Yup!"

I switched it off and stumbled my way to my bed, which was basically a straight shot from the light switch but was still unnerving in an unfamiliar room. My eyes had adjusted to the darkness a little by the time I got halfway, and I could make out the shape of the bed in the moonlight that was dimly filtering through the curtains.

I tucked into bed and lay there, staring at the ceiling, now covered in dark shadows, waiting for the pills to kick in and my mind to quiet.

Allie's breath was steady, peaceful. She'd been so nice today. Not at all like the first time I'd met her, when she seemed so cold.

"Can I tell you something?" I asked.

"Of course," Allie replied, sleepily.

"When I first met you, I thought you hated me."

Allie sat up and leaned on her elbow. "Why would you think that?"

I raised a shoulder and dropped my head toward it. "I dunno. You seemed kind of... cold. Like you hated me, without even knowing me. Which isn't all that surprising when it comes to me, but considering I'm meant to be your Lord God... Yeah, I dunno, maybe I read it wrong."

Allie grunted. She stayed on her elbow, looking at me in silence, for about a minute, before she flopped back onto her pillow. Interesting that she didn't deny it. Even for courtesy's sake, most people would deny it.

CHAPTER
THIRTY-THREE

I WOKE the next morning to plenty of activity within the house and outside. Allie was shuffling around by her dresser, just finishing getting dressed. She'd warned me we'd be up early, but it was still basically dark outside. Not even medication time yet.

Only I didn't have to take medication here. A smile spread across my face, and I stretched my arms out above my head.

"Morning," I said brightly, no longer bothered by the sun not being out yet.

"Morning," Allie replied. "You sound happy."

"Oh, you know, it's a beautiful day to be free."

Allie laughed. "Sure is. Let's hope you still think that after today."

I pulled my arms back in and sat up, leaning on them. *What did she mean by that? What did she and Rose have planned?*

"What do you mean?" I asked, hesitantly.

She glanced at me and laughed again. "I'm teasing. But you've never been on a farm before, so…" she trailed off, then continued since I stayed silent. "Let's just say you're gonna want to have a decent breakfast. I'll see you downstairs soon?"

I flopped back onto my pillow and resumed staring at the ceiling like yesterday.

"See you soon," I agreed, my mind creating potential scenarios for the day. Allie had told me about farm life and what we might get up to, but also said they'd take it easy on me, both with the farm and the whole God thing. But she could have anything planned today—cleaning animal pens, birthing cows... the bed wasn't that comfy but it would be a heck of a lot better than getting cow poo all over me.

But freedom. This was freedom. And the people here loved it. And I could love it.

Stay positive, manifest reality.

I will love farm life.

I took a deep breath in and rolled out of bed. Allie or whoever had set out some clothes for me which were a bit more suitable for farm life than the ones Anne had given me. They were more comfortable than I expected, too. Not the rough made-from-plants-because-we-live-off-the-land scratchiness that I expected. I popped a couple more pills and rewrapped the bottle in my undies.

All set to face the day as best I could, I trudged downstairs to the dining hall. Allie, Rose, Shona and the kids were there. The others had already headed out, I was informed, and was relieved that included Leroy, so I could eat in peace. Allie showed me the breakfast options. They had cereals and toast, along with fresh fruit and fresh milk, all of which I trialled and all of which tasted amazing. I had zero issue having a decent breakfast, just as Allie had recommended.

Before long, Allie and I set off, first to the milking shed, where Allie re-introduced me to Clara, a woman from the night before, whom I barely remembered even seeing, but whom was so utterly smitten to have me there. Clara showed me how to milk the cow and gave me a turn. The feel weirded me out at first, like it was unnatural to be doing that to a cow, but when the milk finally squirted out... it felt good to actually achieve something, to be part of something.

Allie showed me around the rest of the farm, and we helped out (I use the term "help" loosely) so I could have a try of every-thing: feeding the chickens and pigs, weeding the garden, gath-ering fresh veggies, and picking apples from the orchard, even cleaning the coop, pens and sheds, much to my mixed disgust and enjoyment. It was gross, but oddly satisfying. It was honest work, as they say.

We went back to the house for lunch, which Shona and another woman, Fran, had set up for the house residents and Fran's family. We ate, they shared laughs, and treated me like a normal person—no drilling into my past, or watching me when they thought I wouldn't notice.

It was like I was one of them. For the first time in forever, I was part of something good. I belonged, I mattered, just as much as everyone else. Even though they had this claim that I was quite literally a god, there was no extra fussing or different expectations—I joined in with the clean up, the harvesting, the farming. I had to pitch in, just like everyone else.

The duties continued after lunch—cleaning out the stables, grooming the horses. They were majestic creatures, and Allie promised she'd teach me to ride. That was the fantasy—horses always seemed to be reserved for the rich girls, with their fancy houses and perfect lives. Though, Nia was a horsey girl, and she was still down to earth. Probably the only one, aside from people like this who rode for a purpose.

My shoulders sank with the thought of Nia. She'd be in the hospital, all alone. Drawing her mandalas. She hadn't wanted this for me, to get in deep with the Marians. But then, she didn't know that this was what it was like. It was homely, a commu-nity. I had a real chance of being happy there. And if I was happy, then surely she'd be happy for me. As should Aidan. I didn't need hospital or pills after all. Well, besides the ones that helped take the edge off.

Allie called for help with one of the horses, and my attention was pulled back to the present. We worked through until early evening, before heading back to the house with fresh produce to help with dinner. Leroy, Tim and George arrived back at the house at the same time as us, careening past us in Tim's ute, with Leroy driving. He near ran us off the path when he saw me, so desperate to wave and get my attention that Tim had to grab the steering wheel. I smirked when he was scolded back at the house, though it was ridiculous they'd let him drive in the first place.

With full bellies and aching feet, Allie and I flopped onto the couches in the living room. Shona and Lucy tended to their kids, getting them ready for bed, and Rose joined us. Tim lit the fire, even though we didn't need the heat, and we sat watching the flames dance.

As night fell, Tim invited me and Allie out rabbit and possum shooting with his sons, son-in-law, and Leroy. Allie seemed keen, but the thought of Leroy with a gun didn't sit well for me. He'd end up hurting someone, and I didn't want to be around for that.

I played it off as though I was too tired, so Rose got out a book instead.

"How about a story, girls?" Rose asked, expecting the answer to be yes.

Allie obliged. "Sure."

The cover was thick, like one of those old books that get hand stitched. The story was about a young African warrior name Kazi, from the Maasai tribe, who united neighbouring tribes to fight against a common enemy that was taking them out one by one. I waited for the religious preachy part, but it never came.

CHAPTER
THIRTY-FOUR

THE DAILY ROUTINE was much the same as that first day, and I fell into it easily enough. Though my feet and muscles ached, it was a good ache. I was doing something, part of something. I was contributing. I had a purpose.

So much so that it was halfway through the second day on the farm before I realised I hadn't taken any pills since the previous morning. The voices were still there, but not bothersome. They didn't mock me like usual, they were just... there.

Who would've thought some decent work and fresh air was the cure for illness? Almost like there should be a children's story made about it. Call me Heidi.

It certainly wasn't what the doctor ordered, which made it all the more satisfying. I didn't need pills for sleep, I didn't need them for socialising, I didn't need them for the voices. I challenged myself to see how long I could go without, and at the end of my fourth full day working the farm, there was still no need in sight.

Rose read us a story each night. Tucked up on the couch, sharing a blanket with Allie, it was like the childhood I'd never had. Shadows danced on the walls and Rose's face from the flames in the fireplace, giving a warm and sort of magic feeling to the room.

The story book was a very odd combination of people's lives; on my third night there, the story had been about an Egyptian queen, Seshetara or something. On my fourth, about a little Irish boy who grew up to be a copper miner.

Tonight was about a peasant girl in medieval France, named Marguerite. Marguerite wove tapestries for the local lord. She lived a simple life, but was happy enough. I snuggled into the couch and watched the flames in the fireplace as Rose's lyrical voice conjured phantom images in my mind: Marguerite leaving her stone cottage, the kettle on the potbelly, as she ventured off down the dirt path toward town.

I closed my eyes and snuggled further under the blanket, my fingers and toes tingling with its warmth.

And then I was there. The day was grey and overcast, the sky heavy with the threat of rain. I trudged along the muddy streets of my village, my homespun dress and headscarf barely keeping me warm in the chilly air. The work I was on my way to do was both tedious and taxing; I was to weave a tapestry for the lord of the castle, an image of him riding a horse into battle, an image of fiction, for all I knew.

I had done such a task many times before, but it never ceased to amaze me how a single thread could create such beauty, when woven into a design. As I walked, I was lost in thought—a thought within a memory that was being created at that moment —considering the design and the colours I would need for the project. I was grateful for the chance to put my skills to use, as well as for the meagre income it would provide for my family.

The fields around me were green with new life, and the trees were beginning to bud in preparation for summer. I began to pick out landmarks that I knew well; a decrepit old barn belonging to one of my neighbours, an old oak tree standing guard over a pasture, and farther on, the tall stone walls surrounding Seigneur Rochefort's home. My spirits lifted as my destination came closer into view.

As I stepped onto the bridge I fell from my being, returned in an instant to Lena, sitting on the couch in the Marian's farmhouse, my legs tucked under the blanket shared with Allie. I shivered, the chill from the French air still fresh on my skin, and tried to comprehend what had just happened. I looked up at Rose, then over to Allie.

Neither paid me any attention. Neither had any idea that I'd slipped from reality worse than I ever had before, hallucinating living out the life of this Marguerite. I bit into my lip, hard enough to draw blood, which I hadn't done for days. The metallic taste flooded my mouth and was weirdly soothing—grounding. I pulled my hands up to cover my mouth, crossing them over my chest as if that would protect me from myself.

The doctors had been right. I'd been too long without pills. It wouldn't be long before I had a full-blown psychotic episode. As ever, the voices cheered on this thought, willing me to my demise. I mentally recited going into my underwear drawer and downing some pills when we got to our room. I'd take more than usual, to try hold the psychosis off longer while I figured out what to do.

Allie noticed something was wrong before I got to my pills. She stopped when we got through our bedroom door.

"Okay, what's up?" she pressed.

I played innocent. If I told her, I'd be admitting that they were wrong—I wasn't God, I was sick. They might send me away. "Nothing. What do you mean?"

She arched her eyebrows at me. "You've been weird since that story. I didn't ask down there because... well, Rose, but what is it?"

I sucked my bottom lip in, completely ruining any chance I had to keep this secret.

Her voice softened. "You can tell me."

The voices sniggered, rising in their mocking again. They'd let me believe I was healthy and safe in this place, just so they could let me get worse, so bad that I'd have to leave. That if I didn't leave, the Marians would drive me out for being a fraud.

I didn't have anywhere else to go, though. I couldn't even walk to town, it was so far away, and on such narrow roads I'd likely get hit by a car. I was at the mercy of Allie, and her choice to hide my secret.

I took a deep breath in. "That story tonight... it's weird, but... I felt like I was... *there*. Like it was me."

Allie turned to me, grinning. She thought I was crazy. My life with the Marians was over.

"It's not crazy at all," Allie said. "It was you."

"Huh?" My confusion was just as much about the first part as it was the second. I was clearly psychotic, needing to be medicated—I'd had an out of body experience.

"All the stories are about you. They're your previous lives."

"Okay, hold on," I said, trying to determine whether Allie was as delusional as me. "You're trying to tell me that in a past life, I've been a queen of Egypt, a warrior in Africa, an Irish miner, and a French lissier?"

"A French what?"

"A lis—" I paused. That wasn't English. That was a French term, for a tapestry weaver. How did I know that? Unless I knew that through Margeurite. But no, hallucinations only played on what we already knew, whether or not it was in our conscious thought. Rose must have mentioned it during the story.

"A lissier," I said, surety in my situation renewed, despite my longing to be wrong. "A French tapestry weaver."

Allie still had that grin plastered on her face. "Okay, if you say so. And yes, I am telling you that you had all those past lives. Plus heaps more."

I nodded slowly, trying to rationalise Allie's claim—craving to, because it would mean that I wasn't sick. It wasn't outside the realm of possibility that we had previous lives, even when we weren't supposedly God Herself. But those were God's human lives that Rose was reading, or supposed to be, anyway. And when I was there as Marguerite, I'd actually felt it. I'd lived it, like the memories were all sitting there waiting to be accessed, as clear as any memory from my life as Lena.

I realised I was thinking in French, switching in and out between Lena and Marguerite.

"Tell me more," I whispered.

CHAPTER
THIRTY-FIVE

"THIS IS FANTASTIC," Allie said. "Rose is gonna flip."

"Allie," I said quietly, my voice trembling. "I'm really starting to freak out here." The voices rose in my mind, whispering to me in their indecipherable tongue, willing me to scream, to show I was mad, that I needed to be locked up in a hospital with the key thrown away.

"Sorry, sorry." Allie took my hands in hers and led me to my bed. "I know it's a lot to take in."

I scoffed. "Yeah, bit of an understatement." This was the first proper evidence that I might actually be God incarnate, if I believed it was real and not a hallucination. If those were the previous lives of God, and I had lived them... then, by the power of deduction...

"What... what does this all mean?" I asked.

"It means," she said, squeezing my hands, "that you're starting to get hold of your powers. It means that you're gonna be able to change the world. And I'll be right there with you."

That was all a bit too much pressure. I wasn't going to change the world, and definitely not for the better. Nothing ever went to plan for me, never worked out. Even if I tried, I'd only make things worse.

"But what does it... how?" I stammered.

Allie shook her head. "I—we—don't know how, exactly. Just that you will. When the time is right. You'll tap into Everything, every person, every plant, that ever has been or ever will be. Kind of like the Akashic records, only everything, not just life."

"The what?" Some God I was, even the Everything that I was meant to possess was foreign to me.

"The Akashic records. They're a collection of every thought, experience, intention, emotion—everything—of every living thing that has ever or will ever live. But it doesn't matter, you have access to more than that. You'll have access to *Everything*." Allie put emphasis on that word that was steadily growing in enormity.

"Right," I said quietly. "No pressure, then."

Allie laughed and slapped her hand on mine, then put her hands on my shoulders and looked me square in the eyes. "It happens on your terms, okay? Manifest reality, remember?"

Manifest reality, right. Only...

"I don't know that that's such a good thing, when it comes to me. Things don't normally turn out... well... for me."

"Well, then, we'll just have to work on changing that, won't we?" Allie said with a smile. "You've got me, now! I'm with you, okay?"

I took a deep breath in and dipped my head. If I had any shot, it would be with this girl who had far better morals and hope and was so confident in herself. I would've been so much better off—and the world would be so much better off—if I'd had the life Allie had lived. I might not ever have ended up in the psych ward, if Rose had been my minder.

The voices pushed again, taunting me, wanting me to think that everything would be exactly the same, no matter where I was or who I was with, because I was broken and useless and powerless. I clenched my teeth and squeezed my eyes shut, willing them to stop.

"You okay?" Allie asked. I opened my eyes to respond and her face was etched with concern.

"Yeah." I produced a fake smile.

"Tell me." There was genuine care in her voice. "Seriously, Lena. I'm in this with you."

What harm could it do to tell her? "It's just the voices. They got less, since I've been here, but tonight's been... a lot."

Allie gripped my hands again. "Let me help. This used to help me when I couldn't sleep. Guided relaxation, have you done it?"

I hunched down and groaned. "Yes, I have. It's not gonna work. I've tried it."

"Ah," Allie said, holding up a finger. "But you haven't tried it with me. Manifest reality, Lena. This will work. Hop into bed." She strode over to her own bed and sat on it, facing me. I sat where she'd left me, so she gestured for me to get into bed. I obliged—I owed her that much.

"Get comfy," Allie instructed. "Legs out straight, arms relaxed by your side?"

I wiggled into position. "Yep."

"Okay," she continued. "Close your eyes. Now, focus on your breathing." Her speech softened, slowed, pausing between each instruction. "Feel the coolness of the air as you inhale. The warmth of the air as you exhale. Take a deep breath. In, one, two. Hold, one, two. And out, one, two, three, four." She paused before repeating the direction another four times.

I obeyed calmly. I was pretty used to this. As I'd said, I'd tried all this before and knew for a fact it was not going to stop the voices. They laughed and mocked that I was trying to quiet them naturally, that I hadn't learned yet that I had no power against them. I squeezed my eyes shut instinctively, and in vain, as if that would possibly have any impact whatsoever.

Allie told me to imagine each of my muscles was controlled by a switch, and guided me through turning each of them off. I pictured me, as God, accidentally sending blackouts across the country—across the world—because I was doing something as mundane as guided relaxation where I switched lights off in my own body. Supposedly, as God, I'd actually have the power to do that, even by accident.

"Now as you wander up into your mind, you see that instead of a light switch, there's a dimmer."

Huh, that's different.

The voices rose in their demands, surging forward in a mob to try prevent me from getting to the dimmer.

"You wrap your fingers on either side of the dimmer. As you touch it, you feel its power. It has the power to turn down the lights, or the stress, or the volume of the voices within your mind. It has the power to do whatever you want it to do."

The voices yelled louder, indecipherable and angry.

Turn down the voices, I definitely want the dimmer to turn down the voices.

"Right now, this dimmer is for turning down the volume of the voices within your mind," Allie continued. "You turn it ever so slightly to the left, and notice the smallest change."

I did not notice any change.

"You turn it further to the left, turning down the volume of the voices. The voices start to fade out…"

I pictured my fingers on the dimmer, and turning it, and turning it, and…

Oh my God, it worked.

I breathed in sharply.

"… fading further and further, as you turn the dimmer down."

I turned it left. I turned it fully left. I turned it OFF.

Then I promptly fell asleep.

CHAPTER
THIRTY-SIX

I SLEPT LIKE A LOG, as they say. So much so that by the time Allie called my name to rouse me, the sun was streaming through the curtains.

"Huh?" I asked, the world fading back into being. "What time is it?"

"Late," Allie laughed.

"Why didn't you wake me?"

Allie shrugged, heading toward the door. "You looked so peaceful. Besides, Rose wants us here today. She's downstairs, waiting, once you've had breakfast. I'll see you down there."

I flopped my arms onto my pillow above my head, and took a deep breath in. *Peace.* The first night in forever that I'd actually slept well, peacefully, without constant chatter demanding my attention. Even the pills hadn't snuffed them out that well. How did Allie do that?

It didn't matter. She had. My own little miracle worker. And now Rose wanted us to stay back because...

The night before flooded back to me. My life as Marguerite. The Akashic records. Everything.

And along with it, the voices. I grabbed for the mental

dimmer and twisted, twisted, round and round to the left, but it did nothing. It was broken.

I needed Allie.

I groaned and slapped my hands onto my face, covering it. I wanted to scream into my palms. I'd been so close.

But that was it—it wasn't just close, Allie had actually managed to quiet the voices for me. She could do it again. She and Rose could teach me other things, too.

I bolted up and out of bed. I threw on some pants, a bra and top, in my haste getting the top back to front. I flipped it around as I stumbled out of the room and down the stairs, and found Rose and Allie in the living room.

"Good morning," Rose said warmly as I came into view. "How'd you sleep?"

"Morning," I replied brightly. "Great, thanks to Allie."

Allie gave a small bow from her seat on the couch.

"That's great news," Rose said, smiling as she looked back and forth between us. I took a seat next to Allie and she held out her fist for me to bump it.

"Allie suggested you may like to learn more about your past today?" Rose asked more than stated.

"Actually," I said, grimacing. I looked at Allie pleadingly. "I don't know what you did last night, but the voices were gone. I mean, gone, gone. I need to learn how to do that. They're back already." I slumped back onto the couch.

Allie was about to speak, but Rose spoke first.

"The voices aren't necessarily a bad thing, Lena. I don't think they mean you any harm. Rather, the opposite."

With all due respect, lady, you're not in my head. I wanted to say it, was so tempted to, but I was only at this farm because of Rose. I figuratively bit my tongue, physically biting my cheek in its place. The familiar taste of blood flicked my tongue. *Breakfast. And back to my old habits of self-destruction.*

"The voices you hear are actually prayers," Rose said. "From people all around the world."

She'd tried telling me that back in the hospital, only now it seemed far more plausible. Whatever they were, they were annoying. And rude.

"Whatever they are, they never leave me alone. It's exhausting," I said exasperatedly. I turned to Allie and pleaded with my eyes as well as my voice. "Please."

Allie glanced at Rose, advocating for me though still silently asking permission. I followed her lead and pleaded with Rose through my eyes, too.

"Fine," Rose sighed. "I suppose we could look to teach you to focus on one voice at a time, so you could understand what's being said."

"Thank you!" I bounced up and down in my seat, then grinned at Allie.

She laughed, enjoying my excitement.

Rose was smiling, too. "You used guided meditation last night, I hear?"

"Yeah," I confirmed. "But it's never worked before. Nothing has—pills, meditation, therapy. Nothing's worked, until last night." I glanced at Allie again and grinned.

Rose leaned forward. "Tell me more about the voices, Lena. They're always with you?"

"Pretty much always," I said. "It's worse sometimes more than others. Like they're mocking me or something. When I'm already stressed out. They get so loud I can't hear anything else sometimes." Right on cue, the voices laughed at me.

"I feel you may be misinterpreting them," Rose said. "So we need to help you learn to focus, to hear them only when you're ready."

I rolled my eyes, tempted to argue against her misinformed perspective. "Or just blot them out. That works, too."

Rose smiled a fake sweetness. "They're the prayers of people, Lena. Your people. I'm afraid you can't just block them out."

Who are you to tell me what I can and can't do, lady? Apparently I'm God, so I'll do what I damn well please.

Only I couldn't do what I pleased, because I was basically crippled by these voices my entire life. I shot Allie a look. She dropped her gaze to her hands in her lap, obviously knowing what I was thinking and hoping for, but not wanting to speak out against Rose.

Who was the deity here?

"Fine." Rose meant well, but she didn't understand. She hadn't spent her life tormented by an endless chatter in her head. Hadn't endured the migraines and sleepless nights. She'd let me snuff them out, if she'd been through what I had.

"Great," Rose said. "Allie, I'd like you to go next door and pray until I call for you."

Allie nodded once and floated out of the room. She winked at me as she passed. My eyes followed her, staring at the spot she once was, after she disappeared through the doorway, leaving me alone with Rose.

"Lena," Rose said from her chair. "Please close your eyes."

Again, I obeyed, and straightened my back like a good yogi.

"Take a deep breath," Rose started, just like Allie had, only with more expectation. "In, one, two. Hold, one, two. And out, one, two, three, four." She worked through the breathing exercise, and the voices grew louder. I squeezed my eyes shut, as per usual, knowing it wouldn't do anything. I needed Allie to get me to the dimmer.

"Picture the sun above you. Feel its warmth on your hair, your face, on your arms, warming your skin everywhere it touches," Rose continued, pausing often. "I want you to let the sun in, let the warmth in. Feel the warmth seeping through your skin and into your body. Let the sun merge with your being. Let it flow through your body with your life force. Feel the warmth of the sun as it fills your fingers, your hands, your arms, up to your shoulders. Feel your muscles relax as the warmth spreads through them. Feel the warmth spread now across your chest, into your back. Every muscle it touches relaxes down."

Just like other times I had done guided meditation, it was working for everything except settling my voices. I could actually feel warmth and my muscles relaxing. I went with it as Rose guided the sun through my body. Guided *me* to guide the sun through my body.

"Feel the warmth move up your neck. The sun and warmth reach the base of your skull, then flow into your skull, lighting and warming it."

I got little tingles through my hair as my forehead warmed.

"See the sun wash around your skull, and enter your mind, sweeping up all the voices…"

Huh?

"… and sending them flowing out of your mind…"

I pictured the murmur of voices riding a wave of yellow sunlight, washing around like they were on a water slide. The loudness of the murmur changed, rolling along with the wave, different voices growing louder and quieter as the yellow wave of sunlight washed them around my mind and…

"… down through the opening the sunlight came from. The sunlight carries the voices away from your mind."

They were getting quieter.

"Down your neck, washing through your body."

And something else…

"Down through your shoulders, arms, into your hands, into your fingers."

A sort of… static energy. Under my skin. A tingling that felt… good. Powerful.

"The voices wash out of your mind, but one remains. Let the sunlight wash the voices out of your mind, until only Allie's voice remains."

I mentally searched for Allie's voice through the wave. But all of the voices wanted my focus. They clambered against the wave, back toward my mind. I tried to push them away, warring against them. I pictured the sunlight washing through, the voices riding the wave, and it washing back out the bottom of my skull. I tried to bring more sunlight in, to rinse the other voices away, desperate. I listened and searched for Allie's voice.

Manifest reality. Manifest reality. I could wash the voices away. I had, just now.

The more I tried, the more voices seemed to find their way back up from the tips of my fingers, that static energy dissipating, and the familiar roar of the swarm in my mind now mixed with mental wave noises as the sunlight tossed the voices around my skull.

The noise got louder, louder than the voices on their own. The yellow wave of sunlight shifted into a grey ocean wave, breaking apart and tossing onto itself in a stormy open ocean torrent. The voices screamed—people screamed—like I'd just shipwrecked an entire fleet of believers in the middle of the storm, and they were all shouting for their God, begging to be spared. I groaned and grabbed my head with both hands and pressed, the pain from the pressure doing little to distract from the thunderstorm raging inside it.

"Lena?" Rose squeezed my shoulders and pushed me back. I peeked through squinted eyes. Concern was etched on her face.

Damn right, she should be concerned. She should feel terrible. She'd done this. But her suffering didn't stop my suffering. I rolled away from her, off the couch, and stumbled to my feet, still clutching my head.

Her hands grabbed at me again and I shook her off. I stumbled out of the room and over to the stairs. I let go of my head and paused enough to stabilise myself before ascending, supported by the bannister. Rose had enough sense to stop trying to touch me, but I could feel her eyes on me the whole way. The storm of voices calmed the more I focused on my steps. By the time I reached the top of the stairs, I could see properly again.

I stumbled down to my room and pushed the door open. I clambered over to my dresser and fumbled through my underwear until I found the ones that my pills were wrapped in. My pills, my precious pills, that I'd starved myself of for so long, and for what? This false belief that life here could be safe, could be happy. That I could be sane.

I fumbled with the bottle cap, accidentally tightening it as I tried to loosen it, then twisting too hard. The cap flew off and the bottle jerked with the pressure.

The pills spilled out across the floor, just as Allie appeared in the doorway.

CHAPTER
THIRTY-SEVEN

"OH, GOD, ALLIE, I CAN EXPLAIN," I blurted out.

Allie looked at me, then at the pills on the floor, then back to me. She started toward me.

She was coming to slap me. I braced for impact. She hated me, for betraying her again, for lying about not taking meds anymore, for keeping secrets from her, for—

She enveloped me in a hug. A real, true, "I care about you," hug. Her hands pressed against my back, squeezing me, sharing her warmth with me. My tense muscles started to relax, realising that pain was not going to be inflicted after all.

I melted into her arms, my breaths coming in short, hitched gasps. Allie's top was wet and I realised it was from my tears. I wiped my eyes then pulled away, averting my gaze to the floor. I spotted some pills and remembered my shame was spilled out across the floor for anyone to see. I dropped to the floor and began picking them up hurriedly.

Allie crouched to the floor and started picking them up, too. So she could throw them out. Throw all of them out. But it would serve me right. I grasped the bottle, turning it in my hand until the label was facing my palm. That was all I needed, for Allie to find out they were stolen. Stolen from someone else who only wanted to help me, no less.

I was a disgrace. The voices pounded against my skull and eyes, pushing me to let them out, let them scream to the world about how much of a disappointment I was. I hadn't even lasted a week here and already the Marian's would know.

Allie came back to me from where the pills had spilled to, halfway across the room. She held out her open palm, a cluster of small pink pills gathered on her hand. I stared at them for a while, not sure what she wanted me to do.

I raised my eyes to hers. She gave me a slight smile. A pitying smile. She was giving them back to me. Poor, pathetic Lena, who couldn't cope without her pills.

I lifted my palm, and she tipped them onto it. I poured them back into the bottle, along with the ones I had picked up. They were probably covered in dust and dirt and hair and whatever else we had trekked in onto the floor. But they would still work. And I'd still take them, like a trash panda scavenging in the dumpster.

I screwed the cap back on, too ashamed to take any in front of Allie. The voices pressed their non-existent bodies against my eyeballs and skull. They squeezed and prodded my brain. I clenched my teeth through the pain, the bitter taste of blood and failure flooding my mouth.

"Come sit down," Allie said gently. She placed her hand on my shoulder blade and subtly pushed me toward the bed. My legs were like jelly, but I made it over and sat like stone, straight-backed with my hands in my lap and feet flat on the floor.

"What happened?" Allie asked, sitting next to me, her hand now supporting her weight as she leaned on the bed.

I shook my head, unable to speak, unable to even mentally form a sentence that I could then put into audible words.

I missed Nia. I wished she was here, sat right where Allie

was, holding my hand and existing with me as I had yet another breakdown. I couldn't even call her, hear her voice, with my phone dead and no charger. I bit my lip in place of tears, mourning my sad life now and my sad life at the hospital and at what could have been with Aidan if only he hadn't called the hospital. If only I hadn't been an idiot and been drinking with his friend and if I'd just behaved myself for one second instead of always screwing things up and now he was mad at me and wanted to send me away and didn't want to live with me anymore which is how I ended up on this farm in the first place, now having to try to prove myself as something more than I was, because what I really was, was just a broken girl with a broken mind and a broken life.

Allie sat quietly, allowing me the time to process.

No length of time was going to be enough with the pressure and pain the voices were inflicting upon me. I winced and squeezed my eyes shut, then held my hands to my head again, the pill bottle pressing into my temple.

"Do you want me to do the thing again?" Allie asked. "The guided meditation?"

I rolled my eyes back in relief and dropped my head toward her. "Please," I mumbled, afraid that if I opened my mouth too much, blood would come spraying out.

"Okay, lay down," Allie instructed.

I twisted on the bed and shuffled until my head was on the pillow, my legs straight. I tucked my arms onto my chest instead of my sides, gripping the pill bottle in my palm as though covering it with both hands would make the past five minutes disappear.

Allie guided me through my breathing, and switching off each of my muscle areas. I willed her to go faster, to get to my head so I could turn down the dimmer. But it was a process, and I had to trust it—trust her—to walk me through. Rushing might mean it didn't work.

223

My body began to relax, the voices tiring and reducing the force of their banging against my brain and eyes, before we even reached my head. By the time we got to the dimmer, it was as though they were ready for a sleep anyway, and we all drifted off into a peaceful nothing.

CHAPTER
THIRTY-EIGHT

I DON'T KNOW whether I slept, or if that was just what it felt like to not have noise in your head when you're awake. If the latter, I envy everyone who doesn't have to put up with auditory hallucinations, or a constant running commentary, or anything else that doesn't ever let your brain just rest.

When I opened my eyes, with no awareness of how long they'd been closed, beside the sun suggesting it was still mid-morning, Allie was sitting on the couch, staring out the window. She must have heard me move, or a shift in my breathing, because she glanced at me. She turned back to the window, letting me engage with her on my own terms. Oh, how I appreciated her. She cared, she understood, just like my Nia.

I sat up and swung my legs off the bed, relieved that the voices were still quiet, though thought I could hear a slight murmur starting back up again. An ache through my head and eyes persisted, wounds from the morning's battle.

"How long was I out?" I asked.

Allie turned back to me at the invitation to speak. "Not that long. Half hour, maybe?"

I nodded slowly. Rose would be downstairs, wondering what

happened, how I was, when we could try again for me to harness those damn prayers. People could keep their wishes to themselves. This wasn't fair. I couldn't even understand the voices yet they demanded, demanded. *Make your own miracles happen, don't always be relying on someone else.*

I needed to get out of the house. I didn't want to be around for Rose's questions or hopeful eyes. I'd just disappoint her again, and probably suffer more for it.

"Do you think we could go... I dunno," I started, racking my brain for where I wanted to be more than here. *Um, anywhere?* I should've thought more before I spoke, but Allie gave me the space to process. "See the horses, maybe?"

They reminded me of Nia, and I needed more happy. Even though thinking about her was sad, too, because I missed her, it was still happy. She was my happy, my safe place. And being there with Allie... well, she was becoming my safe place, too. The only other person was Aidan, and I didn't know where I stood with him. Maybe he'd come around, since I wasn't his problem anymore.

"Of course," Allie said, and got up slowly. Her whole being oozed calmness, and whether it was some subliminal messaging or pheromones or just human nature and the need to fit in—to relate—her calmness calmed me.

"I don't really..." I started, wanting to say I didn't want to see Rose, but not knowing how to say it... besides exactly like that. "... want to see Rose."

"All good," Allie said, breezing past me to the door. "I'll go check the coast is clear." She peeked out, then turned back. "But Lena?"

I turned to her.

She closed the door and stepped slowly toward me. "I just need to say, before you take those pills..."

Here we go. Heat flooded my cheeks and I dropped my gaze back to my hands. The hands that housed the fugitive pill bottle.

226

Allie came all the way over and crouched in front of me, putting her hands on mine again, like the night before. Strengthening her connection with me. She dipped her head to try to catch my eye, but I fixed my sight on my shirt, too far for her to access.

"It's your choice," she said softly. "All of this, it's your choice. Your powers are real—you have the power to change not just your reality, but everyone's around you. You can tune out the voices because you believe you can. And these pills—they suppress your power because you believe they do. If you take these again, it won't work so well—you won't be able to tune out the voices, just like before, when you said nothing had ever worked before. It's your choice, of course. I'm not going to make that for you. But I believe in you, and I hope you'll choose to believe in you, too."

I lifted my gaze to meet hers, her sweet brown eyes pulling my own toward them, and we sat for a moment, her hands on mine, the voices still quiet, though they pressed at my consciousness, threatening to return.

Were the pills really stopping me from controlling the voices, rather than the other way around? Whatever I believed... I believed I was crazy, I'd been told it so long. And that the pills wouldn't completely stop the voices, that nothing would ever cure me, not fully. That I'd have to settle for being "well enough." Well enough to live outside the hospital, in a semi-normal life, never really being fully normal, no matter how much I wanted it, because my history, my trauma, wasn't normal.

Manifest reality on a massive scale. That's what Allie had said.

"Are you saying that I..." I hesitated. "That I manifested all this myself?"

Allie raised her shoulders ever so slightly, then dropped them back down.

227

"But I put good vibes out. I want to be happy here," I said glumly.

"Manifesting reality is more than putting good vibes out into the universe," Allie said. "You have to put the effort in, as well. Even more than that, you have to believe—really believe—that what you want to come true, will come true. And I mean deep in your soul, believe it. I think you're struggling with that, Lena. You don't believe in yourself. And if you don't believe it deep down, then of course it won't come true."

But what I did believe, deep down, right down in my soul, was that I was broken. I couldn't be fixed. So that—all of that— is what I'd continue to live.

"I'm doomed then. I don't know how to believe in myself. I can't even believe enough to single you out from the millions of voices in my mind. They took over again—I let them take over again—before I could do it."

Allie exhaled with a knowing smile. "You've already singled out my voice, Lena. You did it this morning."

This morning? "Huh? When?"

"When I woke you up. I called your name through prayer. You heard me, and woke up."

What?

I frowned at Allie. "No, you called my name." *Didn't she?*

Allie shook her head, excitement plastered across her face.

My frown deepened. She had, hadn't she? Or had she even said anything? Did she need to say anything? Maybe I just woke up because she was there.

"You're doing it right now, aren't you?" Allie questioned. "You're doubting yourself."

Her truth bomb hit me right in the feels. "I..." I stammered.

"Give me one more day. One day without the meds, for you to see how you feel—what you can achieve, without them," she pleaded. "I'll be here, ready to guide you back to that dimmer switch if you need it, but I reckon you'll be able to do that on your own in no time. Then eventually actually attend to the prayers, too, because it's not healthy. They're a source of power. Think of the difference in achievements between kids who are told they're gonna go far, compared to the ones that are told they'll never amount to anything. Having people believe in you, cheer you on—that's empowerment. And you have literally billions of people believing in you."

I took a deep breath in. That was both heartwarming and terrifying, but she made her case well.

"Okay," I exhaled. "One more day."

Allie grinned and stuck her pinky out for me to pinky swear. I took it in my own, grinning back.

"Deal. Okay, I'll check the coast is clear," Allie said, jumping to her feet. "See you down there in a minute?"

I agreed, and she wandered out of the room. I glanced down at the pill bottle in my hand, briefly considering breaking my pinky swear, just to take the edge off. But Allie had helped me, more than the pills ever had. And if she was right, I might not need to take them ever again. If she was really, truly right, I might be able to have everything I ever dreamed of.

CHAPTER
THIRTY-NINE

AS PROMISED, Allie had made sure the path was clear so I didn't have to deal with Rose just yet. Allie had probably told Rose I didn't want to see her, and that was okay. It'd make sure there wasn't any misunderstanding. I could deal with the fallout later.

Allie and I wandered over to the stables, chatting about random things on the way, now that our serious heart-to-heart was done. She treated me like I was normal, which is exactly what I wanted at that moment. Take the pressure off, and let me come to it on my own.

Allie brought my favourite horse, Butter, the gorgeous chestnut mare, to the stable for me to groom. The rest were out grazing, but Butter didn't mind coming with us. She liked the attention. I collected the grooming mitt and set to work brushing Butter as Allie cleaned up the stalls, letting me indulge in my favourite part of horse care, rather than clean up.

I mulled over our morning conversation, even though I wanted space from it. The rhythmic motion of brushing Butter helped get my thoughts in order, so I played into it.

Allie had said that I'd heard her prayer that morning. That

she hadn't spoken out loud. If that were true—and she insisted that it was, and hadn't lied to me yet—then that would mean I did have the ability to hear a single voice, already, without having to wade through the torrent of voices in my mind like Rose had tried to make me do. Maybe that meant I could do it without pain.

Actually, it did mean that I could do it without pain—I already had. I'd done it without even noticing.

"Do you think…" I started, almost absent-mindedly. I hadn't been ready to put my ideas into words.

"Yeah?" Allie asked.

It was Allie, I could brainstorm with her.

"Well, I'm just thinking, if I've already heard your prayer, then that means I can do it."

"Sure did, and sure can," she said cheerily, still scooping hay into the corner of a stall.

"But when I did it like Rose told me, it hurt," I said, processing.

"So don't do it like Rose told you," Allie said. "You make the rules. You control your destiny. How do you think it should be done?"

My eyebrows knitted together in confusion, taken aback that Allie would so brazenly defy Rose's way of doing things. She was so obedient in her presence.

"I… uh…" I stammered, before thinking it through. I paused to process. "I guess I could just focus on hearing the person's voice, just straight out. Not having to weed through all the others."

"Great, so do that," Allie said. "I'll be outside, praying to My Lady Lena. Come get me when you're ready."

I laughed at how casually Allie turned and left me standing there. She quite literally regarded me as her God, yet could be so casual with me, and treat me just like… a person.

I rolled my eyes and went back to grooming Butter. I envisioned Allie's voice, replaying a couple of our conversations to help, then wondered what she'd be thinking, or praying about.

... *see yourself like I see you, like everyone sees you.*

I froze. Clear as my own narrative stream, her voice rang in my mind.

Her *prayer*.

CHAPTER
FORTY

I WHIPPED MY HEAD AROUND, sure I would see her crouched in the corner, or movement as she ducked away since I'd spotted her teasing me with the whispers. But there was nothing, no one there, except for Butter. And the voice... it was inside my mind, not outside of it. But louder, more like if you're wearing earphones.

And earphones, that was noise from outside your mind, even though it felt like it was inside. Maybe there was some speaker, some way of tricking me so that I thought it was prayer, to manipulate me into believing it so that it would then actually come true.

I ran my hand through my hair, behind my ears, even poked a finger into my ears to check they hadn't slipped something in there while I was sleeping. I searched around the barn. I checked Butter. There was nothing.

I stormed out of the barn until Allie was in my sight, though she didn't see me. I wanted to watch, make sure she wasn't pressing anything, doing or saying anything. Then I focused again on her voice in my mind.

Believe in yourself, so you can bring all the good that I know you can to this world.

No gimmicks—she was scooping hay, with both her hands busy. I marched up to her.

"Are you messing with me?" I demanded.

She turned and raised one eyebrow. "No?" She sounded genuine.

I softened my stance. "Really?"

"Really," she reassured me.

My mouth dropped open a little.

Hers spread into a grin. "You heard me, didn't you?"

I nodded slowly.

She dropped the pitchfork and danced around. "I knew you could do it! Screw those pills!"

I laughed, then. It was weird to hear her say any sort of bad word, even though screw was an entirely innocent word to say in most contexts. I jumped up and down with her, so much that we almost fell over.

It really was Allie's prayer, playing through my mind. No pain, no other screaming voices fighting their way to the top. The rest of the voices remained quietly chattering away in the background, the dial still under halfway thanks to the morning's session.

If I could hear Allie's prayer so easily, then maybe I could hear Nia, or Aidan.

"I want to try something else," I said. "Wait here?"

She waved me inside. "I'll keep praying for you!"

I headed back inside with Butter, without any human distractions.

I replayed conversations from both Nia and Aidan in my mind, just like I had done with Allie. Snippets of chats intertwined with moments of shared jokes and laughter. They got muddled together in my eagerness, so I took a breath and focused. First, on Aidan. I replayed conversations, and when I had his voice clear in my mind, I focused on the now.

Nothing.

Just the hum of the rest of the voices in the background. I tried again, but there was nothing. Silence. What did that mean? Was he okay?

I tried it with Nia, and there was nothing either. Thinking I might have lost the ability, I went back to Allie's voice. Sure enough, her prayers rang through.

… for all the people here, and all over the world, to…

It wasn't a fluke. I couldn't hear them. The two people I wanted to hear from most in this world, and I couldn't. I couldn't see them, couldn't even hear them. I wished they were there, that I could conjure them into reality, more than just in my mind. But my access to my abilities wasn't mine to decide. All-powerful God, and I couldn't even do something so basic as to hear the voice of my best friend or brother.

The other voices rose in volume, reminding me that they were still there. Always there, even if their volume was turned down. They'd be in the background, demanding things from me that I had no power to give. I pictured the dimmer and turned it, but the voices fought back, whispering in their indecipherable tongue, reminding me I was just as powerless as when I first left hospital.

I needed Allie, needed her to anchor me to reality, to talk me off the edge and help me turn down the dimmer. I was nothing without her, and perhaps never would be. But I was starting to believe that maybe, just maybe, she wouldn't be like the others. She wouldn't get sick of me and send me away. Maybe she would always be there for me. So, maybe it was okay that I needed her.

I mentally taunted the voices that they weren't long for this world, then went back out to have Allie help me snuff them out for what was undoubtedly not the last time.

CHAPTER
FORTY-ONE

THE SHADOWED CEILING of my room hadn't changed from the previous night, though I had. We'd skipped Rose's story time—I didn't have it in me to face her, nor more previous lives, yet. I wanted to get a better handle on the voices before I dove further into the labyrinth that was Mary, God Incarnate.

Only, right now, they were quiet anyway. Allie's third dimmer session of the day, the one before dinner, had lasted me through, so much so that I didn't need another one before bed.

Or so I thought. Instead, here I was, staring at the ceiling, unable to sleep despite my mind not being plagued by chatter. Those little pink pills would help me drift off, but I'd promised Allie. And really, I'd promised myself. To believe in myself, at least a little bit.

I glanced toward Allie's bed. The moonlight streamed into the room enough that I could see her fairly clearly. It didn't sound like she was sleeping yet, based on her breathing, but she looked peaceful. She'd forgive me for ruining it.

"I tried to hear Aidan's voice today," I said quietly, as though I was admitting to a crime, but loud enough that she couldn't pretend she didn't hear it, unless she pretended to be asleep.

"Oh, yeah?" Allie mumbled.

"I couldn't. Not a peep."

Her eyes remained closed. "Maybe he wasn't praying."

I frowned. He wasn't religious, so that would make a lot of sense. Though if he was worried about me, wouldn't he be praying for my safety? Even I had a word to God here and there, mostly through blaspheming, but that still counted, right? I said it did.

Even while learning, I still had influence over things. Eventually, what I said would be so. Maybe that's what the feeling earlier in the day was. That tingling feeling, like warmth enveloping me, making me feel... *something*. Maybe Allie would know.

"Can I tell you something else?" I asked.

She chuckled, her mouth pulled into a squashed half-smile against the pillow. "Of course."

"This morning with Rose," I started. "Before I freaked out. She walked me through a guided meditation, the one with the sunshine."

Allie grunted in response, encouraging me to continue.

"She got the voices to wash out of my mind and through my body. And it felt... good. Like... powerful."

Allie sat up, leaning against her elbow to face me.

"I don't really know how to describe it," I continued. "Kind of like, static energy, tingling. I liked it. Up until the voices got out of hand and I lost my mind and... well, you know the rest."

"Huh," she said. "I never had that."

"Why would you?" I laughed. "Do you hear voices, too?"

Allie scoffed. "Yeah, you're right, why would I." She flopped back down onto her pillow.

It was my turn to sit up and lean on my elbow.

"But really, what do you reckon that was?"

"I reckon," she said. "That was whatever you wanted it to be."

"Hmm," I said, contemplating that logic. "I think I'd like it to be my Godpower. Like you see in the movies. Maybe one day, I'll even glow."

Allie laughed. "I feel like you might come to regret that, but okay."

I grinned at having made her laugh. "Regret it? Why?"

"Well," she continued. "Just… a glowing human doesn't exactly scream 'normal,' you know? Might be kind of hard to keep a low profile."

"True, true," I agreed. "Maybe it'll just glow when I want it to glow."

"Or," Allie said, "you may have just stuffed yourself, and now you'll glow whether you want to or not."

I considered this.

"And," Allie continued, "I've just made sure that you're going to glow any time you use your Godpower, because I've influenced your belief about it, because I'm badass like that and totally your mentor."

I scoffed. "With that kind of logic, you sound more like my arch nemesis."

Allie grinned and turned to face the ceiling. "I like mentor better."

"Me, too," I agreed.

We lay in silence for a while longer, me silently coming up with superhero names for us, when I realised I didn't even know her last name.

"What's your surname?" I asked.

"Why?" Allie replied.

"'Cause I need it to come up with potential superhero names for us."

Allie laughed. "The point of a superhero name is to hide your secret identity, not to use your actual name in it."

"Meh." I shrugged. "This is how I do it."

Allie laughed.

"Come on," I pressed. "What is it? Don't make me use my mind reading power on you."

"Have at it," Allie challenged.

"Al-lie," I groaned, stretching out her name.

Allie was silent for a moment longer. "Williams," she said quietly.

"Williams?" I gasped. "Seriously? How crazy is that, that's my birth name, too. We could be related." My brain ticked over as I processed that we could be related somehow; I could have more family. Little Alena Williams could have had a cousin. Alison Williams. Or...

"Hey... I... your full name is Alison, right?" I asked hesitantly.

The air seemed to get heavy as realisation set into my subconscious, feeding my growing dread.

Allie wrestled with her decision to speak, and just before I called her nickname again, she whispered her real name back to me. "It's Alena."

CHAPTER
FORTY-TWO

BLOOD DRAINED from my face and coldness struck out through my limbs. That was too weird of a coincidence. Allie had the same exact name as me? Same age... and now we were both here at this weird cult commune place where this unmarried religious lady had brought us? What was happening here?

"That's my name." The words fell from my mouth and hit the floor dully.

Another pause from Allie. "I know."

The room spun despite me lying down. "We have the same name? How is that possible?"

"Lena, I don't want you to freak out—"

"I am very much freaking out already." I sat up, despite the dizziness. I leaned against the headboard, pulled my knees up, and tucked the pillow across my chest, hugging my knees and the pillow tight.

"Maybe we should wait until tomorrow to talk—"

"Okay, no. I need to know what's going on."

Allie sat up slowly. "Lena, I really think we should wait—"

"Tell me."

Allie inhaled sharply, looked at the floor, then back at me. "Promise you won't freak out?"

"I am already freaking out and this is absolutely making it worse, just tell me!"

"I'm gonna get in so much trouble with Rose."

I stared at her, eyes wide, willing her to put me out of my misery. This clearly was not a coincidence, something crazy was going on here. Something big, based on Allie clearly not wanting to tell me. So what the hell was this? Was Rose collecting Alena Williamses or something? Making her own little collection of imagined Gods, or Marys, or whatever the heck her crazy cult believed?

Allie shifted uncomfortably, glancing at the floor, then me, then the door.

"Allie, I swear to God I will leave."

I will leave. The words echoed in my mind.

"No! Okay, please, you can't leave. I'll tell you."

I stared at her. She took a deep breath, her eyes cast to the floor. "Rose adopted me because she thought I was you."

My head pulled back, brow furrowed, answering my questions in my mind before I got the full sentence out. "Why would she think—" Because we had the same name. "But she —" The same age. "But why would—" She believed Alena Williams was Mary reincarnate. And she wanted to get her hands on me. On Alena. Who was to say I was even the right Alena? There could easily be another one out there. The voices mocked me for being so stupid, for believing such a ridiculous lie.

"Until a couple of months ago, we all thought I was you," Allie continued, peering at me, then casting her eyes to the floor again. "That sounds... I'm sorry. I mean we all thought I was Mary. I know you are you. We just thought... Rose knew..."

Allie fell silent, unable to form her explanation.

"So for your entire life, you and everyone else believed that you were God," I said slowly. "Because you all thought that Rose had adopted me."

Allie nodded solemnly.

"So for *seventeen years,* you were all convinced that you were God."

Allie nodded again.

"You're telling me that Rose and everyone else, not even yourself, couldn't figure out that you weren't God, in all that time?"

Allie sucked in her bottom lip.

"And you're now trying to convince me that you've all got it figured out, and you're one hundred percent sure that it's me, I'm God, all powerful, all knowing?"

Allie looked up at me, eyes wide and brimming with tears.

"I know, Lena, it sounds so silly, and I feel so silly for believing it all those years. I think I knew it wasn't true, but when you're told something your whole life…"

I scoffed. This whole religion was a sham, just like every other. Faith. People put their trust and belief in something with no evidence, and here was my evidence, clear as day, that it was all utter rubbish. Believing something didn't make it true. They'd convinced me, used my desperation to belong some-where, manipulated me into thinking I was more than I was. God didn't walk among us. Why would He? If anything, that was the devil's game.

"So how'd you guys do it? How'd you make me feel that stuff? And hear those voices so clearly?"

My eyes grew wide as I thought of patients claiming staff were hiding medication in their food at the hospital. "Did you drug me? You put something in my food to make me hallucinate. To make me easy to manipulate."

Allie shook her head slightly, eyes pleading, searching for my meaning. "What? No…"

"Allie," I said bluntly, catching her directly in her eyes, saying it aloud to break the pretty lie's spell on me, too. "I am not God. You are not God. For all we know, there is no God."

She flinched at every sentence, each one a dagger in her heart. "You are... I mean—"

"Where's your proof?" I cut in.

Allie looked at me blankly, her mouth open.

I rolled my head side to side and gestured with my hand to get her to speak. "Your proof? That I'm God? Or that some Alena Williams out there is, since it damn well isn't me."

Allie dropped her eyes to her lap. She didn't have any proof. But the name must have come up somehow.

"Is there like, a prophecy or something? Is that why you're all convinced it's someone named Alena Williams?"

Allie shook her head again, still looking at her lap as she fiddled with the blanket. "No, it's not like that."

"What then?"

Allie took a deep breath, then exhaled. I gave her space to speak. "Rose said... Rose knew me—you—Mary—in her previous life. Mary—or Elizabeth, back then—told her that they'd meet again. So I guess it kinda was a prophecy. She said —" a big pause. I stared at her expectantly, so she reluctantly continued. "She said that when they met again, their hearts would beat as one."

I laughed. I couldn't hold it in. This cult was insane. More insane than me. They'd come to find a girl in a literal mental hospital, who had little to no support in her life. Convinced her she was God, drugged her to make her believe it even more, all based on some old lady's insane claim. For what? What was the point in all this? To see how many people would drink the Kool-Aid, and follow me into the afterlife? I wouldn't do it, I'd caught on in time. I wasn't going to lead these lambs to the slaughter. Unless *I* was the lamb. My eyes grew wide again and I dropped my voice.

"Allie... why am I here?"

Allie looked at me quizzically.

"You lot found me and brought me here. You tell me I'm God. But I'm not God, just like you. So what happens at the end of all this? Am I in danger? Do I need to get out of here?"

She stared at me, and the quiet seemed to give her space to process and return with clarity. "You're not in danger. We aren't like that. We all thought it was me for my whole life, and finding out it's not hasn't changed that people love me. If," she put emphasis on the word, "it turned out that you're not Mary either, that won't change the way we feel about you. We care about you, Lena, as a person. Please don't leave."

Please don't leave. Her plea reverberated in my mind. She seemed so sincere in her words, and she did have the proof that everyone still seemed to love and respect her. How she didn't hate me, I didn't know. This must have been so difficult for her, as well, finding out your entire life was a lie. That your whole identity was someone else's, and then meeting that other person. I couldn't even imagine that. But I couldn't share my empathy with her. I had enough of my own processing to do.

I could leave. But where would I go? It wasn't like I had anyone or anywhere left. Aidan had made his choice. Nia would still be in the hospital. And these people, even though they were crazy, were nice to me. I liked this place. If it took them seventeen years and finding a second Alena Williams to figure out the first one wasn't God, surely I could play along for a few years, until I got on my feet enough that I'd never be put back in hospital. As long as they didn't sacrifice me in the meantime.

"So there's not, like, a plan to sacrifice Mary when she turns eighteen, or something? I'm not gonna end up on a wooden cross with nails in my hands?" I didn't really believe it, but the words came out anyway, to emphasise how crazy this place was.

Allie's face screwed up in disgust. "What? No! Why would you... we don't want to hurt you. We don't want to hurt anyone. God is loving, so we are loving."

"God is also a mass murderer," I reminded her. As disappointing as it was to just be plain old Lena, at least I wasn't responsible for the plague or a global flood.

"Lena, just... I know this is a lot to process. Just give it some time, okay? I believe in you. I know that you don't right now, but you will. And I'll believe in you enough for both of us, until you get there."

I scoffed, and rolled my eyes. This was too much. They thought they could manipulate me, trick me into believing I was something more than I was. Well, she was so worried I would leave, then I'd show her. I got up off my bed and grabbed my pillow and duvet.

"What are you doing?" Allie asked nervously.

"I'm not sleeping here with you." I bunched everything up in my arms. The pillow stuck up awkwardly in front of my face. I turned my head to the side so it wouldn't seem like a big deal, then marched toward the door.

"Where are you going?" Allie's voice broke a little in desperation. She had sat up more in bed, like she was going to climb out and follow me. Wouldn't be surprising.

I pawed awkwardly at the door handle and managed to get it open. The duvet and pillows were pushing against it, so I had to grab the door with my foot to stop it closing. This was the sort of time that Allie would normally offer help, but none was forthcoming. Good. She didn't want me to go. Served her right for lying to me.

I managed to get the door open wide enough to get out, and marched into the hallway. I didn't actually know where I was going to go, but didn't want her to know that. I could try an empty room, but if it came to it I could just sleep on the couch. That would be a bit weird, and there'd be some explaining to do either way, but the Marians had way more explaining to do than me.

I opened the door to the spare room next to the bathroom,

not really wanting to go downstairs and risk having to face Rose with all this. The moonlight flooded in through the open-curtain windows, illuminating the room. It was completely empty. No bed, no drawers. The Marians had moved the bed into Allie's room so I'd be forced to spend time with her, and she could keep a close eye on me, probably whispering subliminal messages to me in my sleep to help with their lies.

I left the door open and stomped down the stairs. The duvet had started to slip, so I had to walk down sideways to avoid tripping on it and breaking my neck on the stairs. That'd save them from having to follow through with sacrificing me. Either way, it'd be doing me a favour.

I turned right at the bottom of the stairs and went down the corridor where there was another spare room. The bed was already made up—it hadn't been stripped out to make me bunk with a liar.

The room was chilly, since it didn't have the curtains pulled, nor the warmth of two bodies like our bedroom. I lay the duvet on top of the one that was already there, and puffed up my pillow after dropping it on top of the other one. I pulled the curtains and went back to switch off the light. The room dropped into pitch blackness, but my eyes had started to adjust to the moonlight seeping in around and through the curtains by the time I felt my way back to the bed.

I crawled into bed and fluffed the duvets around me before pulling them up to my chin, trying to regain some warmth as the new, cold sheets sucked my warmth away. Allie best be upstairs thinking about her lies, worrying if I was going to leave for good or not. Maybe I'd leave for evil. I smirked at my own joke.

My spite kept me awake longer than I should've been, until the bed stopped sucking my warmth and instead donated some back. I longed for my pills, the voices now screaming again in my mind, and I wasn't even capable of stopping them. It had all been a lie. A trick. I needed the pills to quiet them and send me to sleep. Heck, at this point I'd even take my regular pills from the hospital. I should've just taken them when Aidan asked me to. I should've done what he said.

I lay there scowling, angry at my life and what it could have been if Rose's claims had been true. I was angry at Rose for dragging me into all this. Angry at Allie for lying to me. Angry at my father for rejecting me before I could even speak, as if he saw me for the monster I would become. Angry at Aidan for choosing the hospital over me, and wishing he would've put me first, for once. Angry at myself for letting it all happen. Eventually, I drifted off into an angry and spiteful sleep.

That night, I dreamed the world burned.

CHAPTER
FORTY-THREE

I WOKE to screams tearing through what should have been the silence of night. Shadows danced across the curtains, twisting into demons come to life. I bolted up in bed, my heart already hammering against my ribcage as I began to process what was happening. I pulled at the curtain. My worst fears materialised in front of my eyes.

The courtyard was engulfed in flames. Orange tongues licked at the dawn sky, crackling with fury.

My nightmare—it was real. I had done this.

I dropped the curtain and dashed outside, grabbing my shoes from the front door as I raced by. I rounded the corner of the house to the courtyard and a wall of searing heat slammed into me. I staggered back as the panicked scene unfolded more clearly. People dashed in all directions, their frantic cries making my heart ache even more. My eyes and lungs burned in the thick smoke.

"Lena!" Allie's voice echoed through the chaos, and I turned to see her rushing toward me. Her eyes were wide with fear and confusion. She threw her arms out. I didn't have time to react before she wrapped them around me. "You're okay." She stepped back and held onto my shoulders. "Where were you?"

I stood like a statue, frozen despite the heat, processing the fire and embrace and guilt and danger. "I—I don't..." My words faltered, barely audible above the roar of flames and shouting. How could I tell her this was my fault?

Allie glanced past me, then rushed to help an older woman struggling beneath the weight of a water-laden bucket. Ash and embers danced on the breeze, finding their way to new things to burn. They were spreading the fire to the other hay bales and straw furniture.

I snapped out of my trance and searched for another bucket. Spotting a watering can first, I seized it with trembling hands, and sprinted toward the water tank. A line of people were passing bucket after bucket for filling. I looked at the watering can, then tossed it aside, thinking how stupidly small and useless it was against the blaze. Just like me.

I joined the line and helped another resident with a full bucket. We followed the masses and tipped it onto a burning haybale, then raced back for a refill. The heat was relentless and unbearable, scorching the hair on our hands and arms, pieces of ash and debris flicking out toward us. My pyjamas burned against my skin, the plastic-like material at risk of going up in flames.

I internally scolded myself for thinking such a thing. That's what had got us into this mess. I had to think we were winning, believe the fire was being extinguished. But from the chaos around me, it seemed more as if it were mocking our feeble attempt to contain it. The fire was spreading faster than we could put it out, fuelled by the dry straw beneath it. A fresh surge of panic washed through me as I realised the fire was closing in on the farmhouse.

No, no. We were going to lose the house, all thanks to my stupid pessimistic thoughts.

Others had seen the threat, too, and all efforts were directed toward breaking the line of fire, desperate to protect the old house so central to the farm and their way of life. The turbulence from the air and heat lifted the embers further and higher than we could physically counter. People threw water as high as they could to dampen the house, but it barely even reached the second storey. We needed rain. And we needed it *now*.

I glanced up toward the dawn sky. Smoke and ash blotted it out, and I had to shelter my eyes from falling debris.

If I could cause a fire with my dreams, then surely I could make it rain. I had to believe. I had to. Like Rose and Allie said— what I believed would come true.

It wasn't like I had to conjure a storm. There was no evidence against there already being clouds in the sky. For all I knew, the clouds were already right above us, full to the brim, just waiting to send rain cascading down.

They just needed a little push.

I closed my eyes, face toward the sky, and pictured the clouds there, dark and full. I pictured the first drops of rain, scarce to start, finding their way from their cloud, through the smoke and ash, and splattering on the ground. Then I pictured the clouds opening up, and a torrent of water plummeting to the earth, soaking the farmhouse and haybales and snuffing out the flames.

A raindrop hit my cheek.

Then another.

I flinched and opened my eyes, searching for visual confirmation of what I had felt.

The air was thick with smoke, but more drops hit my face. I held my hand out, palm turned to the sky, as our salvation rained down from the heavens.

I laughed, then. A disbelieving, relieved, real laugh.

I had done it. I believed, and it had come true. I had saved us.

I held my other hand out, stretched both arms out to each side, and laughed again. Cheers had erupted behind me, back

253

toward the house. I could hear them, now. Cheering for their salvation. Cheering for *me*.

I closed my eyes again and spun, arms stretched wide, spinning and dancing as the raindrops soaked my pyjamas.

"Lena!" Allie's voice screeched in my ear. She grabbed my outstretched arm and yanked me sideways, almost pulling me over. My eyes snapped open and it took a second to process the yellow figures jogging past me, carrying a huge snake.

I followed them with my eyes as the snake twisted, then spewed a torrent of water from its mouth.

Firefighters.

I looked to the sky. No rain was falling.

My heart dropped. I felt dizzy. It wasn't me—I hadn't saved us, after all. I hadn't conjured rain. There was nothing magical or mystical about this salvation. Someone had called the fire service, and they had come to save the day.

CHAPTER
FORTY-FOUR

TEARS welled in my eyes as I surveyed the damage I had caused, and not been able to stop. The fire left the courtyard smouldering and charred. The haybales were gone; furniture was burnt beyond recognition; plants and vegetables reduced to ash. This place was meant to be a safe haven, had been for all these people for so many years. They'd welcomed me into it, and I'd destroyed it in my sleep.

People sat on the ground, exhausted and covered in soot, coughing and wheezing from the smoke. They were silent, besides crying, wheezing, and wiping their eyes. Tim and Rose spoke with the firefighters before they left us in the charred wake of the fire. Allie and I sat next to each other, our shoulders touching as we caught our breath.

I could feel her devastation, emanating from her being. I dared to glance at her. She stared blankly at the courtyard, the place she had grown up, loved and nurtured. A safe place. Until I came along.

"Last night," Allie started, still staring blankly ahead.

I dropped my own eyes to the ground and shook my head. I

didn't want to think about it. About the lies. About the hurt. My anger caused this, but I hadn't been the one to save us.

"I'm sorry," she whispered.

A lump formed in my throat. *She* was sorry? This was my doing.

"I know it wasn't fair to not tell you, I just didn't want to scare you away." She turned to me, trying to catch my eye. "But then this morning, you still weren't in the room, and there was so much yelling, and I didn't know where you were, and I just... I got so scared, you know? I know we had a fight last night, and that I haven't known you that long, but I need you in my life, and I—"

Her sentiment was too much. I didn't deserve it. She'd told me the truth, and she deserved the same, even if it made her hate me.

"I started the fire."

Her mouth dropped open. "You... what?"

My eyes stayed downcast. "From my dream. I dreamed the world was burning, and then I woke up, and the fire was already out of control." I buried my face in my hands. "I'm sorry, I really didn't mean to," I said through my hands, pressing my fingertips into my eye sockets to try stop the tears that were already gathering. I wanted to say more, about how I'd tried to fix things. How I really thought I had fixed it. But I hadn't, and it was even more shameful that I thought I could've. That I thought I could've done anything good, when all I really did was hurt people.

Allie shuffled in her position. The voices reiterated what I was thinking. She was ashamed of me, disgusted by me. She'd leave me. All the Marians would reject me now. I'd be entirely alone in this world. Why not, I'd just as easily abandoned Allie last night, for some stupid lie that wasn't even a lie, she just didn't tell me something to protect me and our friendship, and now I—

256

Allie wrapped her arms around me from my side, resting her head on my shoulder.

"It's okay," she said softly. "That's why we're here, to help you. To learn to control it, to use it safely, all of it."

I gasped, then the tears flowed freely. I squeezed her arm with both my hands, rested my head against hers, and sobbed my fears away.

After I don't know how long, Allie took me upstairs to get cleaned up. I didn't argue. We sat in silence after we'd both showered and changed, me just staring blankly at the ceiling. I could sense her watching me from her place on the couch, wanting to talk. But she let me stay quiet, so I could come to terms with the rollercoaster of emotions I'd been on in the past twelve hours. I'd gone from yesterday believing I was God, to having it torn away from me, to being brutally proven that everything the Marians said was true, only to find that I still had no control at all. How was I supposed to process that out loud?

If Nia was here, I could tell her. I could tell her anything. Or Aidan, even though he already thought I was crazy. What was a little bit more? Maybe he was right, that I needed to be in a mental hospital. Not because I was crazy, but because the medication would dampen my powers, and keep everyone else safe.

But that was exactly Allie's point. I didn't have to use medication to dampen my powers. I had to be the master of my own darn destiny and take control of my abilities, so I could use them for what I wanted, instead of just being a puppet to them, pushed around like the character in a story. And Allie wouldn't be able to help if she didn't know what had happened.

"I was angry last night," I said.

Allie jumped and turned to face me.

"I know, I—" she started.

"I mean, that's why I had the bad dream," I continued. "I couldn't handle my emotions, and then this happened."

That wasn't entirely true. I had invited anger in. I wanted to be mad at Allie, and for her to feel bad for lying to me, and be uncomfortable and suffer in her concern that I was going to leave her.

"I think I'm a bad person," I said.

Allie got up and came over to me. She sat on the edge of my bed while I continued to lay there.

"You are so hard on yourself," Allie said. "And I can't even imagine what you've been through in your life to make you think so badly of yourself."

Tears pricked my eyes. She saw me. She saw my trauma.

"But honestly, Lena." Her tone changed. "We can't just sit here and have a pity party for you. You know, you're not that different to everyone else. We all create our own reality, in a way. If we choose to see the good in people, if we choose to see happiness and light in the world, then that's what comes through. You see the bad in the world, because that's what you're used to, that's familiar to you. But you don't have to live that way."

That was what years of abuse and neglect would do to you. Mix in some teenage hormones, budding Godpowers, and voila —world decimation.

"How?" I asked quietly.

"Well, practise. You have to choose to see good, and challenge the bad thoughts. You'll get there. I believe in you. You just need *you* to believe in you, too."

"I don't want them to be in control of me, you know? I want to be in charge. I don't ever want something like today to happen again," I said sullenly.

"I get that," Allie said. "Remember, that wasn't your fault. And you'll be able to do so much good in the world."

I didn't reply. Maybe someone without so much trauma could do good. Someone like Allie. She was better than me in every way. She'd be better off with this, not me. My mind was damaged, so I damaged things, in turn. She would make a better God than I would. Nothing ever went how I wanted. I'd end up burning the world down, or causing the apocalypse or something.

Allie must've had some sort of mind reading power after all. "Have you ever heard that saying 'don't think about a pink elephant?'"

I smiled. "And then you can't help but think of a pink elephant."

"Exactly. And what you think about comes to life. So, if you're thinking about how you're not capable of turning your life around and being happy, then that's what'll happen."

I grunted. I was doomed. Only, what I thought didn't always come to life.

"I'm not so sure that's always how it works," I said quietly.

Allie looked at me, giving me space to expand on my thoughts.

"I thought about rain earlier," I continued. "To put out the fire. I thought *hard*. I pictured the clouds, and rain falling, and everything. I really thought I made it happen, too. But someone else had called the fire service. It didn't count for anything."

A smirk crept onto Allie's lips. "Here's another saying you've probably heard of: 'God works in mysterious ways.'"

I narrowed my eyes. Did she mean... was she suggesting I *did* have something to do with it?

"What are you saying?" I asked.

"I think you know what I'm saying."

"Humour me," I pressed.

She lifted her shoulders slightly, then dropped them. "You wanted rain. And you got rain. Not the rain you asked for, sure, but think of the purpose behind it. You wanted it to put the fire out, and it did. It was a miracle they got there when they did."

Allie fixed her eyes on mine as she said the last sentence, enunciating each word. She meant it was *my* miracle. The truth

259

started to come into focus: the same self-fulfilling prophecy that had made my life a mess, could make all my good dreams come true, too.

"I'm not saying it'll be easy," Allie said. "But if you put the work in, and believe you can be happy, then you can be."

I bit my lip, but not hard enough to draw blood.

Allie kept her eyes on mine. "Be honest with me—have you been happy here? Because up until yesterday you seemed like you were in a pretty good place."

I nodded. The only thing to make this place better would be to have Aidan and Nia here as well. The farm was great, the people were great... but I had put it all in danger with a dream.

The voices were there with their quiet chatter, reminding me what a risk I was, how dangerous, the lack of control I had over my own mind. I thought of their wave of warmth that Rose had conjured the day before.

"These voices I get—the prayers—I really think they might be linked to my power."

"Well, yeah. They're prayers. They're the proof of all the belief everyone around the world has in you. All the energy and love they're pouring into you."

"But bad things happen when they get loud," I said quietly.

"Is that because you're always thinking bad things?" Allie asked.

I lifted a shoulder and glanced away. *Yes.*

"I'll take that as a yes," she said. "So, if we're gonna practice, we're gonna focus on what you *should* be thinking about, okay?"

"I guess so," I said quietly. Then, again, anger took over. If I was God, I had done all this to myself. Not just the parts of my life when I made conscious choices, or influenced my environment, but all of it. I'd caused myself to be born into a family plagued by mental illness, who would literally throw away their own flesh and blood.

"Why would I do this to myself? Why would God give me

this life, to suffer and hate, and put everyone at risk from my trauma and the bad thoughts that go along with that? I wouldn't wish my life on anyone. But, I did. I put myself here."

Allie sighed. "Living as a human, with people, allows you to fully appreciate the human experience—the struggles, the joy, doubts, love and loss—all of it. It's a choice to understand what it is to be mortal. That's why you don't remember your past lives until you're ready."

"This is way more struggle than joy," I said. And it wouldn't have been if I'd had Allie's life. Maybe this was all a mistake, and she was meant to be the right Alena Williams. Maybe I'd got it wrong when I soul swapped or whatever I did to reincarnate.

"You should hate me," I said dully. "I basically stole this from you."

"You didn't steal anything," Allie said. "I was never Her. I believed it, sure, because I was told so. And I'll still do what I can to make this world better, even if I don't have the same power you do."

"God, this world would be so much better off if you *were* God," I said.

Allie gave a half-hearted shrug. "You've done alright so far."

"Allie, I literally lit the farm on fire."

She waved her hand. "I mean on a bigger scale. Based on what you've been through. And all your previous lives... anyway, I'll be here with you to figure it all out. Because I'm not God, you are."

She sounded hurt.

"That is," she continued, "if you'll have me? You thought last night about leaving."

I shook my head vigorously. "I can't... no, I don't want to. I want to stay. With you. To learn with you."

Allie grinned.

"But the fire..." I hesitated. "Are you going to tell anyone? I don't want them to hate me."

261

"No one got hurt," she said. "And it was an accident. I'm not going to tell anyone, but if you really do want to take control of your powers and actions, then a big part of that is owning up to your actions."

I thought about this for a moment. "We should go help clean up," I said quietly.

CHAPTER
FORTY-FIVE

THE DAY HAD WELL and truly set in by the time everyone had cleaned themselves up and were back outside to start cleaning up the mess, including us. The furniture and barrels were still too hot to touch, so Tim and some others continued to hose those remains down, to keep them wet and stop any stray cinders starting another fire.

While we helped clean up, sweeping the watered-down ash away from paths, I had a realisation that this fire could've just as easily happened at Aidan's if I were there. It could've been worse —I could've killed him.

He'd never believed me about my powers, no one had, but here it was, they were real. Maybe this would keep me out of the loony-bin. I mean, hell, if I couldn't keep myself out, what was the point of the powers to begin with?

Rose came out and called to Tim, so he handed off the hose to Greg and followed Rose around the front of the house. Leroy followed him like the little lost puppy he was, never really thinking for himself.

I needed to stop thinking such mean things about people. Leroy was probably fine, and nice, and it wasn't his fault that he had this obsession with Mary and couldn't separate me from her. He'd literally been indoctrinated into believing in God and Mary —he'd believe or do anything he was told. But then, did that make it my fault that I got weird vibes from him?

I vaguely heard Tim's truck drive away from the house, not really paying it much attention. That was, until people started murmuring and walking toward the front of the house, some even downing their brooms and pausing the clean-up.

I leaned on my own broom and looked to Allie, who'd also noticed the commotion. "What's going on?" I asked.

Allie stopped sweeping, too. "Let's go see."

We leaned our brooms on the side of the house as we passed, and joined the growing crowd out the front of the house, all staring down the long driveway.

There were people down there, and a car on the other side of the gate, but it was too far away to make out who anyone was or what was happening.

I dropped behind Allie as she carved her way through the crowd, trying to get a better position. She spotted Shona up ahead and made a beeline for her, with me in tow. Shona held a pair of binoculars, presumably for visitor-spotting, since they must not have had cameras installed at the gates like normal people would these days.

"Shona," Allie called, and she glanced our way. "What's going on?"

"There's someone at the gate," she said quietly. "Rose told us to wait here."

"Weird." Allie's brows drew together.

Shona raised her own eyebrows and nodded.

I studied the sea of faces, all etched with concern. This really was a quiet little community if someone turning up at the gate caused this much commotion.

"What's the big deal?" I asked.

"We don't know, yet." Shona lifted the binoculars to her eyes. "They're all just talking."

"Can I have a look?" I asked.

"Of course." Shona handed me the visitor-spotters.

I held them to my eyes and took a moment to get the sights positioned, scanning across the grass before finally finding the fence line and following that to the gate. There was one car on the other side of the gate, pulled right up in front of it. I could make out Rose, with her fairly distinctive figure and clothing combo, plus the way she held herself. With her were Leroy and Tim, both with their rifles hanging off their shoulders.

What a warm welcome, taking their rifles down to greet a visitor.

They stood in a sort of semi-circle, a little bit back from the gate. The person standing on the other side was harder to make out because of the car behind them, but it looked like a younger person, a man, or maybe—

Aidan.

CHAPTER
FORTY-SIX

MY PULSE POUNDED, a dose of adrenaline flooding my system. My vision focused even more, though my hands started to shake. I fought to keep them steady as I aimed the binoculars at the person on the other side of the gate.

Oh my Me. It was him.

"Aidan," I said aloud. I absently handed the binoculars to Allie or Shona, not knowing if they even took them or if I just dropped them, before I broke into a sprint toward the gate.

He'd come for me. My brother. My protector.

Adrenaline surged through my legs, pushing me forward. I wouldn't—couldn't—stop. My brother was there, waiting for me at the gate, having driven or flown all this way to find me. How *did* he find me? It didn't matter right now, I just had to get to him. Leroy and Tim were there with their rifles, and surely they wouldn't actually do anything, but what if he felt so threatened that he left? How would I get to him then?

"Aidan!" I screamed, not knowing if he could hear me from so far away. The gap was barely closing. I willed myself forward, and Aidan's figure started to grow clearer, the distance between us gradually shrinking.

"Aidan!" I screamed again, and this time he looked at me.

He rushed to the gate and grabbed the steel poles with both hands, pushing his face through as far as it would go.

"Lena!" he yelled back.

His voice gave me renewed energy and I pushed ahead, though was gasping for breath by that point. The Marians turned to me, and Tim and Rose started toward me. Tim held out an arm for me to slow. I continued at pace, dodging him, straight past him, and skidded to slow myself and give enough time to reach my arms through the vertical bars and wrap them around Aidan.

He did the same, our cheeks pressed awkwardly next to each other through the bars.

"Hey, sis," Aidan said.

"You came for me," I whispered.

"Of course I did." We released our embrace and stepped back. I kept my hands on his arms, and he left his on mine, but we removed ourselves from the awkward squeeze between the bars so we could look at each other face on. We were both grinning like goons.

"How'd you find me?" I asked.

"Nia helped," he said.

Nia. Of course, my other protector. I hadn't even thought of Aidan asking her where I might be. God sure does work in mysterious ways.

We stood there, smiling at each other, squeezing each other's arms, each pleased to know the other was safe. He cared enough to come for me. Then the reality of being separated by bars knocked at me. I turned and glared at Rose.

"Why haven't you let him in?" I snapped.

"Lena, I don't—" Rose started, hands held out in front of her.

"Let him in," I demanded.

Rose hesitated, about to say something else, then sighed and tipped her head at Tim.

Tim went to the keypad on the left side of the gate and tapped five buttons. The heavy gate creaked and began to separate down its middle.

Aidan and I pulled our arms back and I stepped further from the gate, allowing it to swing inward toward me and the Marians. When it had opened enough, I squeezed through and pulled Aidan into a bigger, proper hug. He reciprocated, and for a brief moment, the world outside us ceased to exist. We stood there, hugging, until the gates had fully opened.

I broke our embrace again and turned to Rose. "I'm going to go up with Aidan. We'll meet you all up there."

She gave a placating smile. "Of course. Aidan, welcome to our home. Please, join us for dinner. You're welcome to stay the night, as well."

I glanced at Aidan and flicked my head toward the car. We dropped our arms, and he headed toward the driver's side. I took my position in the passenger's seat, where his sweatshirt already lay. I snuggled it onto my lap. It smelled of him, of family and safety.

Aidan got in the driver's seat, and looked me straight in the eye. "Lena, I'm here to take you home."

Home. What did that word even mean to him? We'd tried that already, and it didn't even take him two hours before he wanted to send me back to the hospital. Panic rose in my chest, and I whipped around, searching for any sign of the police. "What do you mean? What have you done?"

Aidan recoiled. "I haven't 'done' anything. But you need to come back home."

"I like it here," I said sullenly, fiddling with my hands. "I feel like I belong."

"Belong?" Aidan said. "Lena, it's a cult. You don't belong here. You didn't even know these people a week ago."

I exhaled sharply. "It's not a—" I cut myself off, 'cause it kinda was a cult. "It's a religious following." *Following me.* "And it's been more than a week."

He held up his hands. "Fine, just over a week ago, then. Point being, you don't know them, and they don't know you. Not like I do. Come home with me. Let me help."

"Help by sending me back to hospital?" I snapped.

He cringed, and I regretted it for a moment. But it was true. I had trusted him, and he had turned on me. He'd caused all this, really. He'd pushed me out, and the Followers of Mary were waiting there with open arms, ready to accept me as I was.

"No," he said softly. "No, I won't. I'm sorry I pushed you. I just want you to be safe, and I thought that was best, for you to get your meds and everything. But clearly you're really against that, so I'll work with you to figure something else out. Something other than the hospital."

"You're not just saying that?" I asked.

"I'm not just saying that. I mean, honestly, I thought you'd lost it when Ryan said about the religious people—"

"He told you?"

"Yeah, 'course he did. But then Nia said about them, too, so I looked them up, and they're real. They're a huge religion. They're everywhere."

I sat quietly. They were everywhere. They had people everywhere. People ready to jump in to help me by picking me up from a random park; enough funds to fly me across the country on short notice; a huge plot of land to house just a small percentage of their members. And they were all there for me. They'd do anything for me, and wouldn't send me away.

"Would you consider staying here, then?" The question slipped out before I could stop it. I'd wished him here—maybe I could wish him to stay. That way Allie could teach me to control my powers, and I'd have Aidan, too. I pleaded with my eyes. "This place... it's not perfect, but it feels homely, and safe. You might really like it, too, if you gave it a chance."

Aidan furrowed his brow. "I'm here to take you home, not join the cult with you, sis."

My eyes dropped back to my lap, and my hopes with them.

"What even is this place?" he asked.

I lifted a shoulder, half resigned. "It's their commune. It's really nice, actually. So peaceful, and everyone is really nice. You'll like it, I think."

"Peaceful," Aidan said, pausing until I looked him in the eyes. "They had guns."

I grimaced. "Yeah, sorry about the guns. They just use them for hunting."

He didn't seem convinced.

"They're not hurting anyone," I continued. "Come up and you'll see."

Aidan put his hand on mine. "Tell you what, I'll come for dinner, okay?"

My eyes lit up.

"And I'll stay tonight," Aidan continued. "Heck, I don't have anywhere else to stay. I thought we'd be going back tonight. But I'm still gonna want you to come with me. And anything else, hospital or meds or whatever, we can figure it out, okay? You can stay at mine, and we'll figure it out, together."

He squeezed my hand, and I squeezed back. We'd have that time together, at least for tonight. Aidan could see how great the Marian's farm was, we could have a decent sleep, and make those decisions tomorrow. Or the next day... or maybe the day after that.

CHAPTER
FORTY-SEVEN

AS THE DAY PROGRESSED, Aidan's mood got noticeably brighter. The people of the compound welcomed him with open arms, their curiosity piqued when they discovered he was my brother. I downplayed this fact, not wanting Aidan to feel overwhelmed by their admiration and potentially bring up the whole I-am-their-saviour thing.

The tour around the compound had Aidan grinning, particularly at the goats and chickens. He told me how he'd always wanted to have a farm of his own. There was still so much I didn't know about him. Maybe, given enough time, I could convince Aidan to stay here with the Marians. To find a new purpose and life among these people—my people.

The dinner was fairly uneventful, too, and much smaller than my welcome. Just the household and their close friends joined, but the food was still fresh and delicious. At one point, Aidan managed to whisper to me that Leroy gave him the creeps, which pleased me to no end.

Aidan was given a room on the ground floor, the same one I'd slept in the night before. After dinner and socialising, I helped him settle in for the night. We both sat on his bed, cross-legged, knees touching, like we were kids at a sleepover.

"So it wasn't that bad?" I asked with a grin, knowing the answer.

Aidan flashed a coy smile. "For a cult."

"It's nice to have you here," I said. "Thank you for coming."

"'Course. You're my sister," he said. "But listen, even though these people seem nice and everything, it doesn't mean I don't still want you to come back with me. This isn't right for you, Lena."

I dipped my head. I loved him, but his idea of what was right for me was definitely not the same as my idea.

"And what is right?" I asked. "Hospital?"

Aidan sighed. "Look, I'm worried about you, okay? And that's the only way I know how to help. After what happened with Mum, I..."

I stiffened. "What do you mean, what happened with Mum?" The most I knew was that she had post-partum psychosis, got admitted to hospital, and ended her life while she was there. On almost all accounts, I didn't blame her one bit—being in hospital had probably driven her to it.

"You know," Aidan said quietly. "With her psychosis, and then..."

And then that final act. Okay, so we were talking about the same thing, but had a slightly different view on it.

"You think being in hospital helped her?" I asked.

"Well, yeah," Aidan said. "They tried."

"And what if," I said quietly, trying to pull on his empathy for our mother and transfer it to me, while not making him mad like back at his place. "It was *because* she was in hospital that she killed herself?"

He flinched at the words, then shook his head. "No, they—"

"I've been there, Aidan," I continued. "It's not good." My Godbrain might make bad things happen, but of everything, I knew that place did it all on its own. And it would've been the same for Mum, torn from her family. The other thing I knew was there was no way on Earth that I was going back to that hell.

He continued to shake his head. "They're there to help, they—"

"But they don't help, Aidan. People might say they do, but they're just saying it so they can get out. What people need is connection, and family and people around them who love them."

He stared at me almost blankly, my words at war with his belief in the system.

"This place," I glanced around. "This place is good for me. The people are good to me. I'm happy here, and getting healthy, and I don't need meds here because I have a purpose and people who care about me and look after me, without the meds."

Aidan contemplated this for a moment. "But... if you stay here, I won't see you much."

I raised my eyebrows and tapped my fingers on his knees. "You could come live here, too?"

This broke the spell Aidan had been under, and he shook his head with renewed conviction. "I can't just pick up my whole life."

"Why not?" I argued. "What do you really have down there? A job you could get anywhere. A dad you don't even see."

He frowned, unconvinced.

"And besides," I continued. "Rose knew Mum, when I was little. So there's that connection. Maybe there are other people up here who knew Mum, too."

"What do you mean, Rose knew Mum?" Aidan's voice was flat.

"Not that well, sure. But they caught up a few times for coffee when I was a newborn. Before Mum went to hospital."

Aidan stiffened. "This is Rose? The Rose I met tonight?"

"Yeah...?"

"The leader of a damn cult that you have somehow ended up in?" He was processing aloud, but I didn't follow.

"Not a cult," I corrected.

"Lena." He locked his eyes directly on mine. "I don't know much about that time, but I do know that there was some weird lady hanging around before Mum got admitted. She's part of the reason Mum had to go to hospital."

My mouth dropped open, wordless. *Someone else caused Mum to get admitted?*

Aidan continued, our eyes still locked. "Mum was claiming this lady was trying to steal her baby, which to everyone else is crazy, but... if this is the same lady, how the hell did you just happen to end up in her house sixteen years later?"

CHAPTER
FORTY-EIGHT

BLOOD DRAINED from my face as a mixture of fear and anger flushed through me. My mum hadn't been paranoid or crazy after all—she'd been trying to protect me. And she'd died because of it.

Rose had tried to steal me away when I was just a baby, to rip me from my loving family. To suck me into this horrible cult, all for their own gain. Her obsession with me had cost my mother her life, and ruined mine. Ruined it far beyond repair. All the trauma I suffered, all the beatings and foster homes and not knowing who I was, not having anyone who cared—it was all because of her.

Another chill flashed through me as more pieces started falling into place. Rose had got her hands on Allie. Allie said Rose adopted her, but... if Rose thought she was me, then who was to say Rose didn't just steal the wrong Alena Williams? Same age, same features. She took Allie from her real family. It was the only explanation.

Anger swelled within me. I jumped up from Aidan's bed and marched to the door.

"Where are you going?" Aidan called.

"To get some answers," I growled.

I yanked the door open and marched down the corridor toward Rose's room. The light was on, and her door ajar. Then Leroy's voice sounded out from the room, high pitched and whiney.

"He can't take her," Leroy whined. "I don't want her to go."

"He won't, dear," Rose cooed. "She's not going anywhere."

I froze. They were talking about me. Deciding my fate, just like the doctors did. No thought as to what I might want, they just decided for me. Rage renewed in me, and my body tensed, ready to march forward.

The voices swelled in my mind, arguing between themselves, each side trying to be louder than the other—confront the witch. Destroy her hopes and dreams that I would ever, ever support her. Smite her, for all she'd done to me and Allie. For manipulating my life from the very start.

Then, the competing groans and pleas, for me to just go. Get out. Be free, and live my life on my own terms. No more hate, just go.

These voices, that for so long I'd thought were mocking me and my lack of control over my life. But that wasn't true at all. I had the power to change my life how I wanted. More power than I could have ever believed I had, actually. I could march in there, confront Rose and that creep Leroy, or I could go, leave, tonight, without a word of warning. Make them wonder and doubt and live with that unknown that Rose had left me and my brother with our whole lives, wondering what happened to our mother, what she went through, when it was all Rose's fault.

I turned and marched back to Aidan's room, pushing the door open.

"We're leaving," I announced firmly.

Aidan's brow furrowed. "Now?"

"Now," I said, then Allie's face flashed into my mind. That sweet girl, caught up in all of this, none of it her fault, just swept up into the mess that was my life and the carnage that the Followers of Mary had brought to it. I would've been happy without them, if they'd just stayed out of my life. Our lives. If they'd left my mum alone to raise me and love me with Aidan and... even James wouldn't have hated me, if I hadn't been part of the reason Mum died. All of this was their fault. All of it.

Allie would be living happily with her family, too, if she'd been given another name. If the Marians hadn't been so damn selfish that they took what wasn't theirs, tried to play God and manipulate people into what they wanted.

This whole place could burn, for all I cared, and everyone in it. Once I got Allie out.

"Get your keys," I said sharply, and turned to go. "I have to get Allie."

"Wait!" Aidan called, and jumped up. "What's going on? Tell me."

I exhaled sharply, and turned to face him. I briefly considered blurting out everything about how it was true I was their saviour, God incarnate, that they'd built this entire religion around my previous lives, that they didn't intend to let me leave or live a normal life, but it was not the time. We'd have to figure out the rest of that later. We just needed to go.

"You're right," I said. "About it all. These people aren't good people. And they dragged Allie into this, and she doesn't deserve it." I turned back to the door.

Aidan rushed over to me and grabbed my arm. "Wait," he said, quietly. He glanced at the door and went over to close it. "I'm with you, okay? We leave tonight. God knows I want to get you out of here."

I sure did know.

"But, think about this a minute," he continued. "Allie's lived here her whole life, right?"

I stared blankly at him, waiting for him to make his point.

"This is her family. Why would she leave with us?"

279

He didn't know what the Marians had done.

"Let's go, you and me," he said. "She's safe here. But you and me maybe aren't. So let's go, tonight, now. And we'll come back for her."

I scowled at him. How could he say that? Ask that of me? To leave someone who was growing close enough to be my best friend, if not even my sister, for all we'd been through together. But he didn't know all that.

I processed his plea. Allie had lived here her whole life. She believed in this religion one hundred percent. Hell, until a few months ago she was convinced she was God. Even that lie hadn't been enough to drive her away from the Marians. What was to say me telling her she was stolen as a baby would be enough to convince her to come with me, late at night?

The voices stirred in me, and I shook my head.

"No," I said. "She deserves to know."

Once she knew, she'd make the right choice. Just knowing that her parents were out there, waiting for her, she'd go to them. She'd find them. An opportunity to have your parents back—your life back—who wouldn't take that?

Aidan dropped his hand in resignation. "Fine. Go get her, then. I'll get the car ready."

"Quietly, please," I begged. "I don't want to have to face the rest of them."

I didn't know what I'd do if I came face to face with Rose, or Leroy. Might set them on fire with my fury.

CHAPTER
FORTY-NINE

AIDAN FOLLOWED me out of his room and I pulled his door just to, so it didn't make much noise. We snuck over toward the front door, and I turned to take the stairs. Aidan opened the front door just enough to slip out.

I headed straight to my shared room and nudged the door open.

"Allie?" I called quietly, not sure if she'd already be asleep.

The light from the half-moon cast the usual shadows across the room, but I could make out Allie's shape in bed. I snuck over to her bed and dropped down on my knees next to her. I called her name again, and lightly touched her arm.

She groaned and wiped her face with her hand.

"What?" she asked, then saw me in front of her. She propped herself up on her forearm and elbow. "Lena? What's going on?"

I put my hands on the hand and forearm she was leaning on.

"Allie," I said softly. "I'm so sorry to do this to you, but we need to go."

"Go?" she asked, narrowing her eyes. "Go where?"

"We need to leave the farm," I said. "Tonight."

She scowled in confusion.

"Listen," I continued quickly, forcing myself to speak instead of getting slowed down by saying the exact right thing. There was no exact right way to tell someone their entire life was a lie —you just had to get it out. "Rose isn't who you think she is. She didn't adopt you—she stole you. Your parents are still out there, waiting for you, probably not knowing what even happened to you."

Her scowl turned into a strange smile, her teeth reflecting stray beams of moonlight. "What are you talking about?"

I dropped my head, composed myself, then met her eyes again. "Rose is the reason my mum is dead. She tried to steal me when I was a baby. Then, when she found you..." I trailed off, figuring she would fill in the obvious blanks.

She raised her eyebrows at me and wobbled her head, like it wasn't so obvious after all.

"Well, you had the same name... she thought you were me..." I said slowly, still waiting for her to fill in the rest.

She stared at me expectantly, waiting for me to repeat the bombshell revelation. Maybe she was still processing the first time I'd said it.

"She stole you, Allie. Your parents are out there, probably still looking for you." *And what I wouldn't give to have that opportunity.*

Allie sat up and pulled her arm away from me. "What are you on about?"

Still processing, poor girl. It was a lot.

"I'm sorry," I said. "I know it's awful. But we have to go. Now. Me and Aidan are leaving, and you have to come with us. We'll go find your parents."

She pulled her head back in disgust. "Go where?" she repeated.

"To find your parents," I said sharply, beginning to grow annoyed. It wasn't her fault, it was a lot to process. But we had to get out of this place. This sick place that stole and ruined lives for their own gain. I didn't want to be there a minute longer than I had to. And I had to get Aidan out—for all I knew, he wasn't safe there, either. None of my family were safe with Rose.

"Lena, my parents couldn't look after me. Rose adopted me," she said matter-of-factly.

I groaned, frustrated. "That's just what she told you. It's not true—she stole you from them."

"How do you know that?" she snapped.

I recoiled. She was right. I didn't know for sure. It was just the most plausible explanation. Rose had told Allie a story about my life, my parents—a story that wasn't even true. Allie was still stuck to it as if it were her own.

"I—I just—" I stammered.

"You don't know that, because it's not true." She put her hand on my shoulder, reassuringly, like my entire concern was completely unfounded, some messed up belief. A *delusion*. And her eyes… was that… pity?

I recoiled, dropping onto my backside. I shook my head, my own processing taking too long. She didn't believe it. Aidan was right. I'd been wrong. It wasn't enough to convince her to leave. Not tonight.

A beep sounded from downstairs. Aidan had got the car ready. But why would he beep, and wake the whole house? Maybe there was trouble. I had to go. It wasn't safe.

I glanced at Allie sadly, then got to my feet. I leaned on her bed with one knee, and pulled her into a massive bear hug.

"I'll come back for you," I whispered, then ran for the door.

CHAPTER
FIFTY

I BOUNDED down the stairs toward Aidan, growing more concerned every second that something bad was happening, that someone was hurting him. My steps thundered on the wooden stairs, surely waking anyone who'd slept through the beep of Aidan's car horn.

Leroy stood in Rose's doorway, fidgeting with his hands that were pulled up to his chest. He hopped from one foot to the other. If he was there, at least that meant he wasn't hurting Aidan, or trying to stop him from leaving. He turned to speak into Rose's room as I raced to the door. I prayed she wouldn't come out.

"Mary's going away, Mum! Mum! You said she wouldn't leave," he winged.

Damn right I was going away. As far away from this house of lies as I could. I ripped open the front door and stepped out into the dim moonlight. The evening air was cool, scented with pine and moss and a trace of smoke from the morning's destruction. My destruction.

Aidan had backed the car up and had it idling right by the front door, with the passenger door open. He was in the driver's seat, waiting. Safe. Not dragged away to a locked room somewhere, or God knew what else. Well, maybe "Marians knew what else" was more appropriate in that context. I pulled on a pair of my shoes that I'd left by the front door with the others, belonging to people I'd thought would be my family. I launched off the front porch onto the gravel, and almost threw myself into the passenger seat.

Aidan pulled away immediately. The wheels spat dirt and loose gravel as we tore down the driveway. His urgency changed something in me, something that had been lurking just behind my determination this whole time, ever since finding out Rose had manipulated my life from day one.

Fear seeped out from the dark corners of my being, where it had been hiding while my anger flared. The sorrowful voices that had begged me to leave, to go without conflict, whispered and mourned the hurt I had caused.

But it wasn't me who had caused it. It was Rose, and her Marians. I looked over at Aidan. He'd been here, at this strange house, in this compound, which he was convinced was a cult and had every making of a horror movie, where all the audience would have been screaming at him to not go in, not stay the night, didn't he know he was going to get murdered or sacrificed or worse? He was here because of me. *For* me. And he hadn't been far off. Rose had said it: I wasn't allowed to leave. So what would they try to do to us—to him, if he tried to take me?

They'd have to remove the threat.

I glanced back up at the house to make sure no one was following us. *Just let us leave,* I begged.

The Marians were dangerous, and whether I had Godpowers or not, I didn't have control of them yet. I could play pretend, or act tough against a fragile old lady. But when it came down to it, if I had to face off with Tim or Leroy, I wouldn't be able to protect us. I wouldn't be able to do anything, just like at the hospital when the staff lunged on me as a pack and carried me away to inject me with their poison.

We hit a harsher curve in the driveway and skidded on the loose gravel, bringing me back to the present. We careened down the driveway, being quiet no longer our priority. We had to get away before they came after us. The tyres skidded and ripped at the loose gravel, but got us to the gate in quarter of the time it had taken to drive up that day.

The steel gates loomed in front of us, growing bigger and more defiant every second. Blood drained from my face.

"The gate," I said shakily. "It doesn't automatically open."

Aidan glanced at me, then back to the gate. "What—so what do we do?"

Panic clawed at my mind, clouding my thoughts. "I don't know the code. Can we ram it?"

"Can we—no, we can't ram it. There's no way this car will survive that. You don't know the code? What the hell, Lena?"

I dropped my head onto the headrest and hid my face with my hands. "I don't. I'm sorry. I—"

A scene from earlier that day flashed through my mind. Tim typed the code, five digits, right in front of me. The pattern looked like a "C" formation.

"Pull up, I think I can guess it," I said.

"You better hurry," he said, glancing in the rearview mirror. "Lights just came on at the house."

I whipped around and cursed under my breath. Someone had turned the porchlight on. Dark figures stood under it.

You said she wouldn't leave. Leroy's words echoed in my mind, the other whispered voices repeating them in a haunting, awful echo chamber. I shivered, and pressed my fingers against my temple in a vain attempt to make them go away.

Aidan pulled up as close as he could to the gate, even though they swung inwards, to get me as close to the keypad as possible. I opened the door and jumped out before the car had come to a stop. I left the door open and ran to the keypad, the stones scuffing under my shoes. The only other sounds beside the idling car were the chirp of crickets and the faint rustling of leaves in the cool breeze. And my ragged breath.

The keypad wasn't backlit, and was shaded from the moonlight. I could barely make out the buttons, let alone numbers. I felt for them and desperately clicked a "C" formation in the far top right, middle top, then the two under that, and again one to the far right.

Nothing happened.

I swore under my breath again, then raced back to the car. "Give me your phone," I yelled to Aidan.

He fumbled in his pocket, unquestioning. He handed me his phone and I ran back to the keypad, desperately swiping at the phone to turn on the built-in flashlight. The light flooded the tiny black pad, showing wear on four of the five buttons I had pressed. I groaned. The only other button that showed wear had a tick on it.

I punched in the same first four numbers in the combination, following the wear on the buttons. Instead of the bottom right, I pressed the tick. The gate creaked to life.

I ran back to the car as Aidan was slowly reversing, giving the gate room to open enough to let us through. I glanced at the house before diving into the passenger seat. More lights had come on, and people were moving around in front of the house. Toward the vehicles.

"Go!" I yelled at Aidan, not that I had to tell him. He slammed the car into drive, kicking up gravel as the wheels fought for traction. We sped out of the compound, barely missing the gates as they continued to lumber open.

CHAPTER
FIFTY-ONE

THE SILHOUETTES of trees rushed by as we sped away from the commune, and after that, home, wherever that was going to be. I watched the speedometer pick up, my smile spreading as it reached up toward 80kph.

I breathed out and dropped my head back against the headrest. We'd made it out.

A rush of light illuminated the car from behind, hitting the rearview mirror and burning into my soul.

I bolted upright and turned to see that the headlights were gaining on us.

"Oh, God. Aidan—"

"Is it them?" Aidan looked in the mirror, tightening his grip on the steering wheel.

"It has to be. There's no one else around. Can you go any faster?" I glanced back at the speedometer. It was already increasing.

"I am," Aidan said. "What do we do if it's them? Like, are they dangerous?"

What was I meant to tell him? They hadn't been, not in general. But I'd also never tried to escape from them before.

They'd said I couldn't leave—even Allie said I couldn't leave—I was their saviour. They'd housed me and fed me and I'd run away in the middle of the night. They'd be mad. They'd want me back. They'd travelled across the country once, even twice. It wasn't ridiculous that they would again. But they'd surely rather get me back now.

"I—I don't know," I stammered.

"You don't know? You've been living with them. Did they seem dangerous?"

"I don't know," I snapped, unintentionally. "I mean, they've been nice, but I just escaped, you know? I don't know how they're gonna take that."

"They're getting closer," Aidan said, spending more time watching the rearview mirror than where he was going. "What're we gonna do if they get to us?"

"I don't—oh my God, it is them." The headlights sat high, like on a ute. Like on Tim's white ute.

"How do you know?" Aidan asked.

"The car... I'm sure it is."

"What do they want?" He switched from looking in the rearview to wing mirror, with only brief glances at the road itself.

"I don't know!"

Me.

"Should we call the police?" Aidan suggested.

I hadn't even thought of that. The police had never helped me. They'd always thought I was crazy, and redelivered me to the mental health unit. I checked Aidan's phone. "No signal."

Aidan groaned. "They're still getting closer."

I closed my eyes and focused in on Rose's voice in my mind. Maybe if she was praying, I'd know what she was up to. If it was her.

Come back.

I gasped. Her voice rang through so clearly in my mind. I opened myself up more.

Come back, My Lady—Lena—please. Be safe. Let Leroy bring you home to us.

Leroy. Of course it was Leroy, chasing us in the middle of the night.

"What the heck," Aidan cried out from beside me. "Are they —they're coming up next to us!"

I watched, wide eyed and helpless, as Tim's white ute slowly gained speed to hover next to us. This was a straight stretch at the moment but these roads were winding. If someone came around the bend, Leroy would crash. Or they'd avoid him and crash into us.

"Slow down, Aidan! He's gonna make us crash!"

Aidan obeyed, and Leroy slowed, too, still next to us. His window was down, and he started flailing his hand, indicating for us to pull over.

"He's telling us to pull over," I said in disbelief.

"Don't look at him," Aidan said.

I stared straight ahead, praying that a car wouldn't come from the other direction. *Please.*

"If we can get back to town then there's gotta be service there. It's not far now. We can call the cops."

"And just… keep driving with him next to us until then?" There was no shoulder to the road and the deep ditches seemed to swallow the headlights. Paddocks stretched out either side of us. "The road's so narrow."

Rose could keep her prayers. If anyone's, I'd answer my own.

Leave us alone, Leroy, I pleaded.

"If we have—" Aidan cut himself off as he watched the ute drop back toward our rear.

"He's dropping back," I said in awe. It had worked.

A second later he was behind us, driving almost bumper to bumper.

"I know… what's he—" The front of Leroy's car hit the back of ours. "What's he doing!"

"He hit us!" I exclaimed. *This was not what I asked for.* "Is he trying to make us crash?"

"Hold on," Aidan said, shifting the automatic gear stick to low gear. The car lurched forward and screamed in protest, but sped up.

"Don't go too fast! What if there's a corner or some—" Leroy hit us again, matching our speed. The car wobbled. I clung to the arm rest in the door. "We're gonna crash!" *Don't think about a pink elephant, Lena!*

"We're not. We just have to make it to the town."

I winced, wanting this all to be over. How had this turned so badly, that Leroy was now willing to potentially kill me—kill us —instead of letting me leave? If this was it for me, Allie would be left there with those people, not knowing the truth about her parents.

Allie.

Lena.

Was that… a reply?

Lena, please come back. Please come home.

No, not a reply. Just her prayer. She was in on this, too. She didn't want me to be with my brother any more than Rose did. But it wasn't up to them.

The headlights illuminated a bend ahead. "Aidan," I said, panic clear in my voice. "There's a corner. We're going too fast. We're gonna—"

We didn't make it to the corner. Leroy rammed his car into ours, jolting the car sideways. The world outside blurred as we careened off the road, hurtling into the ditch with bone-breaking force. The seatbelt cut into my neck and tightened across my chest, winding me. A wall of white engulfed me, slamming me backward into my seat, my head whipping back with a force dangerously close to breaking my neck.

The car was still. The airbag deflated enough for me to look over at Aidan, whose own airbag had shot him back into his seat. He was leaning on it, groaning.

"Aidan," I called.

He glanced at me, then tried to sit back. Smoke billowed from the crumpled front of our car. I couldn't see where Leroy was.

"Aidan," I said again. "You okay?"

Aidan groaned again and gulped. He shifted his legs one at a time. I did the same. Then noise at my door. I jumped away from it.

Leroy tapped calmly on the window. "Mary." Leroy's voice was a muffled whisper through the window. "I need to take you back."

"No, no," I mumbled. I pushed at Aidan, not breaking my view of Leroy. "Go, Aidan, get out."

He saw Leroy, too, and started to move quicker. He tried the door handle but it wouldn't open. He flicked the locks and tried again. The door swung open and Aidan tumbled out.

With the car now unlocked, Leroy opened my door and grabbed my arm. "Mary, Rose says you have to come back."

"Go away!" I screamed. "Just leave me alone!" I tried to pull away from him and escape over to Aidan's side, but my seatbelt held me back. I clicked it open and tried again, trying to yank my arm away from Leroy's grasp.

Aidan had scrambled to his feet. He climbed back into the vehicle and pried at Leroy's hand. The pressure cut into my arm. I clawed at Leroy's hand, too, but his grip was deathly set, as if he couldn't feel any pain from my fingernails tearing at his skin.

Aidan changed tactics and pulled at my other arm instead. It helped me shift enough to get some leverage against the seats and angle my body to get better use of my legs.

I kicked out at Leroy. One, then two, I managed to get enough force that he had to let go of my arm. He grabbed my

293

foot instead and started pulling me out of the door. I pulled my other foot back and lashed out, right at his face.

His nose shifted beneath my shoe, along with a sickening crack. A gush of blood splattered out of his nose, down his chin and across his shirt. Leroy cried out and grabbed at his face.

I clambered over into the driver's seat to follow Aidan out, leaving Leroy on the passenger's side. Aidan helped me out of the car, up the slope of the ditch and back onto the road.

"Come on, the town's just up there," Aidan wheezed.

I looked up at the light polluting the sky, wishing it was closer. The headlights behind us illuminated the road, casting our limping shadows out ahead of us. My legs hurt, as did my arms, even with the adrenaline pumping through my body.

We were going too slow. Aidan had his arm around my back to help me walk. I pulled away and pushed him forward. "Come, run."

He took my hand and we started to jog, pain screaming through my legs. Aidan was limping, too, but we had to get away. I tasted salt and metal—I was crying, and bleeding.

I glanced back while limp-running, but couldn't make out details well enough without stopping, especially with the headlights shining right at us.

Right at us. Lighting us up, showing Leroy exactly where we were. Ice shot through me.

"He still has his car," I gasped.

"Just run," Aidan commanded.

A loud crack split the air. I ducked instinctively.

Aidan cried out. His hand ripped from mine. Then he went sprawling forward, face first into the asphalt.

CHAPTER
FIFTY-TWO

"AIDAN!" I screamed. I dropped down next to him and tried to flip him over.

It took a moment to sink in. The metallic taste in my mouth briefly masked the growing scent. Dark crimson soaked through Aidan's shirt in the middle of his back. A chill swept through me as I began to understand what was happening.

I pushed again at his shoulder, trying to flip him. I got my arm under him and used my body weight to turn him, mentally begging him to not be dead. *Please, God, no.*

No.

He groaned as I forced him over, through no choice of his own. I shuffled closer to him and lifted his head onto my lap. He panted twice, then his eyelids opened enough for me to see his eyes roll back.

He screamed. Or was it me? Maybe it was both of us. It burned into my soul. It was definitely him screaming. I sobbed over him. My eyes traced down to his belly, blood oozing onto the road. He tried to move his hand to his back, but was too weak, and dropped it to his side. I lifted his hand and held it in mine.

"It's okay. You're going to be okay," I promised. We both knew it was a lie.

Aidan blinked up at me, his eyes turning glassy. His lips moved soundlessly and blood trickled from the corner of his mouth. I cradled his head in my lap, heart shattering into a thousand pieces. *How could this be happening?*

"I'm so sorry," I whispered, clutching him close. "This is all my fault. I'm so sorry."

He coughed weakly, blood spouting from his mouth. He gagged and I lifted his head higher, trying to help him to not choke. He squeezed my fingers in his own, his feeble attempt bringing more ache to my soul.

"Hold on, okay? Just hold on."

He attempted a reassuring smile, then it dropped away as his eyes shut. His breath was raspy, trying to pull air through the thick pool of blood in his throat.

I vaguely heard Leroy approaching, him saying something, but my focus was on Aidan. The murmur was back, mocking, stealing these precious moments with my brother, the only person who had ever truly cared about me, defended me, and now was going to die for me.

Not for me—because of me. The Marians didn't want to hurt me, not physically. They wanted to control me, like everyone else.

I clung to Aidan as his breathing slowed, willing him to stay with me. Begging him not to leave me alone in this messed up world. Aidan was the good one. He didn't hear voices or see things that weren't there. He had a chance at a normal life. A chance he lost because of me.

Hands clamped around my arms, wrenching me away from my brother. He slumped to the ground as I was dragged back, his head hitting the ground with a thud.

No. No, no, no.

I thrashed and screamed, kicked at my captor. At Leroy. I

twisted and clawed at him, shrieking Aidan's name. The rifle hung over Leroy's other shoulder, mocking me as I scrambled to grip the asphalt, shoes skidding. Leroy dragged me further and further away, as if my writhing was nothing to him.

Aidan. I strained my neck, refusing to lose sight of him.

"Let me go!" I shrieked. "Aidan!"

My brother lay motionless.

This couldn't be happening. I screamed, clawed, and kicked. I battered at Leroy with clenched fists, rage and sorrow warring within me. "Let me go!"

He ignored me. Of course he did.

I stretched my fingers out on my free hand, pressed them together so they were straight and solid, wound my arm back, and as hard as I could, drove my pointed fingers into the vulnerable part of Leroy's side.

My fingers crumpled into him, but fortunately he crumpled with them. He let out a wheeze and released his grip on me. I followed up with a kick into the back of his knee and he collapsed onto the ground. He reached for my foot but I pulled it back fast enough, shooting it out again just as quickly, back into his already broken nose. I kicked again, not caring where it landed.

I didn't pause to celebrate my success. I sprinted toward Aidan, my heart pounding. I dropped to my knees beside my brother, gently shaking him, trying to rouse him.

"Aidan, wake up! Please, Aidan!" I begged, my voice trembling. I cupped his face, willing him to look at me. "Stay with me, Aidan. I can fix this. I can fix everything."

The weight of his stillness settled over me, suffocating my hope along with his breathless body.

He was gone.

CHAPTER
FIFTY-THREE

NO. I wouldn't allow it.

I was a freaking god.

No, not just *a* god, *the* God. And if there was ever a time for my Godpower to work, this was it.

Allie believed in me, and that meant something. So many people believed in me. All the people at the commune. All the Followers of Mary. Millions of people across the *world*.

All pouring energy and love into me, for exactly this reason. So I could perform miracles.

I took a deep breath and thought back to the feeling I had when I first released the voices. When I washed them from my mind and through my body on the wave of sunlight. I remembered how it felt, the warmth, control, and sense of limitless power. It had been so fleeting.

That was it. That was my Godpower.

I closed my eyes and breathed in slowly. My breath hitched, trying to stifle sobs, which just served as a reminder that my brother lay dead in my arms. Because of me.

The Godpower had hurt, when I did it last time. Would it

hurt again today? It didn't matter. I'd do it for Aidan. I'd do anything to take this back.

I pictured the sun filling me up from my toes.

Was there a time limit to this? What if I brought Aidan back too late and he had brain damage or something? No, then I'd reverse that, too. I was freaking *God*.

The sunlight filled my calves, then thighs.

I was rushing it. It wasn't going to work. *Go slower. Do it right.*

The sunlight washed around every part of my calves, warming my muscles, easing them.

Okay, now I had it. I worked upward through my body, just as Rose had done, careful to slow myself, to do it right.

I let the sunshine fill me from inside as it beat down on me from above. Up, and up through my body. The darkness in my shoulders was filled with light and warmth as the sunshine wove its way through, touching every inch of me, like a great yellow wave. The wave rose up, up, through my neck, until it tapped on the gateway to my mind. The voices had grown louder in their excitement, ready to be released.

Then the wave of warm, yellow light pushed the gateway open and washed through my skull and mind, collecting the voices in its torrential sweep. They embraced the warmth and the freedom that the sunshine wave granted them. They swam through my body, riding the current, spreading out to every piece of me, every nook and strand of hair.

I gasped at the warmth and power. That familiar, awe-inspiring tingle swept through me and over me and around me and it was me. It could seep out of me, I could float on this aura of pure love and worship and devotion. All that worship, all around the world, all channelling into me, here and now.

Then the scent of blood made its way to my consciousness again, along with its sticky warmth. I looked at my brother, his eyes staring up into the night, lifeless and dull. My own eyes traced down to his belly, where the bullet should have come out, but instead sat lodged in him somewhere.

I put my hands on his belly, roughly where the bullet should have been, and closed my eyes again. I channelled the Godpower into my hands, just like they do on TV. I pictured my power and warmth stitching the tears in his organs back together, forcing the bullet back out. I opened my eyes, expecting a glow around my hands.

There was nothing.

I wedged my hand under his back and tried to feel for the hole in his back, but couldn't. His back and the road were still sticky and wet from blood. Maybe it had worked without the glow, and the blood just didn't go back in. It didn't always, on TV.

I put my hands on his shoulders and shook gently. "Aidan?"

His once-bright eyes continued to stare upward, his mouth and cheeks still waxy with death.

Another breath hitched in my throat. The Godpower started to wane, the tingle retreating from my fingers and toes.

I had failed my brother, more than once, and now for the last time.

I laid on his chest, arms stretched out across his broad shoulders. I brought one hand to his head and stroked his hair gently.

"I'm so sorry," I whispered.

My feet, legs, and up to my hips were cold, the sunshine gone, and darkness spreading further up my spine. Tingles still pricked my arms and cheeks.

No. I had to fix this.

I took a deep breath, steadying myself. This was the moment that defined me—a god among mortals, or a useless, failure of a sister.

I called the prayers back, and their power warmed my spine and returned to my legs. I didn't have to fix Aidan's body. I could shift the entire world to my whim. I had dreamed the world was burning, and made it so. If I made it so all this was just in my mind, that could be so, too. What even was reality if not our perception of our experiences?

I focused every fibre of my being and Godpower, willing Aidan and I to a better life, just the two of us. I took a deep, shuddering breath and summoned a beautiful life together: one where we were safe, happy, and together.

Our big, white villa stood proud against a blue, near cloud-less sky. The birds sang in our trees surrounding our perfectly manicured lawn. Cicadas chirped, the warmth of the sun creating the perfect ambience. The French doors to the lounge stood open, giving an easy sight through to our comfy couches, nice wooden floors, beautiful high ceilings. There were shoes left in front of the doorway—my shoes, but Aidan didn't mind—his were there, too. What did it matter when it was ours? There was no one to tell us how to live, how to be. We were free to be us. Our home was warm and inviting, tucked away from the chaos that had haunted us for so long. In our backyard, an orange tree towered over us, its branches heavy with ripe fruit.

"Catch!" Aidan said, and I looked at him just in time to catch a juicy orange before it hit me. Aidan's eyes grew wide, realising I'd almost been too slow and would've got a face-full, then he laughed. I laughed with him. He went back to foraging, and I examined the perfect orange, feeling its weight in my hand. Perfect.

It was all perfect. The house, the weather, that life. A smile still spread across my face from our shared laughter. Aidan was safe. I'd willed this into existence. I closed my eyes and breathed in the sweet smell of orange and grass and happiness.

But another smell cut through that—the smell of rusting metal. I furrowed my brow and opened my eyes, ready to look for the source of the smell that didn't fit. But instead of the sun-drenched backyard filled with laughter, I found myself back on the cold, headlight-lit road, curled across Aidan's lifeless body.

"No," I whimpered, pulling his body further into mine. "Why didn't it work?"

The Godpower was fading from me. I wasn't as powerful as I thought. I couldn't change time, I couldn't bend reality to my will.

Because I had to believe it. And that story, that life I had conjured, was too perfect. I would never have that life, no matter how much I dreamed of it. That wasn't how my world worked. I couldn't make it right, I couldn't make it perfect for me. I didn't believe in that, not really. It was too good to be true. The only chance I had for this was to make the story real, make it believable.

"I'm gonna fix this, Aidan." I turned my head on his chest to look up at his lifeless face. "Just like I promised."

I closed my eyes again. The memory surrounded me, blotting out the present. I held onto it with everything I had, rebuilding the world until it was exactly as it should be.

"Lena?"

A female voice.

CHAPTER
FIFTY-FOUR

I OPENED MY EYES SLOWLY, the crushing weight of the darkness giving way to the harsh fluorescents overhead. The sterile white walls and faint scent of antiseptic told me I was at the hospital. I blinked a few times, long and purposeful, trying to clear the fog from my mind. Beeps sounded from beside me, and I glanced over at the heart monitor and IV drip by my bedside. I tried to sit up, but my whole body ached.

Why? What happened?

A vague recollection of speeding, and fear, before… before tumbling, pain, and screaming.

Was I in a car crash?

"You're awake," a nurse said from beside me, her gentle, kind voice pulling me further into consciousness. "We were worried about you."

I squinted at her blankly, my eyes still adjusting to the harsh change of light. "What happened?"

"You're in the hospital, Lena. You had an episode," she replied gently, her young face etched with concern. "We found you wandering the grounds, talking to yourself."

Wandering the grounds... the hospital grounds? How was I outside the building? *Why* was I outside?

Flashes of memory flickered through my mind—curled up in Nia's lap, tears streaming down my face... hands, pressing on my arms and ankles as I fought against them... a glass door, and panic that it wouldn't open. But it did, and then—

Everything came rushing back. Running through the streets, Ryan, the Marians, the farm, my powers—*Aidan*.

"Is Aidan okay?" I yelped, a surge of adrenaline coursing through me. I forced myself up onto my elbows, trying to kick myself into sitting position. "Is he safe?"

The nurse hushed and laid her hand on my shoulder to guide me back into bed. "Your brother? He's fine," she soothed. "He called earlier to check on you. Don't try to get up, I don't want you to fall."

Her words sank in, and I sank back into bed with them. Aidan was okay.

I'd done it.

My miracle—it worked. Aidan was safe. The world was as it should be.

It was as if I hit a reset button, and the events of the past week never happened. As if it were all a figment of my imagination, a delusion brought on by my illness.

For Aidan, I would be me again—broken, lost Lena.

I sank further into the pillow, my body feeling both heavy and light, as if caught between two worlds. The beeping and whirring of machines and monitors around me amplified into my awareness. The heart monitor pulsed in time with my heartbeat. The blood pressure cuff compressed my upper arm, my pulse pounding against the pressure. My eyes narrowed, but this time not against the light. They narrowed for the growing dread inside me.

This isn't where I'm supposed to be.

"Where am I?" I whispered, my voice catching in my throat.

The nurse's forehead wrinkled and she leaned in, putting her hand on my shoulder again. "You're in the hospital, Lena. You had an episode, remember?"

I shook my head. "No, no, I mean which hospital? This isn't mental health."

Relief washed over her face. "Oh, you're in the medical assessment ward. You were really unwell, Lena. We need to keep you here for a little while to monitor you until you're well enough to go back to the mental health unit."

Medical ward. Back to mental health unit.

That's what I'd wanted. That's what I'd brought to life. So why was there something gnawing at my stomach, churning unease? Was it just that I didn't want to go back?

But I'd made my choice. I'd sacrificed myself, to keep Aidan safe.

"I'm going to give you something to help you rest," the nurse said, preparing a syringe.

As the medication hit my bloodstream, the edges of my vision blurred. I sank further into the pillow, feeling as though I may fall right through it. The room seemed to sway, as if I were caught in a dream.

I had pictured a world where the events of the past week were all in my imagination—a psychotic experience. That, really, I was just a sick girl with a sick brain who was back in the hospital.

In the mental hospital.

My heart dropped again. Had I been that specific? Had I been explicit, in my belief, that I was back in the mental hospital? I racked my increasingly sleepy brain to remember, but the details remained hazy. It seemed likely, given how vividly I would have to picture it all to bring it to life.

Only, I wasn't in the mental hospital. I was here, in a medical ward. With leads and tubes and IV meds twisted around and pumping into me. This wasn't what I had pictured.

What did it matter? It had worked. Aidan was safe. I would condemn myself to a life as a mental patient, with everyone around me believing that I was just a sick girl with psychosis. That was how it had to be, for him to live. That world was believable. That was my life.

Aidan would go on living his life, blissfully unaware of the gift I had given him. The sacrifice I had made, for him, resigning myself to this place. He could be my protector again. I'd be the helpless, troubled younger sister, whom he could swoop in and save.

But I knew the truth.

The power coursing through my veins, through my being, was more than anyone could ever possibly imagine. I had recreated the world as I needed. With only a thought, I had reshaped the fabric of existence itself. I was no mere mortal, but a deity, capable of bending reality to my will.

In that moment, I knew for certain.

I was God.

AUTHOR'S NOTE

Thank you for reading Follow Me! I do hope you've enjoyed it.

The absolute BEST thing you can do for authors is to shout about our books! If you're able to leave a review on any of your preferred platforms, that would be so appreciated (I'll read every one!). And, of course, tell all your friends!

I've set up a special Behind the Story document for my mailing list subscribers, which describes some background info about the book's content. If you haven't received the link, please email me at hello@rachgrahamreads.com, or sign up for the list at rachgrahamreads.com if you're not already joined!

I'll be sending out early copies of future releases to that mailing list, so get amongst it! Insider goss: there's a Pick a Path/ Choose Your Own Adventure coming your way ;)

You rock!

Much love,

Rach

ACKNOWLEDGEMENTS

The past year has been a wild ride, getting Follow Me written and ready for publication. It started as a means to prove to myself I could write a novel, but once Lena found her voice, it developed into so much more.

Thank you to every single reader who has taken a chance on this new author, and has ended up loving the story and messages within these pages.

A special thank you to Andrew, one of my earliest readers, who loves the book possibly more than I do. Our chats gave me the ego boost and motivation I needed to share this story with even more people.

William, who was the little voice in the back of my head shouting "GIVE ME STAKES!" and helped craft the beginning pages to be more in line with published books.

Every early reader who gave feedback to develop the story more deeply, and pick up on inconsistencies I had missed.

The Psychological Thriller Readers Facebook Group, who are always up for a new book to read, and gave me another massive ego boost with the overwhelming response to this novel, plus the refinement of the front cover.

Noelle W. Ihli, for reading and enjoying Follow Me so much that part of her review now features on the cover (such warm debut-author feels, getting a recommendation from one of the greats!).

Daniel from Avid Readers Club, who loved the story so much that he recommended it to his reviewer and blogger friends, including putting me in touch with Noelle. Your advice around marketing was so appreciated leading up to and beyond launch.

John Marrs, who not only was completely cool with me referencing him and his book Keep It In The Family, but got a laugh out of it as well.

My family, particularly my mother, who listened to me prattle on about the latest update in the publishing saga, and my sister, who read an early version with the reassurance that she was "sure it wouldn't be the worst book [she'd] ever read" (spoiler: it wasn't).

My husband, who let me be throughout writing and marketing, even when it meant he had to watch television in a different room.

Finally, to my wonderful Tiffany, who got sucked into chatting with me about the potential prequels, sequels, and other stories, and now cannot escape. Let's make this thing huge, and get you your trip to New Zealand!

Love you all.

ABOUT THE AUTHOR

Rachel Graham is a mental health nurse living in New Zealand with her husband and two dogs. Her inspiration is drawn from her experiences in the inpatient unit and community, and the stories of those she has worked with. Her writing is informed by her close engagement with people experiencing acute mental illness as they navigate life, relationships, and the mental health system.

Follow her (no pun intended) across all social media: @rachgrahamreads.